Dog's Run

By Nick Russell

Copyright 2013 © By Nick Russell
ISBN:13: 978-1493648443

All rights reserved. No part of this book may be reproduced in any form or by any means, electronic or mechanical, including photocopying, recording, or by any information storage or retrieval system, without permission in writing by the publisher.

Nick Russell
1400 Colorado Street C-16
Boulder City, NV 89005
E-mail Editor@gypsyjournal.net

Also By Nick Russell
Fiction
Big Lake
Big Lake Lynching
Crazy Days In Big Lake
Big Lake Blizzard
Dog's Run

Nonfiction
Highway History and Back Road Mystery
Highway History and Back Road Mystery II
Meandering Down The Highway; A Year On The Road
With Fulltime RVers
The Frugal RVer
Work Your Way Across The USA; You Can Travel
And Earn A Living Too
The Gun Shop Manual
Overlooked Florida
Overlooked Arizona
The Step-By-Step Guide To Self-Publishing For Profit

Keep up with Nick Russell's latest
books at www.NickRussellBooks.com

To Greg White, who does so much and is always there when I need him. Thanks, brother.

Dog's Run

Two boys playing hooky from school to go squirrel hunting found the young woman's body lying facedown in the muddy creek at the bottom of Dog's Run. At first, Wayne DeCross thought it was a dummy and started to approach it, but his buddy Chance Carver grabbed his arm and pulled him back.

"No, Wayne, that ain't no dummy, that's a real woman and I think she's dead!"

"Naaa," Wayne told him disdainfully, shaking the other boy's hand off his arm. "You got too much imagination, Chance. Besides, even if it was a real woman, I ain't scared of no dead body. Are you?"

"I'm not scared," Chance said with a shake of his head, even though he was. "I just don't want to be messin' with no dead body."

"Well what do ya think those squirrels hangin' off your belt are? Ain't they dead bodies?"

Chance couldn't deny the reasoning but he still didn't want to get anywhere near the thing laying in the creek. "That's different. These are animals and pretty soon they'll be food. That there's a dead person."

"Ain't people animals, too?" argued Wayne. "And if we don't get her out of that water pretty soon she'll be food too, for the crawdaddies."

"I ain't touching her!" Chance said. "We need to go tell the Sheriff."

"I swear, you are such a sissypants. Dead is dead, ain't it? Don't matter if it's a squirrel or a chicken or a person."

"Well I ain't never been haunted by no squirrel or a chicken before!"

"And when was you ever haunted by a dead person?" Wayne asked.

"I wasn't. But you ask Pete Ledbetter about gettin' haunted. He'll tell ya! He was haunted by his mother-in-law after she died 'cause they never got on."

"Pete Ledbetter?" Wayne scoffed. "Hell, you know well's I do that old Pete's drunk most of the time, and he's got a worse imagination than you. If he heard a tree branch scrapin' the side of his shack, he'd swear it was old Bessie Green scratchin' on the door tryin' to get in!"

"I don't care. I ain't touching no dead body!"

"Fine, then hold my gun and I'll do it. I ain't scared of nothing!" Wayne said, handing his old Savage single-shot .22 to his friend and walking up to the body.

And there was no doubt that it was indeed a body he determined when he got closer. A hank of long, curly yellow hair waved off to the side in the muddy water and the back of the woman's white dress had ridden up, exposing her upper thighs and the cheeks of her butt. Being a normal thirteen year old boy, Wayne couldn't help pausing to admire the curve of her rear end for a quick moment before he put his hand on her shoulder and tried to pull her over. She was surprisingly heavy for such a relatively small woman. He called out to Chance, "Stop bein' such a baby and come here and help me."

Chance hesitated for another moment, then screwed up his courage. He wasn't a Catholic, in fact he wasn't much for Sunday School of any kind, but he crossed himself like he had seen that priest in the Saturday matinee at the Rigley Theater do last week, then laid the three squirrels they had shot, Wayne's rifle, and his beat up old Savage 20 gauge on the creek bank and joined his friend. The water covering his ankles was cool, but that wasn't what made him shiver.

"Who is it?"

"Don't know," Wayne said. "Guess we'll find out when we roll her over. Here, give me a hand."

They grabbed the woman's right arm and pulled her onto her back and were greeted with the sight of a fat crawdad hanging from the corner of her left nostril by one pincher.

All thought of false bravado disappeared as both boys screamed and ran splashing out of the creek, leaving their guns, the dead squirrels, and the body behind them as they fled Dog's Run.

Chapter 1

Police Chief Lester Smeal took a bite of his meatloaf sandwich and smiled at Mary Jo, nodding as he chewed. "That's just delicious, darlin'," he said as he swallowed.

Mary Jo beamed and said, "I'm glad you like it Les. Anything else I can get you?"

"Well I can think of several things I'd like," the chief said. "But most of them are immoral, and I'm pretty sure a couple are flat-out illegal."

Mary Jo blushed and cackled, slapping his arm playfully. "What am I going to do with you, Lester J. Smeal? You're incorrigible!"

"Yes ma'am, I am," the chief said with a wide grin, before taking another bite. That's just one of the reasons you love me."

"Oh, I love you, do I? I think you're assuming a lot there, big fella."

"Well, if it ain't love, it must be lust," the chief said, drawing another loud laugh from the waitress.

Their daily flirtation was interrupted when the door to the Sunshine Café burst open and two muddy, excited young boys rushed inside leaving a trail of footprints across Mary Jo's linoleum floor.

"What in the world are you boys doing stomping in here like that?" Mary Jo demanded. "You take yourselves right back outside and wipe your feet and then come in and close the door like gentlemen!"

Normally Wayne and Chance were well behaved boys, but this day they were too excited to even hear her, much less obey.

"Chief, we found a dead body! Come quick!"

"What? What dead body? Where?"

"Down in Dog's Run. She's lying in the water and a crawdad was eatin' her face," Wayne said.

Chief Smeal knew the boys by sight, though he didn't know their names. They were like most of the youngsters from Dog's Run; often unwashed, dressed in hand-me-down clothes, and allowed to run free most of the time with little parental guidance. Dog's Run was a shabby collection of shanties and thrown together houses on the east side of Elmhurst. The town attracted refugees from West Virginia, Kentucky, and Tennessee, who came to Ohio looking for work in the factories around Toledo and a better lifestyle than the coal mines and hardscrabble farms they had left behind could offer. Most were decent, hardworking folk, but there was also a hard element among them that included moonshiners, petty thieves, and ne'er-do-wells.

"Slow down boys. Now just where did you find this body, and who is it?"

"She's down in the creek at the bottom of the Run," Chance told him. "Just upstream from the bridge. I don't know who it is, we just looked and ran when we saw the crawdad eating her."

Mary Jo's face had gone pale at the boys' revelation and she said, "Oh my Lord!"

The chief looked at the boys sternly, and asked, "You sure about this? You boys ain't just pulling my leg? Because if you are and you come here interrupting my lunch like this, we're going to have a problem."

Both boys shook their heads vigorously.

"No sir, it's a dead lady and she's layin' there in Dog's Run!"

***

Dog's Run is a steep-sided ravine that begins somewhere just across the line in Michigan and continues southward to the west side of town before petering out at Swan Creek. Chief Smeal parked his Buick Roadmaster under a hickory tree near the bridge and followed the boys down a worn footpath to the water's edge.

"Where is she?"

"Right up there around the bend," Wayne said. "I ain't going no further. I don't want to see her again."

"No, you're both going to show me exactly where she's at," Lester said. "I still don't know what you found, but until I get to the bottom of this, I'm not letting either one of you out of my sight!"

Reluctantly the boys led him upstream and around the short bend, where the chief stopped abruptly. "Holy shit! You boys stay right here and don't you go nowhere, you hear me?"

Both boys nodded emphatically, relieved not to have to get too close to the body again.

Dog's Run

Chief Smeal walked a few yards farther and surveyed the scene. The woman lay twisted onto her left side, her upper torso in the water. Nearby, on the creek bank, he saw a rifle and shotgun and the dead squirrels the boys had left behind. Walking out into the water, he felt it rise to just above his ankles as he squatted next to the body. The crawdad that the boys had seen was no longer in evidence, but small marks on the woman's face told him that it'd been there.

The woman had been pretty in life, but in death there was little left to show of what she had been at one time. Studying the body, the chief noted the dark bruise on the side of her face, that her left ankle was twisted at an odd angle, and that the scrapes and abrasions on her arms and legs had come from something more than crawdads.

"Oh Wanda Jean, what's become of you now?" Lester asked the woman.

***

"I can't tell you right now what killed her," Doctor Albert Crowther told the police chief three hours later in the examining room of his office above the Rexall drugstore. "It's going to take an autopsy in Toledo for that. But I can tell you she's got a broken ankle and a bunch of broken ribs, which probably also means internal injuries. And if you look here," he said, rolling the body onto its side, "it looks like she may have dislocated her shoulder, too. See how her arm rotates unnaturally? And something gave her a good wallop on the side of her head here."

Lester had seen a lot of battered and broken bodies in the South Pacific during the war and more than a few in his time as police chief, but he felt uncomfortable when it was the naked and abused body of a young woman he knew.

"So you think someone did this to her?"

"Well, she didn't do it herself," the doctor said. "Do you know her?"

"Yeah. Her name's Wanda Jean Reider, from out in the Run."

"That explains why I don't recognize her," the doctor said. "I try to avoid that whole bunch out there. Nothing good has ever come out of Dog's Run, and I don't expect it ever will."

Dog's Run

Chapter 2

Alice Reider lived in a four-room, tarpaper-covered house that hadn't seen any maintenance since the day her husband Raymond and his brother Luther had slapped it together. And with Raymond long dead in a head-on wreck on Alexis Road when her youngest, David Lee, was just a baby, and Luther in the state pen over in Mansfield, there was little chance anybody would ever do much to keep it standing upright.

An old, yellow dog growled menacingly when Lester walked past it, but didn't seem to have the energy or the willpower to do much else. The chief mounted the two steps to the porch, feeling them sag underneath his weight. He raised his hand to knock on the screen door, but pulled it back when the door opened and a small boy with a dirty face looked up at him.

"What you want?" the boy demanded.

"Is your momma here?" Lester asked.

"She's in the outhouse. I asked you what you want?"

"David Lee, you mind your manners!" said a slightly older girl as she pushed her brother aside. "Don't pay him no mind. He's a moron."

"I ain't no moron," David Lee said, "I'm the man of the house, so you just get back to ironing and I'll handle this."

"You are too a moron. Now shush your mouth and get out of the way."

Before the argument could continue, a door slammed somewhere in the back of the house and a woman's voice said, "Whatever you two are arguing about, stop it!"

"Ma, the law's here," said David Lee, "and Penny called me a moron again."

"Both of you hush up," said the woman as she came into view. Seeing the Police Chief standing on her porch, she shooed them away and asked, "What is it now? If Paulie's been stealin' or fightin' in school again, you can just keep him!"

"No, ma'am." Lester told her, "It's about Wanda Jean."

The woman's face drew up and she said, "Please tell me she ain't dead."

"I wish I could," he said. "Two boys found her laying in the water at the bottom of the Run this morning."

Alice Reider had had a hard life since the day she was born. The oldest of nine children born to a part-time coal miner and full-time drunk named Wiley Marcrum and his wife Reba. It had fallen on Alice to help her mother with the housework and childrearing almost from the time Alice was old enough to walk. And when her mother had died of consumption when Alice was just fourteen, Wiley had told her there were other duties that she would now have to perform in her mother's place. When handsome Raymond Reider had come along just over a year later, she had jumped at the chance to escape life in the little cabin perched on the side of Badger Holler and run off, never to return.

Life with Raymond had been no walk in the park either, but in spite of his many shortcomings, he never beat her and he usually managed to hold down a job. They had left the West Virginia coal mines and moved north, following the migration of so many from their region seeking better opportunities. They hadn't lived high on the hog, but there was usually enough food to go around and she was able to make clothes for the family on the new Singer treadle sewing machine Raymond had bought her their first Christmas together.

If Raymond had one fault that stood out from all others, it was his penchant for hard liquor. But at least, unlike her father, Raymond had been a happy drunk who loved music and even picked up a dollar or two playing his guitar in the local gin mills from time to time. Alice knew that there were women in those places who would let a handsome guitar picker know that they were available, and she had no doubt that more than a few of them had found their way into the back seat of Raymond's old jalopy. But he always came home to her, and Alice figured that if someone else was spreading their legs for him, maybe she wouldn't have to.

After Raymond died drunk in that car wreck, his younger brother Luther had just expected to assume his role. Since somebody had to earn enough money to pay the bills and feed her young'uns, Alice had just gone along since it seemed like the easiest thing to do. Unfortunately, while Luther was as good looking and charming as his older brother had been, he shared the same love of whiskey but without Raymond's good nature. When he had a few drinks in him, he wanted to fight, and if he couldn't win with his fists or his feet or his teeth, he didn't hesitate to reach for the little top break, nickel plated Iver Johnson .32 he always carried in his hip pocket.

Most times just showing the gun was enough to end a fight. But one night three years ago, Luther had run into a man named Jerry Lee Cousino, who had spent three years fighting the Germans in General Patton's army, and no hillbilly with a little popgun was going to scare him. When the smoke cleared, Jerry Lee lay dead on the barroom floor and Luther Reider soon found himself in shackles and on the way to a lifetime behind bars.

Since then, Alice had scraped by just to keep her kids fed and a roof over their heads. She had no education and could not read or write, but she wasn't afraid of hard work and by taking in ironing, mending, clothing alterations, and cleaning houses for the rich ladies of Elmhurst, and with a little help from the Relief people now and then, they had survived.

Alice's children had not helped either. She loved David Lee just like she did all of her children but Penny was right, David Lee was a retard and was never going to amount to anything. Eight years old and he still peed the bed most nights and was incapable of performing even the easiest chores without breaking something or hurting himself. Why just last winter he had lost two toes on his left foot when he tried to split some firewood!

Penny was ten and she tried, God bless her. She was bossy and headstrong, but Alice didn't know what she'd do without Penny. When she worked long hours cleaning those rich ladies' houses and then walked the five miles home in the blistering summer sun or the cold winter wind, Penny always had leftovers waiting for her, warming on the stove. Alice might have to threaten her with a switching from time to time for her stubbornness, but if a job needed doin', Penny never hesitated to try her best. Alice still remembered waking early one winter's morning three years earlier to find Penny scrubbing David Lee's urine soaked sheets. And Penny was smart as a whip, too! She was always bringin' papers home from school with a gold star on them. Alice might not know what was on those papers, but she knew the gold stars meant her baby had done good.

There had been two little ones that never made it through their first year, between Penny and her next oldest, Paulie, but Alice tried not to think much about them. What's done is done and the good Lord has his reasons for everything. Alice had to believe that.

At sixteen, Paulie was headed for big trouble and Alice knew it. She just didn't know how to put a stop to it. He had already been in trouble with the law for stealing candy and soda pops from Reynolds' Store, and just a month earlier Chief Smeal had kept him in a cell overnight after Paulie pulled a switchblade knife on another kid during a fight.

Alice worried that Paulie was going to follow his Uncle Luther to the pen before too long, unless old Judge Hathaway did the same thing that he did with her oldest, John, and gave him his choice of reform school or the Army. At first that had seemed like a blessing, but last summer an Army sergeant had handed her a folded flag and a bugler played a mournful song as John's casket was lowered into the ground at Memorial Park. Alice had never heard of a place called Inchon, let alone Korea, but she knew that a far off war in that place had claimed another of her children.

And then there was Wanda Jean. Of all her children, Alice had loved Wanda Jean the most, and she had given her the most sleepless nights. The day she was born, Alice knew that Wanda Jean was something special, with her big, green eyes and her hair the color of ripe corn and that beautiful, flawless skin. Most babies came out all red and wrinkly, cryin' and ugly, if she had to admit it. But not Wanda Jean. She had looked more like a porcelain doll than a baby.

Wanda Jean had been beautiful as a baby, and she grew more beautiful every day of her life. She developed at an early age and Alice had tried, Lord how she had tried. She knew about men, starting with her own father, and then Raymond and Luther, and a few others that had come sniffing around, back before work and worry had taken their toll. She watched Wanda Jean like a hawk, afraid she'd come home pregnant some day, with some big, old, bucktoothed hillbilly boy standing there grinning behind her. But it hadn't happened.

Sure, the young bucks of Dog's Run had all given it a try, as did a lot of their fathers, but Wanda Jean wasn't having any of that nonsense. She seemed to realize early on that what she had was a treasure, and you don't sell treasure away cheaply. If Wanda Jean was going to give anybody a taste of honey, they were going to pay well for it.

Dog's Run

The first had been Mr. Bigelow, the principal at the high school, who had complained that Wanda Jean showed no interest in her studies and always seemed to have her head in the clouds. He had called Wanda Jean into his office one afternoon during her second year at the school to lay down the law to her. Alice didn't know what happened behind that closed office door, but Wanda Jean never seemed to do a lick of homework for the next two years and she still graduated with the rest of her class. And that lesson had taught her a lot more than was ever in those schoolbooks.

Oh, she pretended not to know, but Alice knew all right. She knew when her daughter started staying out late, sometimes all night long, and coming home wearing some new piece of jewelry, or when a wad of folded bills mysteriously appeared in the Maxwell House coffee can where Alice kept the bill paying money. She knew when she'd hear the sound of a car driving away late at night, just before Wanda Jean walked up on the porch. But they were never the beat up, old pickup trucks and rusted out cars of Dog's Run that Alice heard late at night. They were new Chryslers and Studebakers and Hudsons, and the men that drove them weren't factory workers with grease under their fingernails or the moonshiners of Dog's Run. No, these men owned shops and practiced law and sat on the City Council. Alice knew this because she cleaned their homes while those men's wives played bridge and sipped iced tea and smoked cigarettes in fancy holders that they held in their gloved hands.

Alice knew she should have tried to steer Wanda Jean in another direction. But what other direction was there for a poor girl from Dog's Run? To end up old before her time, tits sagging under a shapeless housedress and hands red and raw from scrubbing clothes on a washboard? And to be honest with herself, was what Wanda Jean was doing really any different than what Alice herself had done to escape Wiley Marcrum's cabin back in Badger Holler? Wanda Jean was just selling herself to a better class of men for a higher price.

And now here was Chief Smeal standing on her porch with sweat stains in the armpits of his khaki uniform shirt, telling her that Wanda Jean was dead at just nineteen. She knew there was no way to deliver that kind of news easy because it wasn't an easy message he had brung her. But it didn't matter what he said or how he said it after he told her that her baby girl, her precious Wanda Jean, was gone, because the rest of his words were drowned out by a sorrowful wail that could be heard across much of Dog's Run.

Chapter 3

"Is it true her head was bashed in, Daddy?"

"Hush, Loretta. What kind of talk is that for a ten year old girl? And at the supper table no less!"

"Irene said that her brother Donald drove the hearse to Toledo Hospital and he told her that half that girl's head was bashed in. Was it, Daddy?"

"Enough!" Elizabeth Smeal said. "I won't have that kind of talk at my table."

"I think it was a bear or a puma that killed her," eight year old Woodrow said.

"That's dumb, there ain't no bears around here. I bet it was a hobo."

"Now both you kids stop it right this minute," Elizabeth warned. "And Loretta, ain't is not a word. Use proper English at the table, please."

"Anyway, Irene said…," Loretta started, but stopped when she saw her mother glare at her.

"This fried chicken is delicious, Sis," Robert Tucker said, trying to steer the conversation in a different direction. "You really outdid yourself again."

"Why, thank you, Bobby," Elizabeth said to her twin brother. "It's nice to know that somebody at this table appreciates all my hard work. Although, I guess it doesn't hold a candle to the meatloaf sandwiches at the Sunshine Café. Or maybe it's something more than the meatloaf that keeps a man going back there day after day."

"Now don't you go getting all riled up at me," Lester Smeal said. "You know that I don't always have time to come home for lunch. Besides, even if I had time, your special dessert might keep me busy all afternoon."

"Lester!" Elizabeth admonished, her cheeks coloring.

Loretta nudged her brother with an elbow, then leaned in to say in a loud whisper, "They're talking about making intercourse!"

"Loretta," Elizabeth shrieked. "Where did you ever hear that word? I'm going to take you upstairs and wash your mouth out with soap!"

Lester and Robert laughed loudly, only adding to Elizabeth's mortification.

"Hush, you two," she ordered. "It's no wonder my children are growing up wild as Indians and with mouths like sailors with the example you two set. Now finish your supper so I can serve dessert."

At the word dessert, everybody in the room burst out laughing except for Elizabeth, who hurried into the kitchen, but not before Lester caught a slight up-tilt to the corners of her mouth.

***

"So what can you tell me about this dead girl?" Robert asked when dinner was over and they had stepped out onto the back porch to smoke.

"Her name was Wanda Jean Reider, from out in the Run. You might have seen her around town. Pretty little thing, she could sure turn heads. Damn shame, whatever happened to her."

"Do you think somebody killed her?"

"It sure looked that way to me," Lester said. "Doc Crowther said she had broken ribs and internal injuries. It wasn't a pretty sight."

"Any suspects yet?"

"Not yet, Bob. Now stop grilling me. Maybe the newspaper editor doesn't take an evening off, but I'm off duty." He belched, then said, "As soon as I know anything, you will, too."

The screen door opened and Elizabeth joined them, taking the cigarette from her husband's fingers and putting it to her lips. "Lord, I have no idea what's going to become of that girl," she said, exhaling smoke and handing the cigarette back to Lester. "She has no shame. And where does a girl her age even learn about *that*?"

"Well, maybe you should be a little quieter when you serve Les here his *dessert*," Robert suggested.

"Robert Eugene Tucker! Maybe I need to wash *your* mouth out with soap!"

Robert laughed and dodged her playful slap, and finally Elizabeth gave up and joined in the laughter too.

"So what are you two out here talking about, besides intercourse?"

"Actually, Les was telling me how good the meat loaf sandwiches are at the café."

"Shut up, you home wrecker," Lester said. "I've got enough to deal with without hearing from the peanut gallery."

"Speaking of home wreckers, was it really that Wanda Jean Reider those boys found out in the Run today?"

"Yeah. How did you know who she was?"

"Because the telephone was ringing off the hook all afternoon from people who had heard the rumor and were calling to see what I could tell them."

"You see, we don't need your newspaper," Lester said to Robert. "If folks want to know what's happening here in Elmhurst, all they have to do is call my wife."

"Hush, Lester, you know I never tell anybody anything about your work. And Lord knows I sure get asked often enough."

"I know that, Sugar. I was just teasing you," Lester said. "I couldn't ask for a better wife or confidant. Besides, the desserts are pretty damn good around here, too."

She laughed and kicked at him, saying, "Enough already!"

"What did you mean when you called that girl a home wrecker?" Robert asked his sister.

Elizabeth glanced toward the screen door to be sure there were no little ears eavesdropping, then said, "Wanda Jean Reider was a trollop! Last winter Abigail Lyons caught her and Thomas in a compromising position in the back of the store."

"Well, I guess that explains why Tom bought Abby that new Cadillac for Christmas," Lester said.

"And he's not the only one," Elizabeth said, looking through the screen to be sure the kids were still in the living room watching the new television Lester had bought. "I've heard plenty of stories, off the record."

"You're standing here sharing all the local gossip with the High Sheriff and the newspaper publisher and you want to talk off the record?" Robert teased.

Elizabeth stuck her tongue out at him, then said, "I know that she was supposedly *working* at Wilson's Department Store for a month, until Virginia went in unexpectedly one evening when Randal was supposedly staying late to balance the books. The next day Wanda Jean was gone and a week later the Wilson's went to Florida for a week. And that's not all. Edgar Sikes was seen giving her rides out by the quarry, and Rachel Maguire swears she got up to let the dog out and saw Wanda Jean sneaking out the back door of the Smith's place late one night while Betty was in the hospital with female trouble."

"Looks to me like you've got a long list of suspects to work through," Robert told Lester, just as the telephone began ringing inside the house.

"I swear, if that's another nosy woman looking for gossip, I'm just going to hang up on her!" Elizabeth said over her shoulder as she went to answer the phone.

But it wasn't a woman calling to hear the latest juicy tidbit, it was Harold Cote, Lester's night jailer, calling to say that his two patrolmen had trouble.

Chapter 4

"What do you mean they took your badges and guns?" Lester shouted at the two chagrined young officers standing before him in his office.

"There were a dozen of them and only two of us," Billy Shaver said by way of explanation. "There was nothing we could do, Chief."

"There were a dozen of them? That's twelve, Billy. You each had six shots in your pistols, I don't see what the problem was."

"Actually, sir," the other officer, Ted DuPont, started to say, then thought better of it.

"Actually *what*, Ted?"

"Nothing, sir."

"Nothing my ass, Ted. Actually what?"

"I was just gonna say that actually, they were revolvers."

"Revolvers? What the hell are you talking about?"

"Our weapons, sir. They're Smith & Wesson revolvers. A pistol is…."

"I know the difference between a pistol and an revolver, you lunkhead! I don't care if you two were carrying howitzers. How the hell did you let a bunch of drunk hillbillies get them away from you?"

"I'm not really sure," Billy admitted. "We got a call about a fight at the Cherokee Tavern and when we got there I guess they decided to stop fighting with each other and take it out on us instead. Before we knew it they had crowded in all around us and the next thing we knew they took away our weapons and badges. They gave them to Ernie behind the bar and everybody was laughing at us. They said if we came back tomorrow and apologized for breaking up their fun they might give them back."

"Jesus H. Christ! I could do better with two circus clowns with seeing eye dogs," Lester said as he crossed to the gun rack on the other side of the office. He took down an old sawed off Greener double-barreled 10 gauge shotgun and pulled a drawer open to retrieve a box of double ought shells.

"Come with me. Just keep your mouths shut and observe. I'll show you how to be a cop!"

Robert rode in the front seat beside Lester, and the two officers followed in another car. Knowing his best friend and brother-in-law well enough to know when to remain silent, the newspaperman was quiet on the ride to the tavern. Parking beside the front door, they stepped out and the smell of stale beer carried on the waves of loud music wafted out the open door and windows.

"Here boys, stick these in your ears," Lester said, holding out a handful of cotton balls, then heading for the tavern.

The barroom was full of rowdy, drinking men and coarse women, and nobody noticed the police chief and the other three men walk through the door. At least not until Lester reached down and unplugged the Seeburg jukebox and the sound of some lonely hillbilly singing about having the *Lovesick Blues* suddenly stopped.

There were several shouts asking what happened to the music, but things started to quiet down when the crowd saw Police Chief Lester Smeal standing next to the jukebox, cradling the Greener in the crook of his right arm. A few people grumbled loudly, but Lester ignored them as he shifted the shotgun to his hands, holding it with the barrels pointed toward the floor.

He held the shotgun in both hands and looked at it like he had never seen a firearm before, then he pushed the lever on the top and broke the gun open.

"What's he gonna do, Henry?" a woman asked, but her common-law husband ignored her and kept his eyes on Chief Smeal as he plucked a fat paper wrapped shell out of one barrel and held it up to the light, studying it. He held the shell next to his ear and shook it for a second, then replaced it and took the shell out of the second barrel and repeated the process.

The barroom, which had been raucous just moments before, was now as quiet as a tomb. Everybody in the area knew that Chief Smeal was not a man to trifle with. He had won a Silver Star at Okinawa after single handedly killing most of a platoon of Japs that had attacked his position. Then a few days later he had charged an enemy machine gun nest that had his squad pinned down, dropping his Tommy gun when his ammunition ran out and finishing the job with his .45 pistol and a pocketful of hand grenades. There were a number of veterans in the

Dog's Run

Cherokee Tavern that night, but none of them had ever faced a Kraut or Jap that scared them as much as the sight of the police chief and his shotgun did that night.

Lester reloaded the shotgun and closed the breech, then stared at it in wonder for a second before holding it up next to his ear and pulling one of the hammers back, which made an audible click in the silent room. He pulled back the second hammer with another click, then dropped the shotgun down to his hip, the lethal barrels pointed at the crowd. He held the Greener with one hand while he fished his gold pocket watch out with the other and opened it. Then, with a voice that was as quiet and composed as if he were discussing the weather or if the perch were biting out on Lake Erie, he said, "It's five minutes to nine and this place is now officially closed. At nine o'clock I'm going to consider anybody still here a burglar and kill them."

Four minutes later the only evidence of the crowd inside the tavern was the echo of engines speeding away and dust still flying in the parking lot.

"I believe you have something that belongs to these men," Lester told Ernie Hamilton, who stood behind the bar.

"You can't come in here running my customers away like that," Ernie said angrily. "Those boys was just having fun. Nobody got hurt."

"I said I believe you have something that belongs to these officers," Lester repeated.

Ernie reached under the bar and sat two Smith & Wesson Model 10 Military & Police revolvers and two silver badges on the top.

"Boys, get your badges and weapons," Lester ordered.

"What the hell am I supposed to do for the next four hours with no customers?" Ernie demanded to know, "Twiddle my thumbs?"

Lester laid the barrels over the top of the bar and Ernie yelped and jumped backward. Lester ignored him and walked the length of the bar, knocking over bottles and glasses and sweeping them to the floor with the shotgun's barrels. Ernie shouted in outrage, but stopped when the police chief reached the end of the bar and walked back up to him.

"You thought embarrassing my men here and causing me to leave my family to come out here was pretty funny, huh, Ernie?"

"Hey, I didn't do a damn thing!"

"You had their guns and badges, that sort of makes you just as guilty in my mind," Lester told him.

"It was all in fun, man! You got no right to run off my customers and break all that glass like you did."

"You know, I look the other way when you let things get out of hand around here, Ernie. I know these hillbillies and rednecks need a place to blow off steam. And I know a lot of that hooch you sell didn't come in those bottles, it came from a still down in the Run. And don't think I don't know about those two whores you let work out of that room in the back. A man's got to get his ashes hauled now and then and I don't see no harm in it. But when you cross the line, there's a price to pay."

Lester laid the shotgun's barrels across the bar again and said, "Cover your ears and step aside, Ernie."

"You can't…"

"Step aside," Lester said again, then pulled the shotgun to his shoulder. The bartender cursed and moved away, and Lester pulled the trigger on one barrel, the heavy buckshot shattering the large mirror behind the bar, along with a couple dozen bottles of assorted liquor that had been on a shelf in front of the mirror.

"Shit!" Ernie shouted, but nobody could hear him over the ringing in their ears. Lester stepped back, then turned to the brand new Seeburg jukebox, Ernie's pride and joy, and a great source of revenue for the tavern.

"No, please don't!" Ernie pleaded, but Lester ignored him, emptying the second barrel into the machine. Pieces of the jukebox flew in all directions and Ernie howled in outrage. Lester broke the shotgun open again and dropped the two spent shells onto the littered floor.

"Since you don't have any customers, why don't you spend some time cleaning this place up, Ernie? It's a mess!"

Even with the cotton balls in their ears to dull the gunshots, they were back to town before either of them could hear well enough to talk. Lester parked the Buick in the driveway and Robert said, "One thing about you, Les, there's never a dull moment."

The police chief grinned, his white teeth showing in the light from the instrument panel. "It's like trying to put new shoes on a mule, Bob. The first thing you need to do is hit it between the eyes with a two by four to get its attention. After that, the rest is easy."

They stepped out of the car and Lester asked, "You coming in?"

"No thanks, I've still got work to do. Like you said, I'm never off duty."

Lester laughed, then said, "In that case, I think I'll go see if that sister of yours feels like giving me any dessert."

Chapter 5

Sweating and breathing heavily, Lester rolled off his wife and reached for her hand in the dark.

"Fifteen years and you still take my breath away, Lizzie."

"Maybe you're just out of shape from all those meatloaf sandwiches you've been eating," Elizabeth teased.

"Meatloaf's okay, but when a man's got beefsteak at home there's no comparison, baby."

Elizabeth snuggled up to him and laid her head on his chest, smiling, and said, "Well you better not be sampling any of that meatloaf if you know what's good for you, buster!"

Lester said, "You don't need to worry yourself about that. Like I said, when a man's got beefsteak at home…"

"So now you're comparing me to a cow?" Elizabeth teased.

Lester grabbed her breast and squeezed gently, "I've been pulling on these things for a long time now and never got much milk."

"Stop it! Are you ever going to grow up, Lester Smeal?"

"I surely hope not," he told her.

"It's no wonder I never get anything accomplished around here," Elizabeth said, "what with two children and you to chase after."

"And you love every minute of it."

She rolled over onto his chest and kissed him. "Yes I do. I couldn't imagine a better life than what we have together. And I thank the Good Lord every day for it."

They lay quietly for a few moments and then Elizabeth said, "I worry about Bobby, though. I wish he'd find somebody. It's been three years."

"You want to talk about your brother *now*?"

"He seems so lonely all the time. All he does is work and take care of Mama."

"Robert's married to that newspaper of his," Lester told her. "He don't have time for a woman in his life right now."

"Maybe if he had somebody to go home to besides Mama he wouldn't work so much."

"Yeah, or maybe if he had somebody to go home to they'd up and leave him just like Shirley did because he'd still be working around the clock."

"Shirley!" Elizabeth said the name with scorn. "That woman had a heart as cold as ice. I never did like her!"

"You liked her just fine until she left your brother."

"And broke his heart!"

"Don't you be fretting about Robert," Lester told her. "For all we know he's got a secret love life we don't know anything about. He might be with his inamorata right this minute."

"Inamorata? Where in the world did you ever learn a word like that, Lester Smeal?"

"Hey, I'm not just some hick from the Run, you know. I do the crossword puzzle in the *Blade* every Sunday!"

"Well ain't you just mister fancy pants? And wait until I tell Robert you're reading that big city newspaper!"

"Robert reads it, too. He needs to keep up with world events. And as for fancy pants, what was that getup I saw in your bottom dresser drawer? Where in the world did you get that?"

"You were snooping!" Elizabeth said, slapping his chest in mock outrage. "That's a surprise for your birthday."

"That's six weeks away. How about a little sample in the meantime?"

"You just *had* a sample."

"Well, I'm getting' old and forgetful. Remind me."

"Am I that easy to forget?" she asked, positioning herself over him and gently easing down.

"Oh yes, I remember now," he said. "Nice."

"Very nice," Elizabeth said, picking up the pace. "Very, very nice!"

***

A mile away, Robert Tucker cursed as he sweated over his "inamorata."

"Come on, you stubborn bitch," Robert said through gritted teeth. "Just once I wish you'd cooperate and make my life easy."

The worn out old Linotype machine refused his best efforts to free the stuck matrix and Robert finally gave up and walked across the pressroom to where Scotty, the cranky jack of all trades, was loading newsprint onto the press bed.

"I can't move it," Robert said in frustration and Scotty frowned at him.

"Course you can't. You don't know how to sweet talk Old Betsy. She's like a woman. She needs caressed, not manhandled. I'll get it. If you'd just get back upstairs and park your ass at your desk and do your job and leave me alone to do mine, we'd both be a lot better off."

Robert knew better than to argue with the crusty old man who had come with the *Citizen-Press* and outlasted the last three publishers. And as much as his ego disagreed, he knew that Scotty was right. Robert was a much better wordsmith than he was a typesetter or pressman. But he also believed that one key to success in any business was to be intimately familiar with every aspect of the operation so that he wasn't dependent on anyone if things went to hell in a hand basket.

"Just show me one more time," he asked.

Scotty glared at him, but left the press and walked to the typesetting machine. He fiddled with things for a minute, pulled a rag out of his back pocket and wiped something, then held the rag under Robert's face.

"See that? Just like last time! Too much oil. It collects dust and things gum up in the matrix path. Then the magazine won't release it and this is what you get. A machine is like a woman, Bobby. They need a little lubrication to get them going, but too much just makes a big mess."

Robert didn't consider himself a prig, but when he first acquired the newspaper, he'd been put off by Scotty's insistence on addressing him not only by his first name but by the more familiar term that no one but his sister and mother ever used. Then he learned that Scotty had routinely called his predecessors "Asshole" and "Shit-For-Brains" respectively, and felt better about it. Not that Scotty spared him any grief. Like many young officers during the war, Robert had grown a mustache. The first time they met, Scotty had said, "I don't understand why a man'd cultivate something on his face that grows wild on his ass." Robert had shaved the mustache off the next day.

Still, newspaper publishers were a dime a dozen, but good pressmen who showed up sober for every shift were scarce as hens' teeth. Nobody knew the intricate workings of the paper's ancient machinery better than Scotty did, and Robert suspected that if he ever walked off the job, the equipment would just shut down in protest.

"Get your shirt sleeves rolled up and clean this thing up," Scotty said, handing him the rag and a half quart can of gasoline. "You messed it up, not me."

"Thanks, Scotty," Robert said, taking the rag and can from him. "I was just trying to help."

"If you want to help me, the best way is, don't help," Scotty said, shaking his head in disgust as he returned to the press and Robert poured gas onto the rag and started cleaning the Linotype.

All Robert had ever wanted to do in his life was to own a newspaper. He had started out as a printer's devil, cleaning the pressroom at the old *News Messenger*, working his way up to setting type by hand for advertising flyers and handbills. During high school he had covered local sports and school activities, earning a regular byline and enough money to keep himself in Brylcreem and gasoline in his old Model A Ford. During college, at Toledo University, he had made a name for himself covering everything from sports to school politics for both the college newspaper and the *Toledo Blade*. Robert knew he could have had a secure position as a reporter for the *Blade* after college, but he realized that he would never be satisfied working for someone else, even on a fine newspaper like the *Blade*. He longed to see his own name listed as publisher on a newspaper's masthead.

When the war came, Robert had volunteered just like almost every young man he knew, and though his background had earned him an offer to work for the War Department's *Stars and Stripes* newspaper, he had opted instead for an assignment with an infantry unit. On his last day at home before shipping overseas, he had been the best man at the wedding of his twin sister, Elizabeth, and his best friend, Lester Smeal.

As it turned out, Robert had never made it to his assigned unit. A colonel at an office somewhere at Fort Dix, New Jersey had come across his records and ordered him to take over the post newspaper for the busy training base. Eager to get into the fighting, the newly minted Second Lieutenant chafed at the assignment, but his protests fell on deaf ears and he spent the next four years writing puff pieces about training exercises and which officers were holding a reception at their home and which were getting promoted.

Meanwhile, Lester Smeal was killing Japs and earning glory in the jungles of the South Pacific. While Robert was proud of his friend and never resented his hero status, he always felt that he, himself, had never been tested and been allowed to prove himself. He often wondered if, faced with some of the dangers Lester had been in, he would have handled himself as well.

But the war was over, and after going back to the *Blade* for a year, only to be reminded of how much he wanted to run his own paper, he spent the next two years getting his feet wet in small town newspapering at the *Patriot* in Maumee and the *Lake Erie Review* out in Point Place. Then Robert had come home to Elmhurst and purchased the *Citizen-Press* and had never been happier. Yes, the equipment was worn out and he was working long hours six days a week, but he didn't care. In fact, he was so happy that he had not even realized he was whistling a cheery tune until Scotty yelled across the room, "Will you quit that goddamned noise! What the hell do you think you are, a damned tweety bird?"

Dog's Run

Chapter 6

Worry and speculation about Wanda Jean Reider's death was running rampant across Elmhurst and out in Dog's Run. Some claimed a homicidal maniac was running loose in the deep ravine that separated the cemetery from the down and out cabins and shanties of the Run. Others were just as sure that Wanda Jean had stumbled upon a hobo camp somewhere deep in the ravine and been ravished and killed for her trespass. And there were plenty of whispers about how it didn't matter who killed Wanda Jean, it was bound to happen with the way she lived her life. No names were ever mentioned, but everybody seemed to know of at least one married admirer, from the good side of town, who had shown an untoward interest in the beautiful, young woman.

Mothers were keeping their children indoors, and in the nice homes of Elmhurst, men dug long forgotten Lugers and Army-issued Colt .45s that had come home from the war out of footlockers and steamer trunks. Guns were always kept handy in the Run, propped behind a door or hanging on a peg on the wall. But after Wanda Jean's death, the men of the Run made sure they were loaded and ready for action, just in case whoever had killed one of their own came back for someone else.

But all of that changed with the news that Wanda Jean had committed suicide. A young man hitchhiking on Alexis Road had ducked into the woods near the bridge to empty his bladder and spotted a mongrel dog chewing on something. Shooing the dog away, he found that it was a white purse. In spite of the damage done by the dog, he realized the purse was not some castoff piece of trash, but relatively new and from the look of it, expensive. He opened the clasp and found a hairbrush, lipstick, a small mascara case with a mirrored lid, a fountain pen and a note that read:

I'm sorry but I can't do this anymore. Mama, I'm sorry to let you down, but I'm going to a better place and we'll all be together again soon, I promise. Kiss the little ones for me and tell them I love them.

Wanda Jean Reider

"Well, that shines a new light on things, don't it?" Robert said as he read the note a second time. "How do you think she did it?"

"Based on what Doc Crowther said about her injuries and what I saw of her, I think she jumped off the bridge. The water wasn't deep enough to drown her, but I think she was hoping the fall would kill her."

"But she was found a ways from the bridge, wasn't she?"

"Yeah, I went back and looked around and found some blood on the rocks under the bridge. It's about a thirty foot drop and I think she probably knocked herself out and laid there for a while, then came to and wandered off to where those boys found her, where she collapsed and died."

Robert handed the note back to Lester, who said, "Damn shame, a pretty young thing like that. Can you get this here in tomorrow's paper? People are scared to death and I'm afraid somebody is gonna shoot their kid coming sneaking home late at night. Or else go on a witch hunt and string up some poor hobo they find passing through town."

"I'll have it on the front page," Robert promised. "I wonder what makes a pretty girl like that feel like she has to take her own life?"

Lester shrugged. "I gave up trying to figure out what makes somebody tick the day I pinned this badge on."

"Yeah, but still…… there might be a story in all this."

"Now you hold on there," Lester said, raising a warning finger. "I don't hold much truck with gossip, but I've heard some of those rumors Lizzie was talking about last night myself, and probably more she don't know about. I don't like to talk bad about the dead, but that girl had a reputation and dragging it out in the public is just gonna embarrass her mama and whoever she might have been messin' around with."

"You calling me a muckraker, Les?" Robert asked with a smile.

"I'm just saying that some things are better left unsaid, that's all. And keep in mind, son, some of those men Wanda Jean was whispered to be messin' with run the businesses that advertise in your newspaper."

"There are a lot of newspapermen who'd take offense to that," Robert said. "They'd tell you that the public's right to know isn't for sale."

"To know what, Bob? That some little split-tail couldn't keep her legs together? I'm not tellin' you how to run your business, I'm just saying that sometimes discretion is the better part of valor."

"Why, Lester Smeal, you're becoming downright profound in your old age!"

"Old age?" Lester said, "I'm just a kid at heart."

"Uh huh. Maybe in your heart, but your ass might disagree."

"And with that," Lester said, standing up, "I'm going to drag my ancient ass back to work. I'm gonna go have a talk with Wanda Jean's mama, give her this news. I've got a feeling it's gonna hurt her even worse than finding out her little girl was dead in the first place."

"I don't envy you," Robert told him.

"Well, I guess this job can't be all about standing around looking handsome and shooting up jukeboxes, can it? You going to the funeral tomorrow morning?"

"I'll be there," Robert said.

***

Chief Smeal had been right. The news that her little girl had killed herself broke Alice Reider's heart even more than losing her in the first place. Alice had never had a day of schooling and she couldn't read or write a lick, so she had to have the chief read Wanda Jean's note to her twice, then she sat back in the rickety, wooden chair at her kitchen table and closed her eyes.

"You gonna be okay, Miz Reider?"

"I 'spect so, sooner or later. It's just hard to believe my baby'd come to this."

Life had taught Alice that tears shed were a waste of time. They didn't fix a thing and only left her feeling wrung out and worse. But she couldn't stop a single, lonely teardrop from rolling down her cheek. Apparently realizing that she had allowed her weakness to show, Alice abruptly wiped the tear away and stood up.

"I appreciate you bringin' this to me, Chief Smeal. Now, if you'll excuse me, I got chores to do."

"Yes, ma'am," Lester paused in the doorway. "Do you need a ride into town to the funeral home? Or to the funeral tomorrow?"

"I walk to town every day to work and back home again every night. I 'spect I can find my way. But I thank you for your kindness."

Lester didn't know what else he could say to the proud woman, so he just nodded and walked back to his car.

Once the chief's car had left, Alice walked into the bedroom she shared with her girls and got on her knees next to Wanda's narrow bed.

Reaching underneath, she pulled out the cheap, yellow suitcase with the red and blue stripes on it that Wanda had always told her was her hope chest. Everybody in the family had been forbidden to look inside, and when Alice set it on the bed and tried to open it she discovered that the brass locks would not release.

Going back to where she had left Wanda's purse on the kitchen table, she poured the contents out and sorted through them. Not finding what she was looking for, she unzipped a compartment on the inside and felt inside. It contained a matchbook from the Pine Cone Motel, three Trojan rubbers, and a fountain pen. Scooping everything back into the purse, Alice returned to the bedroom and opened the top drawer of the flimsy dresser, pawing through her daughter's silk underwear, nylon hose, and other clothing that Alice knew no decent woman would wear. Not thinking about that, she felt around until she came upon a matchbox secured by a rubber band. Inside were two gold rings, a locket, and a small brass key.

When she unlocked the suitcase, Alice found a few fancy clothes she had never seen her daughter wear, several pieces of jewelry that Alice suspected were worth more than she earned in a month, and a cardboard cigar box held shut by three wide rubber bands. Alice pulled the rubber bands off and opened the box, then sat down on the bed and put her hand to her mouth. "Oh my Lord, child! What did you do?"

Alice may not have known how to read and write, but she had learned to count long ago, when she discovered that even though they were rich, some of the women she worked for wouldn't hesitate to shortchange her on her hours worked or on the two pieces for a penny she earned for doing their ironing.

She counted the money once, then twice, then sat back in shocked disbelief. $11,695. That was more money than Alice had ever seen in her life. More than she could earn in a lifetime of scrubbing floors and ironing and mending some rich ladies' clothing. More than a working man made in three or four years.

Even though she was alone in the house, Alice suddenly felt frightened that someone would show up and demand she surrender the money, which Wanda Jean surely must have come by illegally. Alice needed to think. She put the money back in the manila envelope she had found it in, then looked around the room. Seeing no place that looked safe, she finally just slipped the envelope deep under her own mattress before going back to the box. The only other things in the box were four small books that she recognized as her Wanda Jean's diaries. Even though she couldn't read, she opened the first one, feeling comforted by seeing her daughter's neat handwriting on the page.

Chapter 7

Citizen-Press - June 6, 1951

Death Ruled Suicide

Elmhurst Police Chief Lester Smeal has reported that the death of Wanda Jean Reider, age 19, of Elmhurst, has been determined to be a suicide. Miss Reader, a 1949 graduate of Elmhurst High School, was found in a ravine off Alexis Road Monday afternoon by two boys hunting squirrels. Chief Smeal said evidence at the scene and his investigation have revealed that the victim jumped off the bridge over the ravine, known locally as Dog's Run, then made her way a short distance up the ravine before succumbing to her injuries. Miss Reider is survived by her mother, Alice Reider, brothers Paul and David, and sister Penny. She was preceded in death by her father, Raymond Reider, brother John, and two infant siblings. She was loved by many and her loss is deeply mourned. Funeral services will be held at 10 a.m. Wednesday at Duncan Funeral home, with burial to follow at Memorial Park Cemetery.

***

Funerals of those from the Run were seldom well attended, and almost never by folks from town. But a small crowd of mostly women turned out to see Wanda Jean Reider laid to rest. Looking around him, Robert wondered why so many people from Elmhurst wanted to see a poor, white trash girl from Dog's Run being buried. Sure, Alice Reider had done housework or ironing for many of them and they could explain away their presence by claiming that they were there to give comfort and support to a valued employee. But he suspected that for many of them, it was to be sure the she-devil really was under the ground and no longer a threat.

After the casket was lowered into the ground and the last of the mourners left, some paused to pat Alice on the shoulder and told her to take a couple of days off to be with her family, those floors could wait a while to get scrubbed. Alice stood alone with her younger daughter as the boys wandered off someplace, probably to admire the big, black limousine Duncan's Funeral Home had carried them to the cemetery in after the funeral service.

Alice held Penny's hand and looked down into the grave for a long time, not ready to lose this final connection with her daughter. Finally she broke the silence, "Penny, I want you to promise me somethin.'"

"Yes, ma'am?"

"Your sister was my baby, but she made some bad mistakes and that's what brought her here. I want you to promise me that you won't let yourself be lured away like Wanda Jean did."

Penny wasn't sure what her Mama meant but she knew what she wanted to hear, and said, "No, ma'am, I won't. I promise."

Alice sank to her knees and held both her daughter's hands, looking into her eyes.

"You're the only one I can count on now, baby. John's dead and buried, and David Lee's a retard and he ain't never gonna amount to much because he can't. And I know Paulie's gonna come to a bad end just like your Daddy and your Uncle Luther did. So it falls on you, child. I want you to get yourself an education and be better than all this."

"Yes, ma'am. I won't let you down, Mama. I promise."

Alice hugged the girl tightly, feeling her ribs through the thin dress. Unused to such a display of affection, Penny didn't know how to react, but she knew that her mother was placing a burden upon her that she couldn't carry all by herself. Penny patted her Mama's shoulder and repeated, "I won't let you down, Mama. I promise."

From the curb, Robert watched the scene unfold between mother and child, then turned away so as not to intrude on their privacy.

"You ready?" Lester asked from behind the wheel of his police car.

"Yeah, let's go get some lunch," Robert said, climbing into the seat beside him. As Lester put the transmission into gear and pulled away, Robert turned his head to look back again at Alice Reider standing over the grave of one daughter, while still holding the hand of the other.

***

Two days later, Robert was pounding the keys of his Underwood

Dog's Run

when he heard the bell over the office door jingle. Lillian, his combination receptionist/secretary/office manager, had taken the afternoon off, complaining of a headache, so Robert left the typewriter and walked out to the lobby.

"Mrs. Reider. How are you doing?"

"I saw you at my baby girl's funeral."

"Yes ma'am, I was there. I didn't mean to intrude."

"My other girl, Penny, she read me that piece you put in the newspaper about my Wanda Jean killing herself."

"I'm sorry if you felt it was an invasion of your family's privacy. But there were a lot of people all worried about some maniac running loose, and I was trying to ease their fears."

"You said my Wanda Jean was well loved. That was right nice of you."

"I'm sorry for your loss."

The door opened again and a short, thin man entered the lobby, tipping his hat to Alice. She stepped aside deferentially, but Robert said, "I'll be right with you, Wally."

"No hurry. I was just calling to see if those statement forms I ordered were done yet."

"I ain't in no hurry," Alice said. "You go ahead and take care of your business."

Robert retrieved the printed job from the table behind the counter, handed them to his customer, and collected the money.

After he left, Alice said, "I hear those ladies I work for talking about you. They all say you're a good man. I need somebody I can trust. Can I trust you, Mr. Tucker?"

"I guess I'm as trustworthy as any man."

"Well that ain't sayin' much. But I don't guess I got nobody else I can turn to."

The door opened again and Scooter Smith picked up a newspaper from the counter, gave Robert a nickel and said, "Liked your editorial on the library, Robert. We need to get more funding for it. Less than 3,000 books is an embarrassment."

When Scooter left, Alice asked him again, "Can I trust you, Mr. Tucker?"

"I'm not sure what you're asking me, Mrs. Reider."

She sat a small, cardboard box on the counter and said, "I'm talking about these."

Robert opened the box and saw the four diaries. He opened the top one and scanned a couple of pages, then abruptly walked around the counter, locked the door and hung the "Back In 30 Minutes" sign in the window.

"Let's go back to my office, Mrs. Reider."

* * *

"I know my baby weren't no angel," Alice said. "But she weren't as bad as some would paint her, neither. I can't read or write none at all Mr. Tucker, but I know what most of the letters are. And I see some letters in there that I see on stores here in town. I may not be able to read, but I can count, and I can put two and two together."

"What is it you want from me, Mrs. Reider?"

"I'm just a dumb, old woman from the Run, but I know my Wanda Jean was mixed up in somethin' she didn't have no business messin' with. And now that there insurance man, that Mr. Schefstrom, is sayin' that he can't pay me what I got comin' from Wanda Jean's insurance. I been payin' my premiums regular on me and my kids for all these years, $2 a month, and he says 'cause my Wanda Jean killed herself, the policy is somethin' called voided. I need that money to pay for her funeral."

"Mrs. Reider, do you think Wanda Jean died some other way besides suicide?"

"I can't read, but Chief Smeal read me her note, and I know it was her handwritin',' so I guess she did. But I want to know why. And I think the why is in those books of hers. So my question is, can I trust you, Mr. Tucker?"

"Mrs. Reider, you have to understand that there might be things in these books that you may not be comfortable knowing about."

"Mr. Tucker, I told you I'm a dumb, old woman. But I ain't blind and I ain't stupid. I know there was men Wanda Jean was messin' around with. And I know they weren't men from the Run."

"Mrs. Reider, whatever is in these books could cause a lot of people a lot of trouble, including yourself. Is that what you want?"

"Sir, I was born into trouble and it ain't never left me. I ain't got no man to help out. The first one's dead and the other one's doin' life at Mansfield. One of my boys is lyin' over there in the cemetery under that big flagpole, another's headed for the pen sooner or later, and the youngest is a retard that ain't gonna never be able to even tend to himself. I've got my Penny, and she's a good, little girl and she tries to help, but she ain't no bigger'n a popcorn fart in the wind. And now my Wanda Jean's dead and buried. So what I'm sayin' Mr. Tucker, is trouble's nothin' new to me. Now I'm askin' you agin', can I trust you to do the right thing?"

"I'm not sure I know what the right thing is here, Mrs. Reider."

"Well, you got all that schoolin' and I 'spect by the time you get done readin' them there books, you'll know."

Chapter 8

Lester Smeal loved his Buick. The big Roadmaster's 320 cubic inch engine could rocket him from 0 to 60 in seconds, and the car would do 110 miles per hour when he opened it up wide. More than enough to catch any speeder barreling down Alexis Road, or to chase down the old rattletrap jalopies and pickups the moonshiners in the Run drove.

Of course, that didn't mean that Lester chased down every load of shine coming out of Dog's Run. He would never take a dollar to turn a blind eye to a crime going on, but the police chief was a realist. Even though you could buy a drink in any bar in town, those hillbillies from the Run were weaned on homemade liquor, and the store bought stuff just didn't taste the same to them. And if he was honest, he'd have to admit he enjoyed a sip now and then, too.

The chief wouldn't tolerate the men who took shortcuts and produced poison moonshine, the stuff that could make a man go blind or even kill him. There was no reason to do that when there were plenty of customers and enough money to be made doing things on the up and up. If Lester learned of somebody who, either from laziness, greed, or pure malice, was putting out bad shine, he'd make their lives miserable, chasing them down and confiscating their illicit cargo and the vehicles they carried it in, and hunting down their stills and smashing them with axes and sledgehammers.

And he always made sure his brother-in-law, Robert Tucker, was on hand to cover the bust. Lester figured that as long as he had a newspaperman in the family, why not take advantage of it? Not that he was really taking advantage. After all, enforcing the law was his job and the public had a right to know. So if Robert got a good front page story out of it, and Lester got a little bit of publicity, and the good folks of Elmhurst were reminded that he was on the job, everybody won, right?

Lester couldn't deny that he missed the war sometimes. Not the killing and seeing folks all torn to hell, but there was a thrill in combat that he couldn't deny. And he'd been good at it. Damn good.

Not that he could complain. He had a good life and a good job and a woman he loved to go home to at night, and two precious little ones he adored. And occasionally he had to bust a head or two. Some hillbilly from the Run who got out of line or one of the niggers who came into town to do some work and overstayed their welcome or got into mischief.

Sure, he had made some mistakes in his life and done some things he wasn't proud of. But Lester didn't consider himself a bad man and he wasn't prejudiced like some folks he knew. He'd known some Negroes during the war, mostly assigned to work as stevedores unloading cargo off the ships that supplied his unit. For the most part, they had been good men. But he also believed there was a place for them, and as long as they knew their place, they'd get along just fine.

It was the same with the hillbillies from the Run. In spite of being poor, most of them were decent people. And being poor wasn't a crime. But there was that bad element that liked to get liquored up and beat their women and kids or fight with their neighbors. Hell, fighting wasn't all bad. If it was, men like Rocky Marciano and Jersey Joe Walcott wouldn't be making names for themselves in the ring, now would they? As long as a man was fighting with another man his own size, Lester figured it was better to let them settle it among themselves. But when it was women or kids involved, or some big bully taking advantage, or when the knives and guns came out, he drew the line.

Lester would try to talk sense into a man when he could, but there were times when the best way to get their attention was with the leather sap he carried in his back pocket. Yeah, it was like that old mule he had told Robert about; sometimes you had to smack them between the eyes to get their attention. And if that didn't work, he had the big .44 Special on his hip and the shotgun he carried in the canvas sleeve under the front seat of the Buick.

Lester had only had to shoot one man since he left the Army, a big, old red haired boy name of Tommy Crabb who had come out of the coal mines somewhere down south and got himself a job working on the assembly line at Willys-Overland. One Saturday night two years ago, old Tommy had come home drunk and beat his woman almost to death because dinner wasn't on the table. An old man name of Jubal McKinney, who lived next door, had seen Tommy drag the woman out in the yard and start kicking her as she lay on the ground. Jubal wasn't a man to mess with, even at age 80, and he picked up a 2x4 and smashed the big hillbilly over the head with it. Maybe it was the liquor, or maybe Tommy was just thick headed to start with, but the blow had only infuriated him. He turned his rage onto the old man, knocking him to the ground and kicking the life out of him.

By the time Lester arrived on the scene, it was too late to help Jubal. Tommy was standing in his yard swinging the 2x4 at anybody who came near and had already succeeded in breaking the jaw of one neighbor and knocking another unconscious. The police chief ordered him twice to drop the 2x4, but when Tommy ignored his orders and came at him with it raised over his head, Lester had put three shots into him from the .44.

There hadn't been much of an investigation. After all, it was obvious that Tommy Crabb and been out of control and Lester had only done his job. There was some talk that Tommy's two brothers, Leroy and Willis, had vowed to get revenge on the police chief. Not a man who took threats lightly or who wanted to spend his days looking over his shoulder, Lester had approached the problem head-on. He found the brothers drinking and shooting pool at the Thunderbird Lounge and called them out.

Taking off his gun belt and handing it to Ted DuPont, he had whipped both brothers in the dirt parking lot. Then he had asked them if they preferred to shake hands and let things end there, or if he was going to have to meet up with them again some night. Tommy's brothers recognized a brave man when they met him, and they respected the police chief's courage in hunting them down like that. Besides, everybody knew old Tommy was going to come to a bad end, sooner or later. It was just a matter of when. They shook hands with Lester and let the matter drop right there. Since then things had been pretty quiet around Elmhurst.

But now there was this thing with Wanda Jean Reider. Lester had a bad feeling about it. He knew Wanda Jean got around, and he'd seen more than one, proud Rotary member or church deacon looking at her in a way that a man only did when he knew a woman on an intimate level, or was hoping to get to know her that way. Lester's job was to enforce the law, and one way to do that was to know what was going on in his town. Not just who was having the preacher over for Sunday dinner, or who might push the speed limit a little bit when nobody was looking and he was in a hurry to get to work. No, he made it a point to know which kids might take a five-finger discount at the candy counter at the Rexall drugstore and who was drinking more than they should, or slipping out the back door to meet somebody they shouldn't. Overall, Elmhurst was a quiet town, but every closet has its skeletons. He just hoped that by burying Wanda Jean, they had maybe buried a few skeletons along with her.

Chapter 9

Dear Diary,
People must think I'm nuts scribblin my thoughts here on these pages. But sometimes I think I'll go right out of my mind if I don't get all of this out of me and there ain't nobody else I can tell it to. I don't know how I turned out this way because it wasn't what I had planned for my life. Mama says my beauty is both a blessing and a curse. And I guess I have to agree with her. There's times I wish I were just a plain old girl from Dog's Run, but that ain't me. Ever since I was a little girl I wanted more out of life than having babies and living in some tarpaper shack like my mama has all her life. Now I ain't looking down on Mama, she done the best she could and Lord knows her life hasn't been easy! But sometimes I'm asking myself if easy is really better? I always wonder what would have happened if Mr. Bigelow hadn't done what he did that day when I was just a girl. But the man did give me a choice, the whipping or that other thing, and I'm the one who chose, so I guess he ain't all to blame. And I went back, didn't I? It was easier than sitting there in class all day long learning about a bunch of dead kings and presidents and such or what's inside a frog. What good would that ever do me? Shoot, to be honest I learned more about what was going to help me get ahead in life in those "special lessons" Mr. Bigelow taught me than I ever did sitting at a desk!

Robert set the diary down on his desk and leaned back in his chair, rolling his neck and shoulders and hearing a couple of little cracks as he did it. He looked down at the diary and felt a certain revulsion. He wasn't sure he wanted to know what secrets it held. And if he learned them, what was he supposed to do with them? Then he remembered Alice Reider's last words to him – "*I 'spect by the time you get done readin' them there books, you'll know.*"

But did he *want* to know? Robert had never seen himself as a muckraking reporter practicing yellow journalism. He loved small town life and all he ever wanted to do was run a small town newspaper. It wasn't easy work, the hours were long and there were times that he was bored to death covering the ladies garden club meetings or sitting for hours at City Council meetings where little ever seemed to get accomplished. But it was all worth it for the satisfaction he got when the first copy of a new issue of the *Citizen-Press* came off the press and he held it in his hands, drinking in the smell of newsprint and fresh ink. Every month he had seen his advertising lineage pick up and he had more than doubled the circulation since he took over the paper. Whatever was in Wanda Jean's diaries might imperil everything he had worked for and his very future in Elmhurst. Was it worth it to know? Robert wasn't sure, but he found himself picking up the diary again.

***

Once you get started I guess it just becomes second nature. I still remember the first time somebody paid me for sex. Now when I say paid me I don't mean money. I ain't a whore. Or at least I wasn't back then. I guess that's all changed now, hasn't it? I was just mindin' my own business looking at that locket in the showcase at Riley's Five and Dime. It was about the most beautiful thing I'd ever seen, all gold and with those little diamond chips around the edges. 'Course they weren't real diamonds, just glass, but a 15-year-old girl don't know that. I was just admiring it through the glass when Mr. Riley asked me if I'd like to hold it. I told him, "No sir, I ain't got the money for something that pretty." But he took it out anyway and hung it around my neck and let me look in that little round mirror he had on the counter. Lord, didn't I think I was something special wearing it! And I guess Mr. Riley did too, 'cause he said "See there, Wanda Jean, you look just like one of those Hollywood movie stars wearing that thing. Why, did Miss Marilyn Monroe just walk into my little store? Well no sir, it's Wanda Jean Reider, and I think she's even more beautiful than Marilyn Monroe. And that's a fact!" Maybe things wouldn't have been the same if it wasn't such a slow Tuesday night and nobody else was in the store. But I sure did look good in that necklace, and when he asked me to look at it in the mirror in the back room there, I have to admit I had a suspicion what he was up to. I done those things I did with Mr. Bigelow, but that thing that Mr. Riley had me do, that disgusted me the first time! But I guess a girl gets used to just about anything if she's greedy enough.

Robert had never known James Bigelow except to nod to. The high school principal had been hired from someplace up in Michigan while Robert was away with the Army. He had died of a heart attack the same year Robert took over the newspaper. But Ken Riley was a regular advertiser and served on the same Library Board that Robert did. He had always respected the man for his willingness to work hard to help the library grow and for his business acumen. To think that Riley would trade a cheap trinket for the opportunity to molest a young girl, turned his stomach. He heard footsteps outside his office door, and quickly put the diary away, as Lillian Jackson knocked and then pushed the door open.

"What are you doing in here with the door closed?" She asked. "It's stuffy enough even with the window open!"

"Lillian, did you ever stop to think there might be a reason a door is closed? Maybe I needed some privacy."

"Well I knocked, didn't I?"

"Yes, ma'am, you knocked. But then you pushed the door right open. For all you knew I might've been standing here in my union suit."

"You don't wear a union suit, and if you was standing here in one, it was probably because it's so darned stuffy."

"How do you know what I wear under my clothes?" Robert asked.

"Well I know you'd look pretty funny wearing a union suit and short sleeve shirt like you did the other day when I saw you mowing your mama's grass."

"Well maybe I only wear my union suit for formal occasions like when I'm coming to work."

"How about we stop discussing your underwear and talk about why I came back here to bother you in the first place?"

"That might be a good idea," Robert said. "What do you need?"

"To be honest, I got this picture in my mind of you prancing around your office in a union suit and I plumb forgot," Lillian said. "But give me a minute and it'll come to me."

"Fine, and when it does, please knock before opening my door," Robert said.

Lillian stuck her tongue out at him and started out of the office, then snapped her fingers and turned around. "I remember! Andy Zimmerman from the Chevrolet garage called and said he had one of those new convertibles you been talking about, just come in. What in the world are you going to do with a convertible? You'll freeze your tukas off in one of those things in the wintertime!"

"Maybe so, but when it's hot like this, I can put the top down and let the breeze cool me down while I'm driving."

"If you wasn't wearing a union suit under that there three-piece suit, maybe you wouldn't be so hot that you needed a convertible car," Lillian said as she walked away.

Once she was gone, Robert opened his desk drawer and started to take the diary back out but thought better of it. He wasn't wearing a union suit under his clothes, of course, so he didn't feel hot and sweaty, and he had not been working in the pressroom, so why did he suddenly feel the need to spend a lot of time standing under a hot shower?

Chapter 10

"What's this I hear that you bought yourself a fancy new Chevrolet convertible?" Elizabeth asked, as she passed a platter of pork chops across the table to her brother.

"Now where in the world did you hear that?" Robert asked as stabbed a pork chop with the serving fork and put it on his plate, then passed the platter to his mother. "I didn't buy a new car. Or a used car either, for that matter."

"You know there ain't no secrets in this little town," Lester said. "If we'd have had this grapevine working for us during the war, we'd have whipped those Nips in the first month and not had to use those two big old bombs. What's that they say? The fastest way to get information spread around is telephone, telegraph, or tell a woman?"

"Daddy, did you see any of those Japs that got blowed up by that ole big bomb?"

"Loretta Smeal! What kind of talk is that for the dinner table? Or at any time for a girl your age, for that matter?"

"I just want to know if Daddy seen any of those dead Japs that got blowed up."

"Now baby girl, you know your mama don't like talk like that at the dinner table," Lester told her.

"But Daddy!"

"Daddy never saw no dead Japs anywhere. All I did was empty bedpans at a hospital a long ways back from the fighting."

"Yuck!" said Loretta, "bedpans are nasty. My friend Irene said that you killed a whole bunch of Japs in the war and that you're a hero."

"Irene has a vivid imagination. I think she reads too many of them there comic books. The only kind of hero I am is a hero to my little girl. Am I still your hero, Loretta?"

She giggled and said, "Of course you are, Daddy. Always and forever."

"Now your Uncle Robert here, he's a bona fide hero," Lester said. "Why, one time he captured himself a hundred and seventeen Nazi spies dressed up as circus clowns, and two of those little bitty wiener dogs they had with 'em. Yes sir, they had everybody fooled except for your Uncle Robert."

"That's not true," Woodrow said. "You're making that up, Daddy!"

"I swear on a stack of Bibles," Lester replied. "And you know how he found out they were spies? 'Cause one of those little old wiener dogs weren't no wiener dog at all. No sir, it was a Wienerschnitzel!"

Loretta choked on the milk she had been drinking and coughed as it ran out of her nose, while Woodrow laughed at his father and then at her.

"Daddy!"

"Is true," Lester assured the boy as he reached over to pat his daughter on the back.

"Now you three stop that nonsense right this minute," Elizabeth said. "Can't we eat just one meal like normal people instead of all this chaos and catastrophe?"

"Well what do you expect, Lizzie, when you sit down at the table with a certified, professional bedpan emptier and a genuine Nazi circus clown catchin' hero? You got to expect some chaos and catastrophe."

"Robert," Elizabeth said, turning to her brother, "I am just going to ignore those three, wild Indians for the rest of this meal and talk to you. At least I know I can get some intelligent conversation out of a gentleman like yourself."

"Achtung!" Lester said behind her, and Loretta responded, "Gesundheit," sending her husband and children into fits of laughter, which Elizabeth chose to ignore, although Robert saw the twinkle in her eyes and the corners of her mouth lift.

"How's Mama? I wish she would have felt up to coming to dinner."

"Mama is Mama," Robert told her. "When I came home yesterday she told me I needed to shovel the snow off the sidewalk so the postman could pick up her Christmas cards. Last night she swore that Daddy was taking her out dancing and she couldn't find the sweater she wanted to wear. But this morning we had a nice conversation about the weather and she told me I should get a couple of new ties because the ones I've been wearing are starting to look shabby. You really need to get over and see her, Lizzie."

"I know I need to," she said, shaking her head sadly. "It just hurts so darn much to see her like that, Bobby. I can remember when she used to read to us at night. Robert Louis Stevenson, Tom Sawyer, Jack London. Now she don't know who I am most days, and when she does, she wants me to go take a bath because it's bedtime. Or else she keeps asking me when I'm going to get married and have some babies."

"I know, but you still need to spend some time with her."

"How do you do it, Bobby?" Elizabeth asked with tears in her eyes. "You're such a good son, but I don't know how you can do it day in and day out. I wish I was a better daughter, Bobby, I really do. But I just can't stand seeing her like that."

"Hon, you have to understand that she's probably the happiest person we know. In her mind, Daddy's still with her and they're both still young and healthy, and we're just little kids. She thinks she's at the point in her life where you are today."

"Maybe that's what scares me the worst," Elizabeth said. "She thinks she's where I am today. Does that mean, someday, I'll be where she is right now?"

With that she burst into tears and ran from the room.

***

"I'm sorry to get Lizzie upset like that," Robert said as he rinsed a plate in the sink and set it in the rack to dry.

"You didn't do it," Lester told him. "She just feels guilty that she can't be the daughter she thinks she should be to your mama, and she worries that someday she's going to lose her mind, too. Just give her a little bit. She'll be okay."

By the time the dishes were done and put away, Lester's prediction was proven true when Elizabeth came into the living room and told the children it was time to start getting ready for bed.

"But Mama, I'm not even tired yet," Woodrow said.

"Tomorrow's the last day of school," Elizabeth reminded him. "Don't you want to be wide awake and bushy tailed for that?"

"Mama? If I get all A's on my report card, are you really going to take me shopping at Miller's for a new dress?"

"Didn't I tell you I would, Loretta? You've been studying and working real hard, and that deserves a reward."

"Do I get a reward, too?" Woodrow asked.

"Your reward's going to be a spanking if you don't get yourself upstairs and in the bathtub, young man," Elizabeth said, "now scoot!"

Robert and Lester went out to the porch to have their customary after supper smoke. Watching the fireflies dance around the yard, Lester said, "What's troubling you, Bob?"

"Oh, nothing I guess. Maybe just that talk about Mama. It does hurt me, you know. I try to hide it for Lizzie's sake, but I miss who she used to be."

"I know you do. We all do. But that's not what's eating away at you, son."

"It's nothing."

"Hey, you bullshit the baker and you might get a bun, but don't bullshit me, 'cause I ain't got none. I've known you a lot of years, Bob, and I know when something's eating away at you."

"It's something I need to work through myself," Robert told him. "Once I do, maybe we'll sit down and talk about it. But I don't even know what I think myself, at this point."

"Well, when you're ready, I'm here to listen if it helps you."

"It does, Les. More than you know, it does."

Chapter 11

I don't know how the word got around. Who talks about things like that? Or maybe they just could see something in me. Something that told them I was hungry. Hungry for something more than Dog's Run. Hungry enough to do things. Things that they wanted and were willing to give something to get. I can't imagine fat old Gus Schmidt at the butcher shop thinking any woman would be attracted to him, let alone a pretty little girl like I was. But I remember that it was raining hard and I just ducked inside his shop to get out of the downpour. I'd never been in a place like that and it smelled wonderful! Why, I could almost taste those steaks and sausages just by breathing in that place! Back home in Dog's Run, except for Thanksgiving and Christmas, about the best we ever got was tube steak, or Mama would kill a chicken on Sunday. But that old German had more meat in there than I've ever seen in my life. Like I said, I was hungry. I guess Gus was hungry too, because by the time the rain had stopped I walked out of there with a whole roast beef, some ground hamburger meat, and more hot dogs than I could carry! I can still remember the look on Mama's face when I brought that all home. Oh, she knew. And I think it hurt her, but she didn't say a word, and after that we had fresh meat on the table three or four times a week.

Robert shook his head, wondering what it must be like to be so desperate for a better way of life that a girl would do the things Wanda Jean had just for a full stomach or some shiny bauble. He found himself repulsed by the things he was reading in Wanda Jean's diary, and yet drawn to them. Robert may have been a small town boy, but college and the Army had introduced him to the big city and the ways of city people. He had seen the whores standing on the street corners and at the entrances of alleys on weekend passes to Trenton and Philadelphia. And if he hadn't been so scared by all of the training films and stories about men who caught the clap and had to undergo painful treatment, he might have been tempted.

And he wasn't naïve enough not to know that there were women in the honky-tonks and bars who could be had for a couple of dollars, or even for a few drinks. But they were coarse and usually homely, or wore heavily painted faces to hide their years and experiences. Wanda Jean Reider had been young and beautiful, and Robert knew that if she had been born on the right side of the deep ravine that separated Dog's Run from the good side of town, she might have found herself crowned Homecoming Queen instead of earning her diploma lying on the principal's desk.

He had to get away, so he locked the diary away in his desk drawer and headed out of the office.

"Where are you going?" Lillian asked, as he put his hat on and reached for the doorknob.

"It's hot in here. I'm going for a walk to get some fresh air."

"Maybe you ought to buy one of those convertible Chevrolet's after all," Lillian called after him. "Put the top down and get yourself lots of fresh air!"

The *Citizen-Press* was housed in an old, brick building on Main Street, sandwiched between the dry cleaners and Hickey's Furniture Store. Robert paused as two men carried a mattress out of the store and across the sidewalk to where a Studebaker pickup was double parked.

Thelma Hickey came out of the store and said, "Good afternoon, Mr. Tucker."

"How are you this fine afternoon, Mrs. Hickey?" he asked, tipping his hat.

"Mr. Tucker, I'd like to talk to you about the library. I have some concerns about the type of books Beatrice Hazlet is putting on the shelves."

"Oh? What kind of books is that, Mrs. Hickey?"

Thelma Hickey was a little bird of a woman, with bulging eyes that always seemed to be trying to escape their sockets, and graying hair that she always wore pulled back in a severe bun. She looked both ways to be sure she wouldn't be overheard, and then said in a stage whisper, "*Catcher in the Rye* and those trashy detective novels by Mickey Spillane. Vulgar, all of them!"

"Well now, Mrs. Hickey, I guess maybe Miss Hazlet wants to have a good enough selection to have a little something for everyone."

"Now who's going to read filth like that, Mr. Tucker? Perverts and

Dog's Run

degenerates, that's who! Do we really want to encourage people like that to use public facilities like our library?"

Robert was tempted to tell her that, based upon what he had been reading in Wanda Jean Reider's diary, there were a lot more perverts and degenerates in town than she knew, and they weren't all to be found in the library. Instead he said, "I'll tell you what, Mrs. Hickey, I'll share your concerns with the Library Board when we meet next week."

"Well, I would certainly appreciate that," Mr. Tucker. But in the meantime, what about those books that are sitting right there on the shelves attracting who knows what kind of men, and filling their minds with depravity?"

"Your concerns have been noted," Robert told her, then saw his chance to escape. "I'll certainly pass them on. Now if you'll excuse me, Mrs. Hickey, I see somebody I need to speak with." He tipped his hat again and hurried down the sidewalk to where Adam Schefstrom was just unlocking the door of his insurance office.

Chapter 12

"Good afternoon, Adam. Do you have a minute?"

Adam Schefstrom always reminded Robert of a weasel or a ferret with his pointed face and beady, little eyes. But it wasn't just his physical appearance. The man's personality went a long way toward cementing that impression in Robert's mind. Whenever he shook hands with Schefstrom, he wanted to check to be sure that his class ring was still in place afterward.

"Howdy, Robert. Just getting back from making my rounds. Come on in."

He hung his hat on a peg near the door, flipped on the overhead lights and a fan mounted on a tall metal pole, then sat down behind his desk, waving Robert to a seat opposite him.

"What can I do for you today? Maybe write you a policy on that new Chevrolet I hear you're getting?"

"I think Andy Zimmerman is putting money in the bank before any checks are getting written," Robert said. "He mentioned at lunch, a couple of weeks back, that he had one of those Styleline convertibles coming in and I said I'd love to have a car like that someday. I guess in old Andy's mind, that was as good as a written factory order. I'd love to have a submarine someday, too. But I hope the United States Navy don't show up in town with one on a trailer!"

Schefstrom laughed and said, "That's what we in the sales business call assuming the sale. If we believe it's a done deal and act like it is, the customer will, too."

"Well, that's kind of what I wanted to talk to you about, Adam. Sales. Insurance sales, to be exact."

"Well, you came to the right man, then. You name it, I can handle it for you, Robert. Life, home, business, or automobile. What do you need?"

"I need some background for a story I'm thinking about writing, about how different businesses work. Sort of to educate the public."

"Excellent idea," Schefstrom said. "They talk about that in the trade journals. Everybody wins. The public gets a raised awareness of what a business can do for them, the business gets a little bit of free publicity, and the newspaper gets some good content. That's one of the things I admire about you, Robert. You're a visionary. Why, when Chester Daggett ran the paper before you, all he ever wanted to do was run the same old boilerplate stuff. And Herb McMann before him? Even worse. I mean, how many times do we need to see a picture of Mrs. Foster standing in front of her prized rosebushes on the front page? But you? Every week you've got something different. Some high school athlete, or somebody who caught a mess of catfish, or some kids playing in the park. People like to see that sort of thing."

"That was something Frank McCormack taught me when I was working for him at the newspaper in Maumee," Robert said. "If you put somebody's picture in the paper, especially a kid, not only are their parents going to buy a copy, but also two sets of grandparents and maybe a few uncles and aunts, too."

"You see, that's what I mean about being a visionary," Schefstrom said. "That's what's making you a success."

"Well, I try to get by," Robert said. "Anyway, about this insurance business. I see you running all over town calling on folks. Is that all cold calling, trying to sell insurance?"

"No, sir," the insurance man said. "No, sir, that's servicing my accounts. See, the way it works is, most folks buy a policy and pay every week or every month on it, and I go around and pick up their payments and send them in to the company. That way they don't forget and let it lapse, and at the same time, I'm in their homes and businesses and I see what's going on. Maybe they built on a new addition and need to increase their coverage to protect the added value. Or they've got a baby on the way and need to think about that."

"People buy insurance for babies?"

"Oh yeah! At least enough to cover the cost of a funeral, God forbid anything happens to one of them. And we've even got policies that can be changed into their own names once they're adults, or used down the line to help pay for their education. Insurance isn't just about paying out when somebody has a loss, Robert. It's an *investment* in the future."

"So you go around collecting the policy premiums. Do folks really tend to forget to send in a payment on their policy? I'd think they'd be smarter than that."

Schefstrom laughed and shook his head. "You'd be surprised. They get busy and forget, or money gets tight and I need to remind them that they can cut corners in other places, but once their policy goes past due, they've lost it. And then, to be honest," he paused to look around, even though nobody else was in the office," a lot of my clients are too damn dumb to read and write. Now that don't make them bad people, mind you, but you take the folks out in the Run? If I didn't go collect, they'd never pay. Hell man, most of them wouldn't know what a bill was if it came to them in the mail. But we in the insurance industry don't call it collecting. We're servicing the policy."

"Makes sense to me," Robert said, though he couldn't help remembering that his Uncle Wilbur paid another farmer to bring his bull over to service his heifers every year.

"That's why I've been in the top ten percent of the company sales the last six years. In fact, I'm about to get a sales award at our big meeting in Cleveland next week."

"Do you sell a lot of policies out there in Dog's Run?"

"Sure do," Schefstrom said. "It's not easy, though. Those damn hillbillies would rather buy a bottle of shine than pay their policy premiums. But I remind them that they've got a good standard of life here. Better than they ever had back in Corn Cob, Kentucky or wherever they come from. But if one of them was to get sick or injured and die, they'd lose everything. It's all salesmanship, Robert."

"So what happens if somebody does die? Let's say some old boy wrecks his car or gets pneumonia during the winter. The insurance pays off?"

"That's right. They get a check and pay off their mortgage or funeral expenses or whatever. Hell, for all I know, they might spend it getting drunk, or buying a television set. Makes no difference to me."

"Does the insurance company send them a check or do you pay them, or what?"

"Usually the company sends them a check. But again, you take those folks out in the Run? Most of them wouldn't know what a check was if it came in the mail. And most of them don't have bank accounts either. So I deposit the check into my own account and take the cash out to them myself. It's all about servicing the client. Besides, it gives me a little positive reinforcement and helps builds goodwill in people's minds when they see me at their neighbor's door with cash in hand to help them get through their loss."

"Now, are there exclusions? Let's say somebody has a suspicious fire at their business or house?"

"Oh yeah, the folks who run insurance companies aren't dummies, Robert. They know how to spot fraud and will jump all over it. But we don't get much of that around here."

"What about suicide?

"Well now, that's a whole 'nother thing. Most policies have a three year exclusion for suicide. You'd be surprised how many folks find out they've got a terminal illness and then decide to provide for their loved ones at the expense of an insurance company. So they buy a policy and then kill themselves, expecting us to pay off. It don't work that way. Or, you look back at what happened right after the war. We had fellas who came back all twisted inside their heads, and they just couldn't adjust. So they'd kill themselves. And some of them did the same thing; buy a policy one week and kill themselves the next."

Robert remembered Steve Hudson, a high school friend who had always had a smile on his face and was popular with all the girls. Steve had seen vicious combat and helped liberate some of the worst Nazi concentration camps. He had come home a changed man, moody and reclusive, keeping to himself and never smiling. One morning, a year after his discharge, Steve's father had found him hanging from a rafter in their barn. Robert had been a pallbearer at Steve's funeral, and had always felt that while his friend had never been awarded a Purple Heart for injuries sustained in battle, he was still a casualty of the war.

"A three year exclusion on suicides?"

"Yes, sir, that's the industry standard. To protect the company from fraud."

"Well, let me ask you this, Adam. What about Wanda Jean Reider?"

Chapter 13

One of the things that Robert felt made him a good newspaperman was that he was good at reading people's faces. He always had been, even as a kid playing rummy with Elizabeth. He could tell just by the look in her eyes when she had a good hand, and that same ability had made him a good poker player in college and the Army. So he didn't miss the flicker in Adam Schefstrom's eyes when he mentioned Wanda Jean's name.

"Wanda Jean? That was a mess, wasn't it? Such a pretty girl, and all those ugly rumors floating around town about her. May she rest in peace."

"Did you carry a policy on Wanda Jean?"

"I don't believe so, I'd have to check to be sure. Why do you ask?"

"Well, I was just wondering... her being from the Run and you servicing all those folks out there, and then that suicide thing we were just talking about."

"I really don't recall."

"That's strange. How a smart businessman wouldn't recall if he had a client he called upon on a regular basis to collect from, I mean service."

Schefstrom's eyes narrowed and he asked, "Just what the hell are you getting at, Robert?"

"Well, it's all probably just a mistake or a lack of communication somewhere along the line. But Wanda Jean's mother came to me the other day and said she'd been paying you on policies for her and her kids for years now, and that you told her that since Wanda Jean committed suicide, the policy won't pay off. But if she's had a policy all those years, how does the three year clause come into effect?" He snapped his fingers and said, "You know what, I bet that's what it is. She probably got you confused with Bob Bristow over at Ohio Fidelity. I'll bet he's the one she has her insurance with. I'll go ask him about it. Sorry to waste your time, Adam."

He started to rise and Schefstrom said, "Now just wait a minute! You know what, I do service Mrs. Reider's policies, and I did talk to her about Wanda Jean's. What I told her was that while it was so unfortunate that Wanda Jean had killed herself, at least the three year suicide clause wouldn't come into play. I guess in her grief she just misunderstood me. And to be honest with you, Robert, with me getting ready for that big convention next week, I guess I wasn't really concentrating on our conversation just now. I do apologize for that."

"No harm done," Robert told him.

Schefstrom rose from his desk and crossed the room to a row of file cabinets, where he pulled a drawer open and rummaged for a moment before returning with a folder. "Right here it is, Wanda Jean Reider. Her mama's been paying regular as clockwork since she was five years old. $250 payout. That ought to cover the funeral costs and all, and pay for a pretty headstone for that girl. And even leave some left over. I already sent the paperwork in to the company and should get a check back for Mrs. Reider real quick. I'm sorry she misunderstood me the other day. Poor woman's got a lot of grief to deal with."

"You know what would build you a lot of goodwill and look good on the front page of the paper?" Robert asked. "A picture of you handing Mrs. Reider that $250. It's too bad that there check didn't come in sooner. I could get it the next issue and you could take that paper to Cleveland with you. I bet that'd impress the folks there at that convention."

Schefstrom regarded him for a moment and they both understood the messages sent and received. "Well, hell, Robert, there's no reason that poor woman should wait another minute. I'll tell you what I'm going to do. I'm going to just withdraw $250 out of my account right now, and take it out to her. In fact, I think I'll add in a ten percent gift right on top of that from me, to make up for her misunderstanding what I told her. It won't bring her daughter back, of course, but maybe it'll help her through this rough patch."

"And you call *me* a visionary?" Robert asked, smiling. "I'll go get my camera and meet you at the bank."

***

"I don't know what you done to make him change his mind about that policy, but I sure am beholdin' to you, Mr. Tucker," Alice Reider said as Adam Schefstrom's Hudson backed out of her yard and started down Roan Road, leaving gravel and dust in its wake.

"I didn't do a thing," Robert told her. "I think it was just a case of a lack of communication. Once Mr. Schefstrom understood the message, he couldn't hardly wait to get out here and get that money to you."

"I'd be right proud to offer you a glass of lemonade."

"It's a hot afternoon, Mrs. Reider. I'd appreciate that."

The house wasn't fancy, by any means, and the furnishings were spartan, but it was clean and tidy. The lemonade was very good, with just enough tang, and the Mason jar she served it in was clean.

"I'm sorry it's not cold, what with the funeral and all, I didn't order ice."

"It's perfect," he assured her.

"There ain't much in life that's perfect, Mr. Tucker," she said.

"No, ma'am, I guess you're right about that. But this is darn good."

She looked at the money laying on the table, then said, "You didn't have to do that. You're a good man, Mr. Tucker."

"I do my best," Robert told her.

"I hesitate to ask, but could I trouble you for one more favor?"

"It's no trouble at all. What do you need?"

"I need to go into the funeral home and pay them for my Wanda Jean's funeral and order the gravestone for her. Could I ask you for a ride into town? I ain't never had this much money at one time and it makes me nervous."

"No problem," Robert said. "Let's go."

***

"This is what we call our Heritage Memorial," the tall, hollow faced funeral director said. "A lot of folks like the angels and the lamb there."

"It sure is pretty. How much does it cost, Mr. Duncan?"

"Normally that there stone is $100. Now that doesn't include the inscription, which is $2 per line, or placing the stone in the cemetery. That costs an additional $15 to get it set. But you do have to understand, Mrs. Reider, and I certainly mean no disrespect, that until the funeral itself is paid for I just can't extend any further credit. Now I know you're a regular customer and you make your payment every month just like clockwork. But business is business."

"I understand that," Alice said. "You always take care of my family and do a right nice job of it and I appreciate that." She used the fingers of one hand to count those of the other, her lips moving silently as she did it, then said, "The funeral was $150 and the headstone is $100 plus that there inscription. I want it to say her name, and her birthdate and death date, and then I want it to say, "Resting in Jesus' arms but still in our hearts." Can you do that for $275, Mr. Duncan?"

"Well yes ma'am, I think I can. There's tax and such but I'm willing to absorb that and we can do it for that money. But now, like I said, we need to get the funeral paid off first."

Alice opened her cheap cloth purse and pulled out the bills that Adam Schefstrom had paid her two hours before. "How soon can you get that stone put up on my baby's grave?"

A few minutes later, when the transaction had been finished, Robert held the passenger side door of his car open.

"I can't ask you to carry me all the way back out to the Run after all you've done already," Alice said. "I can walk, Mr. Tucker. I just felt nervous with all that money in my hand."

"You didn't ask, Mrs. Reider, I'm happy to do it and I appreciate the company."

"Well ain't you the dandy? I ain't never had nobody hold a car door for me before 'cept that there big, old limousine of Mr. Duncan's when we was burying Wanda Jean and my other babies."

She was silent on the drive back to Dog's Run, and Robert left her to her thoughts, though he did want to ask her about some of the things he had read in Wanda Jean's diary. But how do you ask a mother questions about the kind of things he had read in there? He pulled up to her house and Alice opened the car door, then turned to him.

"I can't thank you enough for all you've done for us, Mr. Tucker. I used to hope that my Wanda Jean would find a man as good as you. I guess every mama hopes that for her little girls. I don't know what you're findin' in those books of hers, don't know if I want to know, to tell you the truth. And I feel I've placed a burden upon your shoulders that ain't fair. Like I said I'm beholden."

Chapter 14

Penny and David Lee were sitting on the front porch step crying when Robert pulled into the yard. Seeing their mother inside the Pontiac, they ran to her door, both wailing and talking at once.

"What in the world has gotten into you two?" Alice demanded. "I can't understand a word you're sayin' when you're both going on like that. Now slow down and talk so's I can!"

"We been robbed!" Penny said.

***

"Well they sure made a mess of things," Robert said as he drug a mattress outside that had been cut open its full length, what was left of its cotton batting trailing after him.

"Had to be vandals," Duane Collett said, sweating heavily through his khaki uniform shirt as he followed along, doing more pushing than lifting his end of the mattress. "Little bastards tear something up just for the sake of doing it. Damned old hillbilly woman ain't got nothing worth stealing."

"Mind your manners," Robert said. "Miz Reider may be poor, but she's a good woman who's had a rough patch to hoe and she damn sure don't deserve this."

"She may be a good woman alright, but that daughter of hers was pure trash to the bone. Spreading her legs for any man that give her a look."

"I'll mind you not speak that way of the dead," Robert said, but the overweight policeman just snorted.

"Shit, Robert, that hit a little too close to home for you? Maybe you was one of 'em who was screwin' her, too? Can't say as I blame you. I'd have liked to have had a piece of that tail myself!"

"You watch your mouth, boy," Robert said, stopping abruptly and shoving the mattress back at Duane. But with most of its stuffing gone, it just folded up and had little effect.

"Hey man, you got a problem?" Duane demanded, stepping backward as the mattress fell to the ground. "If you think just because you're the Chief's kin you can get uppity with me, you got another thing comin'! I'll wipe the floor with your ass, Mr. College Educated Big Shot Think's He's So Special."

"Anytime you feel like trying that, you just step right up to the plate and start swinging," Robert invited.

"How 'bout right now, asshole? I'll...."

"You'll do what, Duane?" Lester asked, stepping around the corner of the house.

The bluster left him instantly, but Duane wasn't quite ready to back down yet. "All I'm sayin' is that Mr. Suit And Tie here needs to learn a little respect. Shit, Chief, he treats these white trash hillbillies like they're some kind of royalty, riding that old woman around in his car like that. Then he wants to sass a hard workin' lawman like me? It just ain't right."

"You wouldn't make a pimple on a good lawman's ass," Lester told him. "How about you get in your damn car and get on out of here and find yourself some shade tree to take a nap under. You ain't doing a damn thing but getting in the way here anyway."

"Yeah, well maybe I'll do just that. But I'll tell you something, mister," he said, pointing a finger at Robert. "One of these days you and me, we're gonna have us a get together. Yes, sir, we are!"

"Well you know where to find me," Robert said. "Anytime, day or night."

Duane started to reply, but saw the threatening look in the police chief's face and abruptly turned on his heel and stormed to his car, saying over his shoulder, "Cleaning house for a damned old hillbilly woman! What's next, giving shoe shines to niggers?"

"Don't pay him no mind," Lester said as they watched the car speed down the road, trailing a big cloud of dust behind.

"That's about the most useless example of a human being I've ever known," Robert said. "And I've known some pretty poor ones in my time."

"Don't take it personal. Old Duane don't like anybody that ain't carrying a plate of food. He's been pissed ever since the City Council made me Chief. He thought when old Chief Gray retired, he'd get the job. Not that's he's even qualified to be dogcatcher."

Robert picked up the mattress and finished dragging it to the burn pile, where he threw it on the fire, still seething at the encounter with Duane. As he turned back toward the house, Lester stopped him with a hand on his arm.

"What is it, Bob?"

"I'm just pissed off at that son-of-a-bitch," Robert said. "He's got no right to talk that way about a good woman like Mrs. Reider."

"No, that ain't it," Lester said. "Something's been gnawing away at you all week."

"It's just been a bad week. That's all."

"Hell, son, we got to sit up and take nourishment this morning, didn't we? I figure any day I don't sleep in the mud and nobody shoots at me to be pretty damn good."

"I guess that's true," Robert agreed. "What do you think happened here, Les?"

"I don't know. Maybe Duane's right for once in his life and it was vandals."

"You think so?"

"No, not really," Lester said, shaking his head. "I think whoever did this was looking for something."

"Like what?" Robert asked, thinking of Wanda's diaries. Did someone else know about their existence? Know that the things inside those little books could rip the very fabric of Elmhurst wide open and spill out all of its dirty little secrets just like the stuffing in Alice Reider's mattress?

"Isn't it obvious? Somebody saw Adam Schefstrom out here and figured out he must have been paying her that insurance money. I guess they thought she had stuck it away somewhere and were hoping to find it."

"Could be," Robert said, not having thought of that possibility.

"Makes sense to me. Hell, it could have been that older boy of hers, Paulie, for that matter. I wouldn't trust that little bastard as far as I could throw him."

"Neighbors didn't see anything?"

"Folks around here don't see much when it's the Law asking questions. But Miz Reider's pretty well respected in spite of how bad most of her kids turned out. Burt Peters over there on that side's stone deaf and mostly blind. The folks over on this side said they were in town grocery shopping at the A&P and came home to see the police cars here. Nobody's lived in the place across the street for a while now, since the bank took it back."

"Is there anything you can do to catch whoever did this?"

"I don't see how, unless somebody starts jabbering about it. It's not exactly the crime of the century."

"Maybe not in the grand scheme of things. But to that poor woman in there cleaning up that mess, it's pretty big."

"You need to take a step or two back," Lester said. "You're getting too close to all this, Bob. A newspaperman's got to be like a cop or a doctor and keep things at arms length. Otherwise you lose your objectivity. This here's a story, that's all. Don't you go trying to put yourself into the situation on a personal level, you hear me? You can't save the entire world."

"Yeah, I know you're right, Les. I just feel bad for that old woman, is all."

"I do, too, son! Just like I felt bad for all those boys I seen chopped to pieces in the war, or the family of some damn fool that wraps his car around a telephone pole and I've got to come tell them that their husband and Daddy won't be coming home any more. But I can't take that home with me. And neither can you. Otherwise we'd both go crazy in no time at all."

Robert knew his brother-in-law was right. He'd been told the same thing in his first days as a young reporter working for the *Blade*. Get the facts and write the best story about them you could, then move on to the next one. And there was always a next story waiting to be told. But how could he be objective, knowing the things he knew from Wanda Jean's diaries? The men she talked about weren't just fleeting characters encountered as he journeyed through a day. No, they were his customers, his neighbors, even his friends, some of them. He served on the Library Board with some, sat next to others at church on Sunday morning, or had lunch with them at the café during the week. How did you move on from a story that was a part of your everyday life? And if he did tell Wanda Jean's story, what did he have to move on to?

"It's getting late. You headed back to town soon?"

"You go on ahead, Les. I'm gonna make sure Mrs. Reider's okay, maybe see if there's anything else I can do."

"Alright. Guess I've done all I can do here. I'll talk to you tomorrow."

"Give my love to Lizzie and the kids," Robert told him as Lester opened the door and climbed behind the wheel of his Buick.

"Will do. And Bob, remember what I said, okay? Step back and maintain your objectivity."

He started the car, shifted into reverse, and backed out onto the road, then waved as he drove away. Robert watched him a moment, then turned back to the house.

***

"What else can I do to help you, Mrs. Reider?"

"You already done more than enough, Mr. Tucker," Alice said as she swept the last of the flour and sugar into a dustpan with a straw broom. "I ain't never had nobody be as kind to me as you have in my entire life, and I thank you for that. Me and Penny have about got the rest of this mess cleaned up. You go on and run along. I know you must have a lot more important things to do than fuss with all this."

"You sure I can't maybe carry something else out? Or maybe mop up that floor for you?"

"No, sir, we got it."

"Where are you and the kids going to sleep tonight?"

"Well, right here," she said. Where else do ya think?"

"But, the beds... the mattresses are all ripped to shreds."

"Don't trouble yourself about that, now. I've slept on a lot of floors in my lifetime and it ain't never killed me yet. We'll make us up a nice little bed of blankets on the floor and be just fine."

"But Mama, what if Danny Lee wets the bed again?"

"Hush, Penny. How can he wet the bed if there ain't no bed?"

"Aren't you worried that whoever did this will come back?" Robert asked.

"What for? They already know there's nothing here worth stealing. They got no reason to come back."

Robert started to say something more, but Alice propped the broom against the wall and said, "Mr. Tucker, the Good Lord don't give us nothing we can't handle. Now, I've buried four of my babies and a husband and I handled all a that, so I guess I can get through this here, too. You run along now. I appreciate all you done, but you'll just be underfoot."

***

Half an hour after Robert left, Alice told Penny to keep an eye on Danny Lee and went out the back door, walking the worn path to the outhouse. She went inside and latched the door behind her, then leaned down and stuck her arm through the wooden hole and felt around under the bottom of the bench until she felt the thick cord affixed to the underside. Pulling on it, she retrieved the metal box whose handle was tied to the other end and sat it on a piece of newspaper. She kept a stack, she brought home from the houses she cleaned and kept in the outhouse, not to read, but for wiping purposes. Wiping the box off with another piece of newspaper, she opened it and looked at the tightly sealed Mason jar inside. The money and Wanda Jean's jewelry were still there. She breathed a sigh of relief, then closed the box and let it drop below the surface, followed by the soiled newspapers.

Chapter 15

"What are you doing, Bob?"

"I'm just trying to help a lady out who's fallen on hard times," Robert said.

"Did you forget what I told you yesterday about taking a step back and keeping objective?"

"I heard what you said, but darn it Lester, somebody's got to do something!"

"But why does it have to be you, Bob? I'm sorry that lady's having a hard time, too. But I've spent enough time out in the Run to know that those people start having a hard time the day they're born, and it doesn't end until the day they put them in the ground and shovel dirt on top of 'em."

"And that makes it okay?" Robert asked as they loaded the second mattress into the back of the Dodge pickup truck he had borrowed from Dennis Edwards at the lumberyard. "So if someone's born into hard times, we should just ignore it and pretend it's not happening?"

"If I didn't know you better, I'd swear you're becoming one of those Communists or Socialists or whatever they call them. Just put it all in one big pot and let everybody take out what they want. That ain't the American way, Bob."

Robert ignored him as he slammed the truck's tailgate closed. When he started for the cab of the truck, Lester stopped him with a hand on his arm.

"What is it with this woman, Bob? There's a hundred families out there in the Run that don't have it any better than she does. Why do you feel like you have to save her? Why not the folks across the street, or next door, or someplace else in the Run?"

"Why not her, Lester? What makes her less deserving? Because her daughter had a reputation for being easy? What's that about the sins of the father? Is this a case where the sins of the daughter are cast down upon the mother? It just don't seem fair, Les, that's all."

"Hell, son, life ain't fair! If you haven't learned that yet I don't know if you're ever going to. Is it fair that Hitler murdered all those Jews? Is it fair what the Japs did? Hell, for that matter, is it fair what your wife did to you, running off like she did? Or is it fair that your own, poor Mama is so addled she don't know who she is, or who her own children are from one day to the next?"

"Well, we done away with Hitler, and we took care of the Japs. As for Shirley, I'm better off without her, I reckon. And Mama has her moments, I can't deny that, but that's the cards life has dealt us."

"That's my point," Lester said. "Hard times are the cards that lady out there in the Run got dealt! You can't reshuffle the deck and deal again, Bob. Wake up!"

"Why not?" Robert demanded, shaking his arm loose and feeling his face get hot. "Maybe I wasn't some big war hero like you were, Les. And maybe I wasn't man enough to keep my wife happy, or maybe I worked too hard, or whatever it was that made her run off. And maybe I can't get inside Mama's head and un-scramble whatever's wrong in there. But what I *can* do is I can gather up this old furniture that's been sitting around, and none of us is using, and I can take it out there to that poor woman in the Run. I *can* help one person, in one little way, and maybe that won't change the world, but it might just make *her* world a little easier to live in!"

"Whoa there, Hoss! You got no cause to go off on me like that. You need take a deep breath and clear your head."

"What I need to do is take this stuff out to the Run. Now, if you're done telling me about all my shortcomings, that's what I'm going to do."

The two friends stared at each other a moment longer, with jaws tight, then Lester stepped back. Without saying another word, Robert opened the door and climbed behind the wheel of the truck.

***

In her usual taciturn way, Alice Reider acknowledged the gifts Robert had brought by saying, "That's very nice of you, sir. I 'preciate it but you don't got no need to be goin' out of your way like this. There ain't no way I can ever pay you back."

Her son Paulie was less appreciative, shunning Robert's help as he

Dog's Run

drug a mattress off the back of the truck and carried it into the house. When he came back outside, Robert was setting an old wooden chest of drawers on the ground.

"So what's your game, mister? What are you after here?"

"What do you mean?" Robert asked.

"Well, I can't figure you out. You don't even know us and you keep showing up here doin' stuff that nobody asked you to. Are you one of the guys who was bangin' my sister and now you got a guilty conscience about it? I can't see you be'in' after my old lady, so it's either that you're a pervert who's got your eye on my little sister, or my little brother, or me. And if that's it, you're gonna get your ass whupped real fast."

"You've got a dirty mind and a dirty mouth to go with it, don't you?"

Paulie wore his hair slicked back with no part, with thick sideburns, a wisp of mustache on his upper lip, and a perpetual sneer. Life was hard in the Run, and even harder if you are Wanda Jean Reider's kid brother. He learned early on, that swift and aggressive response to any perceived insult or threat went a long way.

"How about you don't worry 'bout me and look out after yourself, if you know what's good for you."

"Are you threatening me, son?" Robert asked.

"I ain't your son, asshole, and I'm just lettin' you know that I got my eye on you. Like I said, I can't figure you out. But when I do, you and me will have another talk."

"Maybe, instead of thinking about me, you ought to put some thought into who came in here and busted up your Mama's place the other day. Or here's an idea, how about you quit trying to impress me with what a tough guy you are, and actually do something to help your Mama out for a change?"

"Like I said, I ain't your son, so I could give a damn what you think. Here's what I'm gonna do. I'm gonna carry this here dresser inside, then I'm gonna go over there to the shithouse and squeeze me out a big, old turd. And I might just name it after you!"

He lifted the dresser and carried it, bowlegged, to the house. Robert watched him go, then shook his head and got in the truck and drove back to town.

Chapter 16

I remember when I was a little girl Mama telling me that I had to save myself for the right man. She'd tell me I needed to find a young man away from the Run. A man that wore a tie and drove a nice car. Oh, Mama, if you only knew how many of those kind of men I found! Men with fancy cars and fancy clothes and foldin' money in their pockets. Yeah, I found 'em even though I didn't go lookin for 'em. But what Mama don't understand is that men like that, they'll take a girl like me for a ride at night when nobody can see, and they'll say all kinds of sweet things. They'll even give you nice things to get what they want out of you. But they don't marry girls from the Run. No, they marry girls just like themselves. Spoiled girls that live in nice houses and get their hair styled at Mabel's Salon of Beauty on Third Street. And there's something else I learned. Those men may marry those nice girls, but even after they do, they still slow down and invite me for a ride when they see me and nobody else is lookin. I gave up on those young men pretty quick. I figured out that if I'm gonna let a man use me, it might as well be their daddies, cause a man's just a man when he's on top of you gruntin away or has you on your knees doin' that other thing they all seem to like so much. It don't matter if he's 20 or 50. Except those old men own businesses and call the preacher man by name on Sunday morning after being with me Saturday night, and they're a lot more generous than their sons are.

    Robert shook his head in disgust. Not every entry in Wanda Jean's diaries was about her sexual encounters. Indeed, like any young girl, she had written about things like movie stars and music and her dreams of having a family someday. But he noted that there was never any mention of some boy she might have a crush on, or of girlfriends she might share girly secrets with. But even those normal entries somehow seemed to lack the happiness he would have expected to find in a young girl's diary. There seemed to be something tired, even jaded, in what she wrote. And those more normal entries were earlier on. The more he read, the less there were of them, and the more Wanda Jean seemed to focus on the seamier side of her life. Maybe because that *had* become the focus of her life.

I swear I had every intention of changin my ways when I applied for that job at Wilson's Department Store. I saw that sign in the window that said "Salesgirl Wanted" and all I did was go in there to apply for that job. But I noticed that Mr. Wilson's eyes never made it all the way up to my face from the minute I sat down. He said the job was in Ladies Foundation, and then he made some remark about maybe some ladies didn't need any extra support and he made that little laugh of his. But I just smiled at him and sure enough he hired me right there on the spot. And it was a good week before he did more than just say hello and ask me how I was doing. Then I was back in the stockroom sorting through a box of brassieres that come in, and the next thing I know he's behind me and has his arms around my waist, and he tellin' me how maybe I should model one of those red ones for him. 'Course, he didn't want to see me in a brassiere, he just wanted me out of mine. I tried to tell him no, but he was sayin how there's a lot of girls who wanted that job and how he really gave me a chance, what with me not having any experience and all. Then he said there was a very nice bonus in it for me if I was the kind of employee who showed her appreciation for the break he gave me. That was the first time I actually took cash money off a man. $20. That was more than I was makin in a week. And I found out something. Two things, actually. If a man gives you a gift, that's nice. But with cash money you can buy whatever you want, not just settle for whatever he gives you. The other thing I learned is that once they pay you that cash money, they don't even pretend about what's happening between you any more. You're bought and paid for.

Robert heard the telephone ring out front and Lillian answer it, and a moment later she pushed his office door open without knocking. He barely had time to shove the diary out of sight and was just about to scold her, when she said, "That was Chief Smeal. Your mama's been hurt!"

***

"We got a call from Mrs. Alexander next door. She said she was sitting in her living room reading a magazine and she heard some noise outside. She looked out the window and saw a ladder propped up against the side of the house and didn't give it much thought. Then a minute later she heard your Mama talking and she looked outside because she wondered what you two were up to. She thought it was strange you'd be home doing chores around the house in the middle of a workday. That's when she saw your Mama up there on the ladder and rushed outside. She said Dorothy was chattering away like she was in the middle of a conversation, talking about needing to paint the eaves and clean the gutters. She said she tried to get her to come down, but Dorothy acted like she didn't even hear her. Then she said something about needing paint thinner, and Mrs. Alexander said she stepped sideways right off the ladder and came crashing down."

"It's all my fault," Elizabeth sobbed. "I should have spent more time over there. Oh, Mama, please don't you die on us!"

"Now don't you go making mountains out of molehills until we know something," Lester said. "She may not be right in her head, but your Mama's healthy as a horse, otherwise. Hell, Lizzie, I wouldn't be surprised if she outlives us all!"

Before anybody could respond, the examination room opened and Doctor Crowther came out.

"How is she?" Elizabeth asked in a trembling voice.

"She's going to be just fine, Elizabeth," he said patting her hand. "She got the wind knocked out of her, and a few scratches and bumps and bruises, but otherwise she's okay."

"Can I see her now?"

"Sure you can, dear. Just go right on in. Nurse Hughes is just cleaning her up a little bit. You're Mama's a bit confused right now, but I'm sure she'd appreciate seeing you."

Elizabeth hurried into the examination room, but the doctor stopped Robert and Lester with an upraised hand. "Give them a bit to get her tidied up. We need to talk. Let's go in my office."

Dog's Run

Chapter 17

They followed him into his office and took seats across from his desk. Crowther took off his glasses, wiped them on his tie, then held them up for inspection. Satisfied with what he saw, he put them back on and said, "I've known Dorothy Tucker since we were school kids. Her and my younger sister Joyce were best friends growing up. In fact, she gave a nice little talk at Joyce's funeral and sang a pretty song for her. I've always admired Dorothy and the way she handled things after your Daddy died, Robert. A lot of women with two little kids to raise would have married the first man that came along asking, but not Dorothy. She worked hard over there at the telephone company and provided a good home for you and your sister. Never took a dime of charity either. So please understand that what I'm going to say now comes from both my perspective as a medical doctor, and as a lifelong friend."

Robert nodded, but did not reply, and the doctor regarded him for a long moment.

"Robert, you're a fine man, but you can't do it all. You're running the newspaper and sitting on the Library Board and half a dozen other things, and that's all well and good. Elmhurst needs men like you. But your Mama needs more. This thing today. We all know it could have turned out a lot worse. Could have been a tragedy."

Robert shifted uncomfortably in his chair.

"Dorothy is never going to get better. We all know that. Unfortunately, she may get worse. The time has come to consider alternatives."

"We're not sticking my mother in one of those old folks homes!"

"Listen to me, Robert…"

"There's nothing to discuss," Robert said, shaking his head stubbornly. "That woman has lived in the same house for over forty years. She raised Lizzie and me there and it's her home. I'm not throwing her out with the dishwater."

Lester put a hand on Robert's arm. "Take it easy, Bob. Nobody's doing anything just now. But let's hear the man out, okay?"

Robert started to object, but Lester squeezed his arm firmly. "Just listen to the Doc, that's all. We can't make informed choices if we don't know what our options are. Nobody's gonna cart your Mama off nowhere."

Robert remained silent, but sat stiffly in the chair.

"There are alternatives to a live-in residence setting. What about some sort of assistance to help you? To be there when you can't be?"

"Lizzie can pitch in more," Lester said.

"Lizzie's got two kids to raise," Robert said. "And besides, you know how hard it is for her to deal with Mama the way she is. She comes away all upset and frazzled."

"Don't underestimate your sister," Lester told him. "She comes from strong stock."

"I know that, Les. But you saw how she was the other night."

"Have you considered some sort of live-in assistant?" the doctor asked.

"You're talking about a babysitter?"

The doctor shrugged and said, "You could call it that, I guess. It's…"

"It's humiliating, is what it is," Robert said. "Take an independent lady like that and start treating her like a child! Besides, even if I agreed, I can't afford to pay a nurse to be there all the time."

"She doesn't need a nurse," Crowther said. "Just somebody to look after her when you're out. To keep her safe and out of mischief. A *companion*, if you will."

"A babysitter!"

Before anything more could be said, there was a knock at the door and the doctor's nurse poked her head inside. "Mrs. Tucker is all cleaned up, and she'd like to see Mister Robert."

***

At 61, Dorothy Tucker was a pretty woman with graying hair and smiling blue eyes. Even though she was tall and buxom, she had always been light and graceful on her feet. She was sitting up in bed, wearing a wide smile, when Robert and Lester came into the room and started chuckling.

"Look at the long faces on you two," she said, pointing. "You boys look like you lost your best friend!"

"How are you, Mama?" Robert asked, kissing her cheek.

"I'm just fine, Robert. I'm just not sure what I'm doing here."

"They said you fell off a ladder, Mama. What were you doing up there anyway?"

"A ladder? Nonsense! Who told you that?"

"Mrs. Alexander saw you fall. You about scared the life out of her."

"Oh pish! Gladys Alexander always makes a big deal out of everything. I wasn't up on any ladder. I think I may have tripped over a throw rug or something."

"Mama, do you remember getting the ladder out of the shed?" Elizabeth asked.

"The ladder?"

"Yes, Mama, the ladder. The one you fell off of."

"Oh, the ladder! Yes, I was helping your Daddy clean the leaves out of the eaves. If you don't do it this time of the year, you're asking for trouble all winter long. Take care of the little things before they become big ones, your Daddy always says."

"So you were up on that ladder?"

"Well of course I was, Elizabeth. Didn't I just say that? Your Daddy can't do it all by himself, can he?"

"Mama, I'd have helped Daddy when I got home," Robert said. "You didn't need to get up there on that ladder."

"Oh Robert, you're working so hard on your studies. You don't need to be worrying about all that. And besides," and she lowered her voice to a stage whisper and looked around before she spoke, "I think that Shirley Barnes has a crush on you. You should walk her home from school one of these afternoons. And don't forget to carry her books! That's what a gentleman does."

"Yes, ma'am, I'll do that," Robert said, patting her hand.

"And you," Dorothy said, pointing at Lester, "Now that you and Elizabeth are engaged, you need to start thinking about getting a better job, Lester. Now, I know you love working with your Daddy at the greenhouse, but it's going to be difficult to support a family on what you earn there. I could ask Mr. Tucker to talk to Mr. Rheiner at the post office, if you'd like, and put in a good word for you."

"That would sure be nice of you, Miss Dorothy. I'd appreciate that."

"Well, then, consider it done!" Dorothy said, folding her hands in her lap. "Now you'd better run along home, young man. Elizabeth has homework to do. But I'll look the other way while you give her a peck on the cheek, if you'd like."

"Thank you, ma'am, I'd like that just fine."

"Speaking of going home, how'd you like to go home, Dorothy?" Doctor Crowther asked.

"I believe I'm ready, Albert. It's late and I've got kids to feed. You give my love to Madge, and if you see that sister of yours, tell her I've got that dress pattern she wanted to borrow."

"Now, you're going to feel a bit stiff and sore tomorrow," the doctor said. "I could give you some pain medication, but really, Bayer aspirin will work just as well."

"That's fine, Albert," Dorothy said, wincing slightly as Elizabeth helped her out of bed.

"Are you okay, Mama? Are you hurting?"

"No, I'm fine dear. Just old age creeping up on me, I guess."

Robert held her arm as they walked out to the car and he helped her inside.

Elizabeth opened the back door and Dorothy asked, "What are you doing, dear?"

"I'm going to ride home with you and help you get settled in."

"Oh, there's no need for that. I'm just fine."

"It's no problem, Mama."

"Well, if you insist."

"I do, Mama."

***

Two hours later, with her mother comfortably ensconced in bed, Elizabeth kissed her goodbye and promised to come by in the morning to check on her. Robert walked her out to his car and gave her the keys.

"Is she going to be okay, Bobby?"

"She'll be fine. Doc said she doesn't have any serious injuries at all."

"She's so addled right now. It seems like she gets worse every week. She didn't even know who I was when I first went in to help the nurse with her."

"Lizzie, she'll be fine," Robert assured her again. "This morning she made me breakfast and we had a nice chat before I went to work. She just gets forgetful later in the day. Now go home before your kids forget who you are."

"I love her so much, Bobby. I do! But I don't think you realize how bad she's getting. Maybe because you're around her every night, it doesn't seem so much. But I can see it."

"I'm not stupid, Lizzie. I can see it. But I think you're blowing things out of proportion."

"I never said you were stupid, Bobby! Please, let's don't quarrel."

"You're right," Robert said, kissing her cheek, "We're all tired and upset right now. Let's talk about this later, okay? But for now, go home, Elizabeth. Your kids and Lester need you."

He watched her back out into the street and drive away, then turned back toward the house when a voice called out from next door, "Robert? I'm so sorry. I tried to get her down off that ladder."

"It's not your fault, Mrs. Alexander," he said, crossing his neighbor's yard to stand at the bottom of the porch steps. "I should have locked the shed so she couldn't get inside it."

The round little woman who had been like an aunt to him all of his life said, "Then what, Robert? Are you going to lock every door in the world? I try to keep an eye on her, but…"

"It's okay," he said, interrupting her. "Listen, I'm beat. Let me get inside and check on Mama. I appreciate all you do, Mrs. Alexander. I really do."

"Well, if she needs anything, you just give me a shout."

"I'll do that. But we'll be fine. Really, we will."

He went inside and heard his mother calling him.

"I'm right here, Mama," he said, going to her bedside. "Do you need anything? Are you in pain?"

"No, I'm just embarrassed for doing such a fool stunt like getting up on that ladder. I don't know what I was thinking. I'm sorry to worry everybody like I did."

"It's alright, Mama. Just promise me you won't do that again, okay?"

"I promise. Now give me a kiss and I think I'll get some rest."

He kissed her cheek and tucked her in, then switched off the bedside light. As he started to leave the room, she spoke again.

"Robert, I'm not sure about something."

"What's that, Mama?"

"That nice blonde woman who rode home with us from Doc Crowther's? She looked familiar to me. Have I met her before?"

Chapter 18

After that first time with Mr. Wilson in the back of the store, I'll be honest and tell you that I felt pretty low. Sure, I liked that money he gave me, but I couldn't fool myself any more about what I was. I was a whore. No different than some whore standing on a street corner on skid row in Toledo. No, I wasn't standing on a street corner and I didn't go lookin for the men. But they were always there. That silly Mr. Wilson, after he give me that money the first time, you'd a thought I was his personal property! Anytime a man came into the store and I even smiled at them or said hello he was right there making sure they wasn't gettin any of what he was payin for. 'Course, that didn't slow me down any. More than once I'd be in the back room with him and then go right down the street to the Five and Dime just as Mr. Riley was lockin the door, and we'd go back in that back room of his and I'd do that thing he liked so much and walk out that door with even more money in my pocket! No, I can't say I'm proud of myself, but it does feel good to help Mama out with the electric bill and to buy my little sister Penny a pretty dress or some toy soldiers for David Lee. Mama says the Good Lord made each of us like we are for his own reason and it's not ours to question why. So I decided that if he made me a whore, he must have his reason for it, and I take some comfort in that.

***

I took Penny and David Lee to the movie today to see Gene Autry in Silver Canyon. He sure is a good actor! Penny loves the movies, especially the ones where the cowboys sing like Gene does. David Lee can't follow the story, but he likes it when they get to shooting! I remember a movie we saw a while back where one of those villains had notches carved in his sixgun handle for every man he killed. It made me wonder what people would think if I carved a notch in something for every man that's had me. Why, I could start with a big old pine tree and have myself a walkin stick by the time I was done!

His mother had seemed more clear-headed Saturday morning, though she was stiff and sore and didn't want to get out of bed except to have Robert help her down the hallway to the bathroom. Once she was back in bed, he brought her a tray with oatmeal, toast, and coffee.

Robert had spent the morning piddling with chores around the house, but was growing restless by the time Elizabeth arrived at noon. Assuring him that she had things well in hand, his sister shooed him out the door. Robert drove around town for a while, trying to shake off the unsettled feeling that had been with him all morning. Finally, he stopped at the diner and got a plate to go and went to his office. He had just finished his lunch when he heard the bell over the front door.

When he went to the counter he found a scraggly looking man dressed in bib overalls and wearing a straw hat.

"Are you the newspaperman?" asked his visitor.

"Well, this is a newspaper and I'm a man, so I guess so," Robert said. "What can I do for you, sir?"

"It's about that girl that got herself killed the other day."

"Wanda Jean Reider? Police Chief Smeal has closed that case as a suicide."

"Yeah, well Chief Smeal weren't there."

"What do you mean?" Robert asked. "Were you there? Do you know something that he doesn't?"

"Not sayin' I was and not sayin' I wasn't," the man told him. "But if a feller was somewhere around that bridge that night and he saw somethin' but didn't want to get involved with the law, what would he do?"

"Well, it seems to me like he'd come to the newspaper office and strike up a conversation with the man in charge."

The man scratched his neck and then said, "See, here's the problem. I kinda had a few run-ins with the Law myself and I try to avoid messin' with 'em. I hear you and the police chief are kinfolk, so I'm going out on a limb just talkin' to you as it is."

"I didn't get your name, sir," Robert said extending his hand. "But I'm Robert Tucker, owner of the newspaper."

The man seemed to think about it for a moment, then reached out a grimy, calloused hand with broken fingernails and shook Robert's.

"Conrad Phillips."

"So, are you telling me you know something about Wanda Jean's death?" Robert asked.

Phillips worked his mouth a time or two and then said, "Well now, like I said, I try to avoid John Law when I can 'cause they's always caused me trouble. So what I'm gonna tell you ain't something I'm gonna sit down and repeat to Chief Smeal."

"We're just two guys having a conversation off the record," Robert told him.

Phillips looked around, as if to be sure they were alone in the office, then said, "I make a little 'shine now and then. Sunday night me and my cousin Rex was parked there off the side of the road by the bridge, back there in the trees, waitin' for a feller from Norwalk who was supposed to meet us there to pick up a few bottles. That's when we seen it."

"What did you see?" Robert asked him.

"We saw this woman walkin' across the bridge and a car stopped next to her and this feller got out from the driver's side and they had themselves a big old argument, screamin' and cussin' and all that. Then that feller, he thumped that gal upside the head and she just fell down right there on the side of the road. Next thing we knew, he looked around to be sure no cars was comin', and then he picked her up and set her on the rail of the bridge and then pushed her over!"

"Did you see who the man and woman were?" Robert asked him.

"No, sir. It was dark and I couldn't make out no faces."

"What about the car? Could you identify it if you saw it again?"

"No, sir, it was a big, black car, that's all I can tell you."

"What happened then?"

"What happened was as soon as that car hightailed it toward town, we got the hell out of there! Like I said, I've had my trouble with the law before and I don't need no more."

"Mr. Phillips, if what you're telling me is true, you and your cousin witnessed a murder. It doesn't matter what problems you've had with the law before, you've got to tell Chief Smeal about this."

"No, sir!" Phillips said, shaking his head adamantly. "I ain't talkin' to the police and if you bring my name into it, I'm gonna swear you're lyin' and that we never even met."

"Then what do you expect me to do?" Robert asked. "Why even come in here and tell me all this if you're not willing to talk to Chief Smeal about it?"

"You're a college educated man and I ain't nothin' but a hillbilly from the Run," Phillips said. "You figure out how to tell him what he needs to know and keep my name outta it. And as for why I'm tellin' you in the first place is because Wanda Jean may not of been nothin' but a whore to all these rich folks here in town, but out there in the Run, she was one of our own. And for all her good looks she weren't stuck up. She'd always smile and say hello or wave when I passed by. I knew I never had a chance with a woman like that and I never even tried. But she was the best thing I ever saw in the Run, and she deserves more than what she got."

"What about your cousin, Rex? Will he talk to me or to the Chief?"

Philips shook his head again. "Chief Smeal is about the best law we've ever had around here. Yeah, he'll thump a head now and then when it needs thumpin', but I ain't never know'd him to be mean just for the sake of bein' mean. Now Chief Gray who come before him? That man was pure mean. I saw him go out of his way to run up on the side of the road and run over a little dog one time that weren't doing nothin' at all. And he liked beatin' on folks, him and that fat deputy of his. They took pleasure in it. So yeah, Chief Smeal's a lot better. But he's still the law and it's still the Run and those two ain't never gonna go together any better'n dogs and cats do. Now I've told you all I can tell you and all I know. I got it off my chest and it's yours to do with what you see fit."

With that he turned and walked out the door.

Chapter 19

Except for being together at Doctor Crowther's office after his mother's accident, Robert had avoided Lester since their argument Friday morning. He wanted to forgo the traditional Sunday afternoon dinner at his sister's house, but as luck would have it, for the first time in over a month, his mother wanted to go and spend time with her grandchildren.

Dinner was civil, though strained between the two men. Loretta and Woodrow loved having their grandmother visit and she doted on him, insisting on cutting Woodrow's roast beef even though he was fully capable and would have objected if his mother had done the same thing. After they had finished the fruit salad Elizabeth had prepared for dessert, Dorothy insisted on helping with the dishes and the children went outside to play, leaving Lester and Robert alone at the table in an uncomfortable silence.

Sensing something was wrong between her husband and brother, Elizabeth urged them to go sit on the porch and smoke. Lester sat in his rocking chair watching his children frolic on the wide lawn, while Robert lounged on the porch swing, lost in his own thoughts.

After a long time, Lester broke the silence. "I never knew you resented all that stuff that happened when we was in the Army. I never asked to be no hero. Hell, I ain't one. I didn't do nothing a thousand other guys didn't do and I don't know why I got singled out for it. There's been a lot of times I wish I hadn't been."

"I was out of line," Robert said, "and I'm sorry I said that. You deserve that medal and I'm ashamed of myself for what I said."

"You know, friends can disagree, but that don't change who they are. Just 'cause I don't think it's a good idea for you to be messin' around out there in the Run don't change who we are, you and me."

"I know that, Les. And I'm sorry we argued. But I just can't turn my head and look away when I see something that needs doing."

"You wouldn't be the man you are if you did," Lester said. "I just don't want to see you getting hurt."

"How can I get hurt by just being nice to somebody, Les?"

"You don't understand those people out there in the Run," Lester told him. "There's people out there that would just as soon stick a knife in your ribs for two bits you have in your pocket as to say hello. And the other side of that coin is that there's folks right here in town that would stick a knife in your back just as quick. You're putting yourself between two different worlds, Robert. Their world is as different as us and the Japs were. People say, how could they do the things they did during the war, but it's because they're different people and they don't think the way we do. It's the same with the folks here in town and those out there in the Run. They're different as night and day."

"You can't be saying that everybody in the Run is bad and anybody here in town is good," Robert said.

Lester shook his head, "That's not what I'm saying at all. What I'm trying to tell you is they're different. And you're putting yourself in the middle and that ain't no good place to be, because then you become a target for both sides. What you see as helping, some folks will see as meddling. Now, I know your intentions are good, but I can guarandamtee you that there's going to be some out in the Run who think you're just some rich man getting involved where he don't need to be. They'll be questioning your intentions and wondering what it is you really want. And there are people here in town, people who own businesses and advertise with your newspaper, who look down their noses at the folks out there in the Run. And when they look down those noses, who do they see right up front where he's got no business being? You! That's what I mean by you getting hurt. No good can come of this, Robert."

Robert started to object, then remembered his conversation with Paulie Reider when he had dropped off the furniture. If Paulie's reaction was typical of what people in Dog's Run were thinking of his good intentions, maybe Lester had a point.

Before he could decide what to say, the screen door opened and Dorothy brought out glasses and a pitcher of lemonade.

"Here Mama, sit here beside me," Robert said, patting the swing beside him.

"Oh, we really should be getting home," Dorothy said. "It's Sunday and I promised your sister I would put a Toni permanent in her hair for school. You know she's sweet on that nice boy, Lester Smeal, and she's

Dog's Run

got her fingers crossed he'll invite her to the prom."

A pained look crossed Elizabeth's face, erasing the comfort the family dinner had given her.

"It's okay, Mama, we can stay a while longer."

"No, we really do need to get along, Robert," Dorothy said, then turned and shook her daughter's hand. "Thank you so much for your hospitality. I do hope you'll bring your family by next Sunday and let us return the favor. I just know you and my daughter, Elizabeth, would get along famously. She's quite a bit younger than you, but she's such a darling. I'm so proud of her. Of course, any mother would be, don't you think?"

Elizabeth blinked back tears and smiled bravely. "We'll have to do that sometime. I'd love to meet her. She must be a wonderful daughter to hold such a special place in your heart."

"Oh yes," said Dorothy. "You know what they say, a son will hold your hand for just a little while and then he grows up and leaves you. But the love between a mother and daughter grows stronger every day."

Robert steered his mother to the car and got her settled in the passenger seat, then went back and kissed his sister's cheek.

"I'm sorry, Lizzie."

She shook her head and held up her hand. "Don't, Robert. I know she doesn't mean to hurt me when she gets like this. I keep telling myself we had a few good hours today and I'm grateful for that."

"She loves you, you do know that, right?"

Elizabeth nodded, not able to hold the tears back any longer. "Yes, she loves me. She just has no idea who I am."

Robert started to say something to her, but the car's horn honked and Dorothy leaned over the seat to call out the driver's window, "Robert we really do need to run, your sister's waiting for us."

With one last look toward Elizabeth, Robert turned and went to the car.

Dog's Run

Chapter 20

Robert had a restless night and woke up grouchy and with a headache on Monday. As happened often with his mother in the mornings, Dorothy seemed perfectly normal as she chatted over breakfast, reminding him that he needed to stop at Randy's Barbershop to get a haircut, and wondering why he felt the need to work so hard. Robert replied in monosyllables, his mind elsewhere. When he finished his coffee he kissed her cheek and told her he'd call to check on her during the day.

When he pushed the starter button on his old coupe, the motor turned over sluggishly and he held his breath until it caught. He wasn't sure a new convertible was in his future, but maybe it was time to stop by and see Andy Zimmerman and maybe inquire about what he had in stock in used cars. He had seen a nice looking 1949 Ford Tudor sitting on Andy's lot the other day.

But not today. Robert had wrestled with the information Conrad Phillips had shared with him all weekend. He knew he needed to tell Lester about it. In spite of his warnings about meddling in affairs out at Dog's Run, murder was murder, and Lester needed to know. *If* a murder had actually been committed. How credible a witness was Phillips, a man who admitted to being a moonshiner with a criminal history?

Robert left town and drove past the cemetery, crossing the bridge over Dog's Run and turning onto Roan Road. He found Alice Reider hanging laundry on a clothesline, propped up by two shaky wooden T-shaped posts.

"Morning, Miz Reider. How are you today?"

"Fine, Mr. Tucker. What brings you out here today?"

"I need to ask you something."

She paused in shaking out a shirt. "This about those books of Wanda Jean's?"

"No, ma'am. This is something else. Do you know a man named Conrad Phillips?"

Alice scowled at the mention of Phillips' name. "Guess I know 'bout everybody hereabouts. Even if they is some I'd prefer not to."

"Is Conrad one of them you'd prefer not to?"

"Conrad Phillips ain't no worse than some, ain't no better'n than a lot more."

"What do you think of him?"

"Thought I just told you that."

"Yes ,ma'am, I guess you did. Do you think he's honest?"

"Ain't nobody in this world honest all the time, Mr. Tucker. You know that."

"Including Conrad Phillips?"

"Including everybody. We all 'bout as honest as we need be. No more'n no less."

"Yes, ma'am, I guess you're right. You've got work to do, I won't be troubling you any more. You have yourself a good day," Robert said, tipping his hat.

As he turned away, Alice said, "You don't seem like one who favors gossip. So I 'spect you had your reasons for askin' about Conrad."

"There's some who would say my entire business is about gossip in one form or another," Robert replied.

"I reckon some would say so," she agreed. "Anyway, like I said, Conrad ain't no better than a lot, and he ain't no worse either. He grew up minding his Daddy's stills and ain't never done no other work in his life. Some see that as a sin, but it ain't no worse than the man who stands behind a bar and sells liquor is it??

"No, ma'am, I guess it isn't."

"I used to hate Conrad because it was his shine my husband Raymond was drunk on when he got himself killed in that wreck. But truth is, if it weren't Conrad's liquor, it woulda been somebody elses."

"I guess that's true."

"You asked me if Conrad was honest. I don't know that I'd loan him any money, if I had any to loan. But I will say that after Raymond died, he came by and apologized to me for selling him that shine. There's others that would have pretended they never heard of him. I guess that says somethin' 'bout the man."

"Yes, ma'am, I guess it does. Thank you for your time." Robert tipped his hat again and walked back across the yard, while Alice went back to hanging laundry on the clothesline.

Dog's Run
***

He drove through the Run, passing rundown houses and shanties where dirty children played in the yards and hungry dogs barked at his car, a few chasing it a few yards before giving up and laying back down.

Robert reached for a cigarette and realized he was out, so he pulled into the dirt parking lot of Reynolds' Store. He went in for a pack of Chesterfields, passing a group of three or four teenage boys who were lounging in the shade on the side of the building. When he came back outside, the door of his car was open and a pair of legs stuck out.

"What the hell are you doing?"

Startled, Paulie Reider banged his head on the dashboard and cursed.

"You trying to hotwire my car? Get out from under there!"

"Don't you be accusin' me of stealin'. I was just lookin' at your piece of shit car, asshole."

"Uh huh. You always look under the dashboard first when you admire a car?"

Paulie smirked at him and said, "There ain't much to admire about this old clunker. If I *was* to steal it, I'd have been doin' you a favor."

"You think you're pretty funny, don't you? Maybe Chief Smeal won't think it's such a laughing matter."

"He said he was just lookin' at it," said one of the boys that Robert had seen earlier, and he realized that they had formed a circle around him, with Paulie still standing in front of the open car door.

"Yeah. Like I said, I was just lookin' at it. Now, I think you owe me an apology, Mr. Newsaperman."

"Get out of my way," Robert said, and started to brush the boy away when he heard a sharp click and Paulie waved a switchblade knife in front of him.

"This here's that guy I was tellin' y'all about. Can't decide if he's a pervert after my little sister or one of those queers got his eye on my brother and me."

"Cut his ass, Paulie," somebody said behind him, and Robert heard another boy laugh as he felt them tighten the circle around him.

They were all about fifteen or sixteen years old, but these were not children. They had all grown up under rough circumstances, where violence and even bloodshed were taken for granted. Paulie moved a step closer and the knife was inches from his face. Robert felt his bowels turn to water, but he knew that just like dealing with a mean dog, showing fear would only make matters worse.

"Get out of my way, Paulie."

"Oh yeah? What if I don't? What you gonna do?"

"I'm going to stick that knife so far up your ass it's going to take a team of doctors a week to get it back out."

"See, I told you he was a queer," Paulie said to his friends. "Right away he wants to stick something up my ass!"

They laughed and Robert was deciding what his best move would be when a gunshot rang out. Standing in the doorway of his store, Mel Reynolds pumped the action of the Ithaca sixteen gauge shotgun and said, "That one was in the air. The next one won't be. Ya'll get on out of here and leave that man alone."

"We was just havin' fun," a boy the size of a college linebacker said, "weren't no harm done."

"Ya'll go have your fun someplace else. Not on my property. Now git!"

Paulie folded the knife and slipped it back into his pocket and smiled at Robert. "Watch yourself, asshole. I'll be around."

The boys sauntered away and Robert said, "I appreciate the help. I sure needed it."

"You keep poking your nose around here in Dog's Run and you're gonna need more help than I can give you," Reynolds said. "This ain't no place for you, sir. You'd best stay in town and away from here."

"You're not the first person to tell me that," Robert admitted.

"Yeah, well maybe you'd better start listening." And with that the storekeeper went back inside and closed the door.

Chapter 21

"What? Are you nuts?" Lester shouted. "Didn't I tell you to stop messing around out there in the Run? You just couldn't leave well enough alone, could you?"

"I didn't hear this out in the Run," Robert said. "I told you, a man came into my office and told me about it."

"And you can't tell me who this man is?"

"That's right, he made me promise to keep his name out of it."

"He made you promise to…. Jesus Christ, Robert. You come in here with some cockamamie story that somebody told you, you won't tell me who it is, and you expect me to believe it?"

"I think you need to at least look into it."

"Look into what? Some mysterious man tells you that he saw some man and some woman get in a fight and the man throws her off the bridge. But he couldn't see who the man was, he couldn't see who the woman was, and all he knew was that it was a big, black car. Is that it? That's what I'm supposed to look into?"

"So you think it's just coincidence that a man and a woman got in a fight on the bridge and he threw her off the day before Wanda Jean Reider was found dead by that same bridge?"

"I don't think it's coincidence at all. I think it's bullshit."

"Lester, a young girl is dead. Doesn't that matter to you at all?"

"Of course it does!" Lester said, pounding his desktop with his fist. "Are you accusing me of not doing my job? 'Cause if you are, me and you are about to go at it, brother-in-law or no brother-in-law!"

"All I'm saying is…"

"All you're saying is bullshit! Now, that girl killed herself. You saw the goddamn note she left. And now you come in here with this fairytale you want me to believe because some man whose name you won't tell me, and who you never heard of a week ago, told you it was so."

"Yes, I saw the note. And yes, it was in Wanda Jean's handwriting.

But that don't mean somebody didn't throw her off the bridge."

"And this fairytale of yours don't mean… wait a minute. How do you know what Wanda Jean's handwriting looks like anyway? Next thing you're gonna tell me she was writing letters to the editor, or covering the Art Club meetings for you."

"Of course not." Robert knew he had said too much, but couldn't figure out how to backpedal.

"Robert, how do you know what Wanda Jean's handwriting looks like?"

"I read the note, remember? You handed it to me."

Lester rose from his seat and leaned forward over his desk, palms down on top of it. "You listen to me boy, and you listen real good. I don't care if you are Lizzie's brother. You're getting in way over your head and you need to think real careful about how you answer this next question. How do you know what Wanda Jean's handwriting looks like?"

"What does it matter? The point is, the girl is dead and she may not have killed herself."

"You know more about this than you're tellin' me and I want to know what it is."

The two men glared at each other, the only sound in the room a fly buzzing overhead. Robert wasn't sure why he was unwilling to tell Lester about the diaries. It wasn't like he cared about the men Wanda Jean had written about, and her own reputation was tarnished long before her death. But still, he felt protective of her somehow, even though he couldn't explain why.

"Look, Lester, I came in here to tell you what was told to me because I trust you. What you do with that information is up to you, I guess."

Lester sat back in his chair and regarded his longtime friend. "You just said you came in here because you trust me, Bob. But you won't tell me who it was that gave you that information and now you won't tell me how you know it was Wanda Jean's handwriting on that suicide note. So maybe you don't trust me so much after all. Which is it?"

"The fellow I talked to said he'd deny it if I told anybody we talked. So knowing his name isn't going to make any difference."

"It might. If it was someone credible, that would make it a lot more believable than if it was some barfly just spoutin' off for the sake of being heard."

"Lester, you and I have a unique relationship. We've been best friends since we were kids, and now we're family. But at same time, you're the Chief of Police and I own the newspaper. There are things you know about that go on in this town that you keep to yourself, because you've got good reason to. I've never asked you to tell me something you couldn't, because I wouldn't put you on a spot like that. But right now the table's turned and I'm in that spot."

Lester regarded him in silence for a moment. "Let me ask you this, Bob. Do you think this guy was telling you the truth?"

"I think he saw just what he told me. There isn't any reason for him to come and tell me about it if it wasn't true. If he wanted to get somebody in trouble, or frame them, he'd have told me who it was he saw out there. And if he was trying to get credit for something or just attention for himself, he wouldn't have insisted I keep his name out of it."

Lester closed his eyes and thought for a moment, then opened them and said, "Let's go for a ride."

***

They parked Lester's police car at the foot of the bridge and walked out a distance.

"I found where she landed right about down there," Lester said, pointing into the ravine. "There was blood and some hair on those rocks. So that means she had to have jumped right about here. Do you see any blood on the railing or on the pavement here anywhere to prove what that fella told you?"

Robert studied the rail and surrounding area, just as Lester had done the day Wanda Jean's body was found. And just like the chief, he found nothing to support Conrad Phillips' story. But just because there was no evidence didn't make it untrue.

He walked off the bridge and past Lester's Buick to a small cluster of trees, where wheel ruts indicated automobiles had parked in the past. The ground was littered with cigarette butts and broken beer bottles.

"He said he was parked back here," Robert said.

"Lots of people park here," Lester said. "Lovers makin' out, kids drinkin' or whatever. Look at this place. It's a mess."

A sweat bee buzzed around Robert's face and he batted it away with his hand. "If a guy was backed in and parked here, he'd have a good view of the bridge just like that man said he did."

"Okay, Bob. Let's assume that what he told you is true, and I ain't saying it is. But if it was, what do we have? He didn't see the people's faces and all he could say was that it was a big, black car. What am I supposed to do with that?"

"I don't know, Les. But if there is a possibility that somebody really did kill that girl, don't you think it needs looking into?"

Lester took a deep breath and spent a long moment looking back toward the bridge. "Okay, you win. But I have to have something to go on, Bob. If I could talk to this fella he might remember something else, you never know. Will you do this for me? Will you try to get hold of him and convince him to sit down and talk with me? Tell him I don't care what he was up to that night out here, as long as he wasn't involved in whatever happened to that girl. Will you do that?"

"I will, Les. I'll do my best. And thank you."

"You don't need to thank me for doing my job. But if this is a wild goose chase, and I still suspect that it is, I'm not going to appreciate having my time wasted."

Both men were quiet driving back into town, neither willing to test the fragile truce between them. Lester dropped Robert off at the newspaper office and drove away without a parting word.

Chapter 22

I don't know when things started turnin' this way. Maybe they was destined to all along. I read in a magazine article one time that we all have a fate that's waitin' for us and there ain't nothing we can do about it. I don't know. Maybe it started way back there with Mr. Bigelow in high school and just followed its natural course from there. Sometimes I wonder what would'a happened if I had pushed his hand away that first time he put it on my knee and told me that a pretty little girl like me needed to think about her future. But what would that future have been? Married young to some factory hand and with a passel of kids? Worn out like my mama by the time she was 30? Or maybe workin' behind the counter at Riley's Five and Dime? Then again, if it hadn't all started with Mr. Bigelow, wouldn't I have found myself in the same place, right at Riley's? Now, Mama's Bible says otherwise. It says that we can confess all our sins and be washed in blood. I'm not sure if I believe all that Bible stuff or not. But I got a feeling that my fate was already set in stone the day I was born.

***

Lester Smeal knew his town and the people in it, and given what he had learned from Robert, it didn't take him long to figure out that Conrad Phillips had been the mysterious visitor to the newspaper office. Besides young lovers and teenage boys drinking, Lester knew that the grove of trees just off Alexis Road near the bridge was a common rendezvous spot for moonshiners and their customers.

A quick look through the duty roster told him that Billy Shaver and Duane Collett had been on duty the night in question. When he called both officers in and inquired, Duane said he had spent most of his time on the west side of town, where there had been complaints of hooligans stealing gasoline out of cars and racing their old jalopies near the high school.

Billy said that he remembered seeing Phillips and his cousin, Rex Hooper, coming out of Dog's Run and turning right on Alexis Road in the direction of the bridge sometime around 11:30, when he had driven back to town to use the bathroom at the police station and eat the fried egg sandwich his wife had packed in his lunchbox.

Phillips was one of the bootleggers that Lester tended to ignore as long as he kept himself within reason and didn't cause trouble. He made good shine, treated his woman and kids well, and wasn't above leaving an occasional Mason jar of his best product on the back steps of the station every so often. While they were far from friendly, the lawman and the outlaw had a grudging respect for each other.

He decided he needed to pay a call on Phillips, but first he had a meeting at the mayor's office to discuss the City Council's latest budget and to see if there was any room in it for a radio system for the department. Having to find a telephone and call in hampered his officers' abilities to respond quickly to emergencies and do their jobs. Little did he know that that meeting would keep him from talking to Conrad Phillips forevermore.

***

Robert had just finished a meeting of his own, this one with the Library Board, when he returned to his office and Lillian Jackson told him that she had received a telephone call about a shooting in Dogs Run. While the sound of gunfire wasn't unknown in the Run, it usually happened on Friday and Saturday nights when the hillbillies had gotten themselves liquored up, not on a Monday afternoon.

"What happened? Was anybody injured?"

"Marlene Sawicki, from across Alexis Road in Polack town, said she was over in the Run visiting her sister Kathleen, who married one of the Sawyer brothers, I forget which one, and that some moonshiner resisted arrest and got himself killed."

"Where did this happen?"

"Marlene said it was in the woods back off Alger Drive somewhere," Lillian told him.

"I'm on my way," Robert told her, running for his car parked at the curb out front. The engine turned over sluggishly again, and he banged the dashboard with his fist. "Come on, not now! Start, dammit!" The ancient coupe grudgingly responded and the tired, old engine came to life. Robert shifted into gear and stomped on the accelerator, pushing it far beyond its limits, but it held together, at least for a while longer.

***

Robert had a bad feeling, and it was confirmed when he turned onto Alger Drive and saw red police lights flashing a mile ahead at the end of the road. He threaded his way past people standing in the road, arms folded in anger, looking toward the activity. Parking on the shoulder, he grabbed his camera and started to follow a well beaten trail into the woods when a young county deputy sheriff he didn't know, who was arguing with two women, held up a hand to stop him.

"Ya'll can't go down there, this is a crime scene."

Before he could say anything else, one of the women screamed at the deputy, her face red with rage, "That there's my brother ya'll killed back there and he weren't doing nothing wrong! I just want to see him."

"I'm sorry, ma'am, I got my orders. Nobody goes back there until the investigation is finished."

"What investigation? All you're gonna do is cover it up and make Conrad look like he was at fault!"

Robert's heart sank when he heard the victim's name.

"Listen, lady, I can't let you in there. That's it! Now you move along before you get yourself in trouble, too."

"You evil bastard, I hope you rot in hell," the woman said, spitting at the deputy's feet as she turned and marched away.

Turning back to him, the deputy said, "You heard me, you get along, too now."

Robert fetched in his pocket and pulled out his press pass. "I'm with newspaper."

"Don't matter who you're with, you ain't going down there."

Robert had dealt with enough officious types to know the routine and knew that the young deputy wasn't going to let him pass. But he had also dealt with enough of them that he knew that there was more than one way to skin a cat.

"I understand, you're just doing your job, Deputy…?"

"Deputy Watkins."

"Let me ask you this, Deputy Watkins, can you tell me anything about what's going on back in there?"

"No, sir, you have to talk to Chief Smeal and he ain't here yet."

"Chief Smeal? Why not Sheriff Miles?"

"This here is actually within the Elmhurst city limits and not our jurisdiction," the deputy told him. "They just sent me an' Deputy Collins out here to assist in crowd control."

"Well, I can see why," Robert said. "Some of these folks seem pretty steamed up. It just don't seem fair that a city cop shoots somebody and you boys have to stand out here in the hot sun takin' abuse while they're back there in the shade of the trees where the action is."

"No, it ain't fair, but what can I say?"

"I'll tell you what," Robert said, "sometimes I get pretty sick and tired of hearing about how you county men are just a bunch of cowboys and the city cops always seem to get all the glory. Yet you're the ones doing all the dirty work."

"You noticed that, did ya? Pisses me off."

"Pisses me off, too. What's fair is fair, and that damn sure ain't fair. You men are just as qualified as Chief Smeal's guys, and I know for a fact that they get paid $10 a week more than you men do."

"Qualified? Have you seen that fat ass Collett?" he asked, jerking a thumb over his shoulder toward the path. "He's a disgrace! Half the time he's parked somewhere asleep, and when he ain't, he's struttin' around like the cock of the walk. I knew it'd come to this with him sooner or later?"

"Come to what?"

"Why, killing that man! That's what! There wasn't no need for that."

"I don't know," Robert said, shrugging his shoulders. "Somebody said he was a bootlegger."

"Bootlegger my ass! Sure, Conrad Phillips made a little shine, but he weren't no Al Capone, for Christ sakes! I've stopped that old boy three or four times with a load of shine and he was always a gentleman. "Yes sir" and "No sir" and never a bit of fight in him. And now old Fat Ass Collett says he attacked him? I don't believe it for a minute."

Robert looked down the path. He didn't believe it either.

"Do you think they'll nail Collett for it?"

"Hell no! I've heard Chief Smeal's a good man, but there ain't no way anything will ever come out of all this. It'll get swept under the rug, sure as shittin.'"

"Man, I wish I could get back in there and take a picture or two," Robert said, shaking his head. "If I could get something in the paper, maybe they couldn't cover it up like that. What this town needs is to get rid of that bastard and get a dedicated officer like you in his place. Somebody who deserves that extra $10 a week and would earn it."

"You'd do that? You'd put a story in the newspaper about how Collett killed that man for no reason and try to get him fired?"

"If those are the facts, I damn sure would," Robert declared. "Just like you have a duty to uphold the law, I have a duty to tell folks what's going on in this town so they know about men like Collett."

Deputy Watkins started to say something, then stopped and looked around before lowering his voice, "I can't let you go down that there path. But if a feller was to, oh, say walk down there by that big old weeping willow? Why'd, I'd probably be busy keeping an eye out for Chief Smeal and never notice if he slipped past me. And once he was there in the woods, I figure what a man does is his own business."

Robert looked confused for just a moment and then broke out in a big grin. "Yeah, I bet a guy could do just that! Tell you what, Deputy Watkins, I don't want to bother you any more. I see you've got a job to do here. I think I'll just get out of your way."

"You do that, and have yourself a good day. And that's Watkins. Deputy Leroy Watkins, in case you ever need anything."

"Deputy Watkins. I'll remember that," Robert promised, then walked away. Behind him he heard Watkins tell two boys who had strayed too close, "You kids git on out of here now, there ain't nothing for you to see here."

Chapter 23

Robert cut through the trees and within a minute or two came upon the path, then followed it a short distance to where he found three Elmhurst policemen and a Sheriff's Deputy standing near the body of Conrad Phillips. The dead man lay on his side just off the path, his face turned toward the ground, the front of his overalls and the grass around him soaked in blood. A single shot Stevens .22 rifle lay nearby.

"Well look who's here! Mr. Newspaperman!" Duane Collett said. "Come to get you a big scoop, didya'?"

"I'm sorry, Robert, this is a crime scene. You're going to have to leave," said Sam Carpenter, a longtime Elmhurst policeman who Robert remembered had caught him and Lester speeding down Alexis Road one night when they were seniors in high school. A man who understood youthful foolishness and that boys had to blow off steam now and then, Sam had given them a stern lecture and sent them home without running them in. But today he was all business.

"Can you tell me what happened here?" Robert asked.

"You'll have to wait for Chief Smeal to give a statement. He should be here any minute. But in the meantime…"

"Awww, let him stay," Duane said. "This is about the biggest news to hit this town in a long time. Be a shame to cheat him out of a story like that. Here, Mr. Newspaperman, you want a picture for the front page?" Duane asked with a big grin.

He drew his pistol and walked up to the body, where he put a foot on its shoulder and posed like a proud big game hunter showing off a trophy buck. The other Elmhurst officer, Travis Westfall, and the deputy scowled in distaste, and Sam said, "Damn it, Duane, show some respect! The man's dead!"

"Yeah, and I killed him. One less lowlife around here to worry about."

Duane was obviously pleased with himself and enjoying his

moment of glory. "Go ahead, take my picture. I'll buy a couple 8x10s from you to put in my scrapbook."

"Duane, I said to get your damn foot off that man!"

"I don't recall anybody dyin' and leaving you in charge, Sam. Come on, Mr. Reporter, take my picture!"

Though Robert was revolted by the obscene display, he raised his camera and took two quick photographs, drawing a stern look from Sam. "I thought better of you than that, Robert."

Before Robert could reply, a shout came from behind them. "What the hell are you doing, Duane? Get away from there and act like a professional, even if you aren't one!"

Lester's face was red and there was fire in his eye. Robert recognized the look and faded back, trying to look inconspicuous.

"What's the big deal, Chief? You killed a lot more Japs than this old hillbilly. You gonna tell me you never struck a pose of two?"

"No, I never did. I was too busy trying to stay alive. And even if I wasn't, my Mamma and Daddy raised me to show some respect."

"What's to respect? A damn moonshiner who broke the law and resisted arrest? He got what he had comin' to him."

Lester started to say something, then seemed to be aware that Robert was standing there. "Get the hell out of here, Robert. You know better than to be here!"

"Just doing my job, Les."

"Git!" Lester ordered, pointing down the trail.

"Can I at least get…"

"I said git," Lester interrupted. "You come by the station later and I'll have a statement for you."

Knowing that kinship only went so far, Robert nodded and headed back toward the road, passing two ambulance attendants carrying a stretcher coming the other way.

***

The crowd was in an ugly mood and Robert received hostile glares when he got back to the road.

"You the newspaperman, right? You here to cover this up?"

"He's the Chief's brother-in-law. You bet yer' ass he's gonna cover it up!"

"It jest ain't right! A good man shot down in cold blood like that.

Dog's Run 107

Hell, I knowed Conrad since we was kids. He don't deserve this."

Robert stopped and said, "I'm here to get the story and print it in the newspaper. If it turns out that the dead man was resisting arrest like they say, that's what I'm going to print. And if what you all say is true and he was murdered, I'll say that, too."

"Yeah, sure you will. Ya'll from town are all the same. Rich people lookin' after rich people and don't give a tinker's damn about anybody out here in the Run."

"Well, sir, I'm sorry you all feel that way," Robert said. "But you're wrong. Yes, Chief Smeal is married to my sister, but that don't color my thinking when it comes to the news. And I believe that Chief Smeal is a good man, kin to me or not. If this wasn't a justified shooting, he'll get to the bottom of it."

"Buncha' bullshit," said a rail-thin man with a big wad of chewing tobacco bulging his jaw. "There ain't never been any justice for us folks here in the Run and there ain't never gonna be, no matter what this fancy man says!"

There were angry grumbles of agreement in the crowd and Robert started to think about things like mob justice and lynching when somebody spoke up.

"Now ya'll just hold on for a minute there. First of all, half a' ya' can't read anyway, so you wouldn't know what he wrote anyhow. And he may be a city boy, but he done right by Miz Reider. That counts for somethin.' So 'fore you go off brandin' him with the same iron, maybe you oughta wait and see."

"Like you know so much, Charles?" said a tall man with a huge belly straining at the buttons of his dirty shirt.

Charles was a foot shorter and weighed half as much as the big man, but he wasn't one to back down. "Shut your mouth, Pete. No good's gonna come out of this with that kind of talk. Now I told you, this here man done right by Miz Reider. That says somethin' in my book. And you know he's right about Chief Smeal, too. When's the last time he come down here bustin' heads like old Chief Gray used to?"

"Law's the Law, don't matter who's wearin' the badge," Pete argued.

"Yes sir, and stupid's stupid, don't matter whose mouth it's comin' outta.'"

"You callin' me stupid?" Pete demanded.

"Hell no, boy! You *are* stupid. You're just too damn thick headed to know it."

Several people in the crowd snickered, and Robert wasn't sure if the two men might come to blows, but they were interrupted when somebody said, "Here they come with him."

Conrad Phillips' body was covered with a sheet and the crowd parted as the two stretcher bearers passed through. A stony faced Chief Smeal and the other lawmen followed quietly. Several men took their hats off, and Robert saw both grief and anger in the faces of the men and women gathered about to watch the grim passage.

As they started to load the stretcher into the back of the ambulance, a thin, haggard looking woman burst through the crowd. "Let me see him! I want to see my man!"

Sam Carpenter tried to stop her, but she pushed him away and grabbed the sheet covering her husband's body. Pulling it down far enough to expose the dead man's face, she wailed, " Noooo, Conrad, nooo! Please don't be dead. Please don't. Me and the kids need you. We love you! Please, Conrad, no!"

Sam wrapped his arms around her and gently tried to pull her back, but the woman resisted with surprising force for somebody her size. "Let go a me, you murderin' bastard!"

"Calm down, Mrs. Phillips," Sam said. "This isn't helping anything."

"I said let go a me!" She screamed, pushing herself away. "I swear by my husband's blood that ya'll ain't gonna get away with this! Y'all are gonna to pay. If not in this life, in the next."

She spit on his shirt, and Sam stood quietly, absorbing the abuse. Around them the crowd began to murmur again, the tone of their voices laced with anger and hatred at the establishment that kept them downtrodden and the men who enforced that establishment's law upon them.

"Next life's too long to wait," someone shouted from within the crowd. "How many of us are they gonna beat up or kill before somebody puts a stop to it?" Heads nodded and Robert heard people saying "that's right" and "it's 'bout time we put a stop to it."

Sensing that things could get out of hand very quickly, Lester said in a loud voice, "Okay, that's enough of that! This here shooting is going to be investigated and I'll find out exactly what happened here. Until then, y'all need to calm down. Ain't nothing going to be accomplished by that kind of talk."

"Ain't nothin' gonna be accomplished nohow," someone retorted. "Yeah, you're gonna to investigate all right, and then your gonna sweep

Dog's Run

it right under the rug!"

"Now you just shut up, Avery," Lester ordered. "Don't be telling me how to do my job."

"Your job is to take care of all those snooty, rich people in town," said a tiny little woman with a thick mop of dark, curly hair and a baby held in one arm. "Y'all think you can come down here and just beat us and kill us anytime you want and it's okay! Well it ain't, and y'all ain't gonna get away with killin' Conrad like ya done."

"What's your name, ma'am?" Lester asked.

Though the woman wasn't much more than half his size, she didn't back down from the big police chief. "Why? You gonna shoot me next?"

"Ain't nobody else getting shot out here today," Lester said.

"Yeah, but what about tomorrow? Or next week?"

"I asked you for your name, lady," Lester said.

"It's Judy Miller. And I ain't afraid of you!"

"I can see that, Miz Miller. And I don't want you to be afraid of me, or of any of my officers. Our job is to enforce the law, not beat up or hurt innocent people."

"Yea? Well you tell that to Conrad! Tell that to his wife and his little kids left without a daddy!"

"Like I said, I'm gonna investigate this. And if there was any wrongdoing, I'll deal with it."

"And just how you gonna deal with it?" somebody shouted from the crowd.

"Shit, same way they deal with everything concerning their own. Give him a pat on the back. Just one more poor, dead hillbilly from the Run they don't have to mess with no more."

Lester was smart enough to know that there are times when words are not going to do any good, and this was one of them. "Well, I damn sure can't accomplish anything standing here. Now y'all just go on about your business and I'm gonna go on about mine of looking into what happened out here today."

Leaving the crowd to disperse on their own, Lester and the other officers got into their cars and left the scene.

Dog's Run

Chapter 24

Lester was furious. He knew that Duane Collett was trouble the first time he laid eyes on him, back when Lester had come to work as a rookie policeman right after the war. Duane was fat and lazy, but Lester could tolerate that in his fellow officer. What he couldn't tolerate was the fact that Duane was a bully.

He had never seen the man try to exert any authority over someone who was capable of standing up to him. But if it were a high school kid, or some poor hillbilly from the Run, Duane wasn't above using a little extra force if he thought he could get away with it. Lester remembered one incident soon after he joined the police department that still brought bile to the back of his throat.

Doodie McRae was a harmless, retarded man who made his living picking through other people's trash cans for whatever piece of junk he might be able to sell for scrap, or just to add to the litter piled up around his old shack. Doodie was partial to old newspapers and magazines, but would carry away anything that caught his eye and the rickety, old, wooden Radio Flyer wagon he always pulled behind him was usually piled high.

Early one morning Lester and Duane had come upon Doodie pulling his wagon down the alley behind Friedman's jewelry store and Duane, behind the wheel, had honked the police car's horn and waved Doodie over.

"What ya got there?" Duane had asked.

"I got some newspapers an' some pop bottles I'm gonna cash in and this here," said Doodie, proudly holding up a flimsy wooden countertop display for Timex wristwatches that he had found in the trash behind Friedman's.

"What you gonna do with that?"

"I got me some pretty rocks and some arrowheads I'm gonna put in it," Doodie told him.

"Did you break into the jewelry store and steal that?" Duane asked with a sideways grin at Lester.

"No, sir, I found it right back there in the trash!"

"I don't know about that, boy," Duane said. "You look like one of those cat burglars. You sure you're not a burglar?"

"No, sir! All I did was find it, just like I said."

"I'll tell you what, I need to take a look at that," Duane said, heaving himself out from behind the steering wheel. "Got to inspect that for fingerprints. Give it here and let me look at it."

"I didn't steal it, you can ask Mr. Friedman about that. But you can look at it if you want to," Doodie said, handing him the display.

Duane pretended to study it carefully from all angles, then said, "Hold up yer right hand so I can see your fingers and study them for prints."

Doodie did as instructed, and Duane chuckled and said, "Well, ya dumb ass, I can't rightly see your fingerprints if you're wearing those damn gloves now, can I? Pull those things off."

Doodie pulled off the cheap, brown, cotton work gloves he wore winter and summer and held his hand up again.

"Damn, boy," Duane said, "your hands are just as dirty and filthy brown as those gloves are! Don't know why you even wear them! Don't you ever take a bath?"

Doodie shifted uncomfortably from foot to foot but didn't reply.

"Okay, let me see the other hand. Okay, now slap them together like you was clapping, and then hold them both out. That gets the blood flowin' and makes it easier for me to see your fingerprints."

Doodie did as he was told, and then Duane said, "Now I want you to wave them around over your head like you was swattin' away a bunch of skeeters."

"Okay, you've had your fun," Lester had said. "Let him go, Duane."

"You telling me what to do, rookie? You might want to think twice before you start giving me orders!"

"That's enough," Lester said. "You go on now, Doodie."

Dropping his arms back down to his sides, Doodie asked, "Can I have that back now?"

"What, this?" Duane asked. "No, boy, this here is evidence. I still ain't sure you're not a cat burglar. I need to send this to the FBI have them check it out."

"But I ain't no cat burglar," Doodie protested. "I found it fair and

Dog's Run 113

square right there in the trash!"

"Sure you did. And I'm the Lone Ranger and that there's Tonto in the car. No, boy, this here is evidence and you can't have it back. Why, you should just be glad I don't run you in right now. But I might come lookin' for ya after I hear back from the FBI."

"I said that's enough!" Lester had said, getting out of the car on his side. "Give it back to him and let's go, Duane."

"Or what, Mr. War Hero? What are you gonna do about it?"

"You're about to find out," Lester warned him, starting around the back of the car.

"Okay, okay! It ain't worth arguin' over. I was just having some fun with the dummy here. Ain't that right Dummy Doodie? Here, have your piece of junk."

Doodie reached out for the display, but Duane dropped it and then smashed it beneath his heavy work boot, grinning at the unfortunate man before him. "Aww, shit, boy, that was an accident! Sorry about that."

He laughed and got back in the police car and slammed the door, then leaned out the window and said, "Hey, Doodie, clean that mess, up will ya? Looks like shit. Makes me think I'm at your place with all the crap you got piled around out there."

Laughing at his own humor, Duane pushed in the clutch, shifted into low gear, then revved the engine and popped the clutch, running over Doodie's wagon and leaving splinters and twin strips of rubber down the alley in the police car's wake.

***

"I want to know exactly what happened out there today," Lester said.

"Like I told you, I was driving through the Run when I saw Phillips looking suspicious."

"Looking suspicious, how?"

"He was walkin' down the road there with that rifle, and when he saw me comin,' he turned away real quick and started down that path. So I stopped and yelled for him to come over and asked him what he was doing. He told me he was lookin' for a dog that had carried away one of his chickens."

"What was suspicious about that? It's not illegal to carry a rifle.

People do it all the time."

"Well, everybody knows Phillips was a moonshiner."

"What's that got to do with it? I never knew him to give anybody any trouble."

Duane's eyes narrowed. "Are you questioning me, Chief?"

"That's exactly what I'm doing. A man's dead and I aim to get to the bottom of it."

"Well that's bullshit! Who do you think you are, treating me like some damn no 'count hillbilly out of the Run? They make you Chief and suddenly you're better than the rest of us? What ever happened to respect for your fellow policemen?"

Lester shot out of his chair and leaned over his desk, his face nearly purple with rage. "You listen to me, you sack of shit. I've seen drunks laying in the gutters down on skid row in Toledo who deserve more respect than you do. You're an embarrassment to that badge you're wearing, and if you don't tell me exactly what happened out there in the Run today, I'm going to rip it off your shirt and then mop the floor with your ass! Now out with it!"

"All right, all right, calm down," Duane said, leaning back in his chair to put some distance between himself and his boss.

"Don't tell me to calm down. I…."

"Okay, okay! Like I said, I saw Phillips and asked him what he was up to, and he said he was chasin' some dog. But he was actin' all hinkey and it made me suspicious. So I told him to give me the gun. He told me no, he wasn't giving his gun to nobody, and that he wasn't breakin' any laws and to leave him alone."

"Then what happened?"

"He asked why I was busting his chops, and I told him again to give me the gun. He said the only way I was takin' it away from him was to take it off his dead body and started walking down that trail into the woods. I figured he had a still back there and got out of my car and started to follow him. I told him he was under arrest and to drop the gun. That's when he turned around and pointed it at me, so I shot him. Simple as that. It was self-defense and he was resisting arrest."

Knowing how fiercely independent the people were in Dog's Run, and how resentful they were of anyone telling them what to do, Lester could believe that Phillips would not have wanted to surrender his rifle. But his past encounters with the man had also shown the moonshiner to be an easygoing fellow who would avoid a confrontation if at all possible.

Especially with someone wearing a badge. Lester was convinced there was more to the story than Duane was telling him.

"And just what was he under arrest for, anyway? Like I said, it's not illegal to carry a rifle."

"No, but it is to ignore an order by a policeman."

"You said he pointed the rifle at you?"

"That's right."

"I've never known Conrad Phillips to do something like that."

"Well, he won't do it again, that's for damn sure!"

Lester wasn't buying Duane's story, but he had no way to prove the man was lying either, since there were no witnesses to the shooting. There was nothing he could do at the moment, but he didn't plan to let the matter rest. Sooner or later, he'd nail Duane Collett's ass to the wall.

"Okay, get out of here. And stay out of the Run for a while, until things cool down. The way they're all riled up over this thing, if you show your face around there we'll have more trouble."

"No skin off my nose," Duane said. "That whole inbred bunch out there can go to hell for all I care."

Chapter 25

"That's it?" Robert asked, incredulously. "That's your official statement?"

"What more do you want from me, Robert? Those are the facts as I know them right now. Conrad Phillips was being questioned by Officer Collett for acting suspiciously, he pointed a rifle at the officer, and Officer Collett shot him in self-defense."

"And you're buying that story, Les?"

"I'm giving you what I know at this time. If more information develops, I'll look into it further."

"What suspicious activity was Phillips up to in the first place?"

"He was walking down the road carrying a rifle," Lester said, knowing that Robert's response would be the same as his had been at Duane's explanation of how the confrontation began.

"So what? Kids carry rifles and shotguns all the time down there to go hunting, let alone grown men. Hell, when we were kids it was nothing for us to walk a couple of miles to Swan Creek and go hunting. Nobody ever stopped us."

"Yeah, well, for whatever reason, Officer Collett said it looked suspicious to him and he stopped to ask Phillips what he was doing and it went bad from there."

"Les, you know as well as I do that Duane Collett is bad news. I don't believe a word of his story."

"Nether do I. But you know as well as I do that as long as his Uncle Harvey is a senior member of the City Council and owns half the county, my hands are tied until he really steps over the line."

"Murdering a man in cold blood isn't stepping over the line?"

"Now who said anything about murder? You need to slow down there, Robert. I don't doubt that there are other ways this thing could have turned out. Should have turned out. But I can't prove Duane actually murdered that man."

"So now what?"

"What do you want from me, Robert? I just told you, that's all I have. Nobody's come forward saying they saw anything."

"Given what happened to Conrad Phillips, can you blame them?"

"What are you getting at? What's that supposed to mean?"

"Don't tell me you can't see it. It's plain as the nose on your face, Lester. Conrad Phillips came to me and told me what he saw the night Wanda Jean Reider was killed. I told you, and now he's dead, too."

Lester's voice was tight when he asked, "Are you saying that *I* had something to do with that man's death?"

"Of course not Les! But do you think it's just coincidence that it happened right after I talked to you about it?"

"I think you're looking for a conspiracy that don't exist, that's what I think. You need to realize who you are, Robert. This ain't the big city and your newspaper's not the *New York Times*. Hell, it's not even the *Toledo Blade*! You need to stick with covering the American Legion meetings and the high school football team. You start stepping on toes around here and somebody's going to stomp right back with a lot bigger shoe."

"It that a threat, Lester?"

"Hell no, it's not a threat, it's a statement of fact, son! Listen, Robert, we're family. And we're friends. And I want to keep it that way. But you need to step back like I told you before. I'm already hearing folks asking what's your interest out there in Dog's Run. Now, it might not be right, but there is a prejudice in this town about the people who live out there, just like there is against niggers. Hell, even against the Polacks and Dagos over there on the other side of Alexis. And the people who read your newspaper and run the businesses that buy the ads that pay your bills aren't out there. Those folks are right here in Elmhurst. But if they begin to think you care more about what happens out in the Run than what happens here in town, they're gonna let you know it. Why do you want to take a chance ruining everything you've been working hard to build up for the sake of a bunch of damn hillbillies?"

"Don't you even care that a man got killed out there today, Lester?"

"Of course I care! But I wasn't there and all I've got to go on is Duane's statement. And until I have more, if I get anything else, Duane stays on the job and there isn't much I can do about it."

"Well, there's something *I* can do about it," Robert said, standing up.

"Now, I'm warning you, Bob, don't go back out there to the Run and start stirring the pot and interfering in a police investigation!"

"What investigation, Les? You just told me you can't do anything?"

"Stay out of the Run, Bob. I mean it."

Robert walked out of the office without answering him.

Dog's Run

Chapter 26

The other day I was at Hastings Soda Fountain and I saw Naomi Fulton and Elaine Englehart, but they acted like I didn't exist even though we was in the same classes all through school and Naomi and I used to be friends before... well before I started down this road to purgatory I'm on. Now they act like I'm invisible. So I ignored them right back, and when I was walkin' out I heard Elaine whisper "Has she no shame?" Oh, it was real hard not to turn around right there and tell her if anybody should be ashamed it was her for havin' a daddy who offered me $10 to let him do his business with me on a bench there at the park just last Monday night! But she's such a fat head that it wasn't worth my time.

***

Rex Hooper lived in a shack made of unpainted lumber scraps he had scavenged here and there, the whole affair listing heavily to one side and looking like the next strong wind could blow it over. A pack of growling, snarling, mixed breed dogs greeted Robert with raised hackles when he stopped his car in front of the house. He was afraid to open the door for fear of being mauled. Even with the windows rolled halfway up to keep them from jumping inside to get at him, the dogs still stood on their hind legs and snarled in at him with bared fangs.

The barrel of a shotgun poked out the shack's door and a voice shouted, "Whoever you are, git the hell outta here before I blow you in half and let my dogs eat what's left!"

"Mr. Hooper? My name's Robert Tucker. From the newspaper? Can we talk for a few minutes?"

"I got nothin' to say to you. Now git on outta here like I said!"

"Please, Mr. Hooper. All I need's a few minutes of your time. I just want to ask you…"

"Don't ask me a damn thing! I seen what talkin' to you got Conrad.

Now this is your last warning!"

Robert wasn't sure which he feared more, the vicious dog pack or the gaping maw of the shotgun. But he was fairly certain that Hooper wouldn't shoot him while he sat in his car, if for no other reason than that to do so, he would have hit a couple of his dogs in the process.

"That's why I'm here. I want to see that the man who killed Conrad gets what's coming to him."

"He wouldn't have got himself killed if he'd have minded his own business. And that's jist want I aim to do, mind my own business."

Robert knew that family relationships went deep into the marrow of the culture of the people who lived in Dog's Run, and asked, "No matter what started it, if you and Conrad were kin, isn't his death your business?"

There was no response, and Robert took advantage of the silence to press his point. "Mr. Hooper, I know that there's a lot of distrust of the police out here. And a lot of it is for good reason. But I want to help set things straight. Will you give me that chance?"

The silence continued for another moment, then the gun barrel disappeared and a string bean of a man in a sleeveless T-shirt stepped into the doorway. He still held the shotgun cradled under one arm and stared at Robert for another minute, then shouted, "You dogs go on now, go lay down!" On command the growling ceased and the dogs slunk away to lie in the shade of the house.

Robert still wasn't sure they wouldn't attack as soon as he opened the car door, but Hooper said, "If you want to talk, let's talk. But I ain't doin' it standin' out here in the yard."

One dog, a large black and white mutt, stood up and growled through bared teeth when Robert approached the house.

"Blackie, you shut up now," Hooper said and the dog lay back down, but kept her eyes on Robert.

The inside of the shack was filthy and reeked of body odor, booze, and smoke. Hooper sat down at a cheap, wooden kitchen table, propping the shotgun up against a stack of wooden crates that held jars of canned peaches, tomatoes, and other foodstuff. He motioned toward a chair across from him and Robert sat. There was an open Mason jar filled with moonshine on the table, along with a blue tin can of Bugler tobacco and an orange cigarette roller.

Once Robert's eyes adjusted to the dim light provided by a couple of yellowed windows, he could see that Hooper's eyes were red rimmed, though he wasn't sure if it was from grief over Conrad's death or the whiskey he had been drinking. But the man's hands were steady as he put loose tobacco into the roller, licked a gummed paper, and rolled a cigarette.

Robert pulled a pack of Chesterfields from his pocket and offered one, but Hooper waved him away.

"I don't smoke those tailor-mades, got no taste to them," he said. "And now they're talkin' about puttin' filters on 'em? Like smoking through a Kotex!"

Robert watched him expertly roll half a dozen cigarettes, until Hooper broke the silence.

"You said you came to help set things straight about Conrad. How do ya plan to do that?"

"Were you there when he got shot yesterday?"

"If I was, that lard ass cop would be just as dead as Conrad is."

"Do you think Officer Collett shot Conrad in cold blood?"

"Don't *think* it, I know it. I told Conrad to mind his own business, but he couldn't do it. He had to go shooting off his mouth. Now see what it got him?"

"Conrad told me that you and him were parked out by the bridge the night Wanda Jean Reider died."

"I ain't talkin' about any of that. That girl ain't none of my business. Wasn't Conrad's neither."

"But you obviously think whatever you two saw out there led to Conrad's death."

Hooper didn't reply, just took a swig from the Mason jar and continued rolling cigarettes.

"Mr. Hooper, Conrad told me that you saw Wanda Jean getting assaulted, and that somebody threw her off the bridge."

"Maybe Conrad just had a imagination he let run wild."

"Maybe so. But if what he told me led to his death, I don't think so."

Hooper rolled three more cigarettes in silence, then said, "Me and Conrad was like brothers ever since we was kids. But I always told him he needed to mind his own business and let other folks mind theirs. Whatever happened out there at the bridge weren't none of our business. Wanda Jean was going to end up dead one way or another. If she didn't get herself killed like she did, it would have been some jealous wife shooting her."

"You said she got herself killed, Mr. Hooper. But the police said she committed suicide. You saw something out there. What was it?"

"What it *was* ain't none of my business. How many goddamn times I got to say that? Now you told me ya come out here to set things straight about Conrad, but all you're doin' is asking the same damn question over and over. Which I ain't gonna answer! So either git to the point or git the hell outta here."

"The point is that the two are tied together, Wanda Jean's death and Conrad's. You know it and I know it. But how can I set things straight if you won't cooperate? Give me *something* I can work with, please!"

"And end up dead myself? No, sir! Like you said, you and me both know the two is mixed up together. So you do with it what you will. But I'll tell ya something right now. If I see that murdering prick that killed Conrad out here agin,' I'm gonna shoot him myself. And you can take that to the bank with ya!"

Hearing her master's raised voice, Blackie walked in the open door of the shack and growled at Robert again.

"I've said all I'm gonna say," Hooper said, putting his hand on his shotgun. "Now, I don't like you and my dog don't like you. That's two votes agin' your one, so I think it's time for you to hit the road."

Robert wanted to pound the table with his fist and demand that Hooper tell him what he and Conrad Phillips had seen at the bridge that night. He wanted to shake the man and drag the truth out of him. But he knew that anything he said or did was only going to get him hurt or killed. He thanked Hooper for his time and walked out of the cabin and back to his car, feeling the shotgun and the dog's eyes on his back every step of the way.

Chapter 27

Naomi Fulton and Elaine Englehart ain't the only women around here that shun me. Except for Mama and my aunt Georgia and my little sister Penny there ain't no woman in this town will even give me the time of day. But I don't care because they're all a bunch of Dumb Dora's anyway. And Naomi and Elaine and the wives of those men I see and do things with, they ain't a bit better than me when it comes right down to it. We all trade what we got for what we want. Only difference is they get a ring on their finger which is supposed to make it look alright. But the jokes on them because I got a whole bunch of rings for every finger and I don't have to answer to no man like they do!

***

You should have seen Virginia Wilson's face when she come prancin into her husband's office that night and caught us! I don't know which was funnier, his or hers. I swear Mr. Wilson turned about three shades of white and she was three shades of red! He was trying to fix his trousers and I think he was in such a hurry that he caught himself in his zipper. Then she started screamin at him and throwin things and I decided it was time for me to get out of there. The next day when I came in to work, Sheila McKenzie, Mr. Wilson's secretary, met me at the door and give me a check for $50 and said my services was no longer needed and this was my sevrince pay. Of course I knew better. My services are always needed. Or wanted anyway. The Wilsons went out of town for a while but a few days after they got back home I was sittin in the park and who should pull up in that big old Oldsmobile of his but Mr. Wilson! We went for a ride up there into Michigan and he pulled into an empty church parking lot of all places. And I have to say the back seat of that big old car of his was actually more comfortable than doin it on the desk in his office!

Robert put the diary down, wishing, not for the first time, that Alice Reider had never brought them to him. He had grown up in Elmhurst and it had always felt like home to him. Now he wasn't sure if he knew his own hometown or the people who lived in it. How could men he knew and respected, men he did business with, lead such sordid, double lives? How could they use a poor, young woman from the Run like they did, and then go home to their wives and children and sit around the dinner table at night and look them in the eye?

He was finding it harder and harder to act civilly when he met the men Wanda Jean had been involved with on the street or stopped into their stores and shops to do business. Her mother had told him that she thought he'd know what to do with the information in Wanda Jean's diaries once he had read them, but he didn't.

His first visceral reaction was to reprint the whole of the diaries, verbatim, and expose the dirty underside of his community to the world. But the more practical side of him asked what good would come of that? Families would be torn apart, lives and reputations ruined. And for what? To avenge the honor of a young woman who was dead and gone? A young woman who apparently didn't worry about her honor when she was alive?

And then there was the whole mess that had happened out in Dog's Run the other day. Robert was convinced that Duane Collett had murdered Conrad Phillips in cold blood. Which meant that Phillips had been telling the truth about what he saw at the bridge the night Wanda Jean had died. And that Duane had wanted to shut him up, either to protect himself, or somebody else.

Lester had said that his hands were tied when it came to the shooting unless somebody came forward with more information. And Robert knew that nobody else in the Run was going to risk their lives to report anything they saw, if there were any witnesses. But Robert's hands weren't tied, and while he still didn't know what to do about the diaries, he knew what he had to do about Duane Collett. He turned toward the Underwood typewriter on his side desk.

***

"Are you sure about this?" Scotty asked. "Because if you do this, the shit's going to hit the fan."

"You don't think I should?"

"It's not my place to decide what you put in the damn paper. My job's just to make sure the thing gets printed."

"But?"

"But Duane Collett is a first class son-of-a-bitch and it's time somebody knocked the goddamned wind out of his sails. And in spite of being a college boy and all that, I think you must have a great big pair of iron balls to want to print this. We might just make a real newspaperman out of you after all."

Chapter 28

Scotty had been right. The minute the next day's edition hit the streets and newsstands, all hell had broken loose. Robert went into the office two hours early to be ready to meet the flack he knew was coming.

"What have you done?" Lester shouted, accosting him as he unlocked the door. "Are you out of your goddamned mind, Bob?"

"Good morning to you, too," Robert said, "How's your day going so far?"

"How's my day…? I'll tell you how my day's going! The mayor woke me up this morning screaming over the telephone. Three councilmen called before I was shaved and dressed, including Harvey Collett, who demanded that I personally go around town and collect every copy of your newspaper and burn it. People are talking on every corner. You have unleashed a shit storm on this entire town!"

"Good. Back in 1861, Wilbur F. Storey, the owner of the *Chicago Times*, said "*It is a newspaper's duty to print the news and raise hell.*" Mission accomplished."

"This isn't funny, Bob! If I thought I could find them, I would round up every copy and burn it."

"Wouldn't do you any good," Robert told him. "I sent it to the *Blade* and the Associated Press. By suppertime, the whole world is going to know all about Duane Collett."

"Goddamn you, Bob, why? I thought we were friends."

"We *are* friends," Robert told him. "But we disagree on what needs doing in this case. I didn't write a bad word about you. All I said was that you are investigating the shooting."

"You didn't have to write a bad word! You did it with a picture! Look at this. What kind of a police chief does that make me look like?"

Robert looked at the new edition with the bold 72 point headline *Officer Kills Elmhurst Man* spread across the width of the front page. Just above was a five column wide centered photograph of Duane Collett, posing with his foot on the shoulder of the man he had shot, proudly displaying his revolver and with a wide grin spread across his face.

"It makes you look like a police chief with a bad officer who needs to be fired, and probably charged with murder."

"You know that if I could have fired Duane long ago, I'd have done it."

"I know. But now I don't think even his Uncle Harvey can cover for him on this one. So actually, I'm doing you a favor. The City Council *has* to do something about him and it's out of your hands. Now, if you'll excuse me, my telephone is ringing off the hook."

And it continued to ring all morning long. The minute Robert or Lillian ended a call and hung up, another one came in. The calls came from as far away as New York and Boston, where newspaper reporters wanted more information about the rogue police officer. Also as nearby as Michaelson's Cigar Store, just down the block, where Gary Michaelson called to cancel the advertisement he had run in every edition of the *Citizen-Press* for the last four years. "Duane Collett and me grew up together," Michaelson told him, "and I don't appreciate you trying to railroad him for killing a criminal."

"He's not the only one," Lillian said. "Catherine Oswald at the bakery called and said not to run her ad anymore, and Mr. Griffin at the stationary store said he was pulling his advertising until you printed a retraction."

"Kind of hard to retract a photograph," Robert said. "On the other hand, Dennis Edwards at the lumberyard called to tell me he was behind us a hundred percent, and Theodore Gardner wants me to come by the Sinclair gas station to pick up an ad. And Andy Zimmerman wants to increase his ad from a half to a full page. Of course, I think he's just doing that to try to sell me that convertible."

"Well, if I was you, I wouldn't be riding around in no convertibles right now," Lillian told him. "You might want to get yourself a Sherman tank instead."

"So do you think this was a bad idea, Lillian?"

"Bad idea? I love it! I haven't seen the people in this town so stirred up since the war ended."

Besides the telephone calls, people were stopping in to purchase extra copies of the newspaper, some to compliment Robert on the photograph, and others to complain.

"It's about time somebody did something about Duane Collett," said Burt Foster. "He pinched my kid brother for speeding one night last August, and I'll admit that Douglas had a couple of beers in him. But he never had a fight in his life or argued with anybody about anything. Collett pulled him out of the car and handcuffed him, then shoved his face down on the hood so hard he bloodied his nose and knocked out two of his teeth!"

"I think going away to college turned you into one of those communists Senator McCarthy is talking about," shouted Timothy Madison, who had been in Robert's high school class and now worked as a maintenance supervisor for the railroad. "Siding with that white trash out in the Run over a respectable lawman! Cancel my subscription. I won't support yellow journalism like that. I'm a God fearing, red blooded American."

When Robert walked the two blocks to the Blue Elk restaurant for lunch, an equal number of people on the sidewalk nodded or said hello as did those who turned away or glared at him. He chose a booth and had hardly sat down when a big bellied man lumbered up to his table and said, "You've got a lot of goddamned nerve coming in here, you son-of-a-bitch!"

"Last time I checked it was a free country," Robert said.

"You made my brother look like a goddamn Nazi or something with that picture you run of him in the paper."

"Well, Duane asked me to take his picture for the front page and even said he wanted to order a couple of 8x10 prints, so I assumed he was pretty proud of himself. He sure looked like it in that picture, didn't he?"

"You think you're pretty funny, don't you? How about I knock your damn teeth down your throat and we'll see how big you smile then?"

He grabbed Robert's shirt collar and jerked him out of the booth, toppling his coffee cup as he did so.

"I'm gonna break every bone in your body and then I'm gonna stomp what's left into jelly!"

Robert choked as his air was cut off and tried to pry the big man's fingers loose, but they were clamped like a vise as the other man drew back his fist to punch him. The blow never landed.

"Let go of him right now Arnold," ordered Sam Carpenter, who had seen the altercation through the restaurant's window as he walked past and came to Robert's rescue.

"Kiss my ass," Arnold Collett said. "I'm gonna pound him into mush!"

Robert's face had turned a deep purple as he struggled to breathe. Sam drew his revolver and leveled it at the big man in a two-handed combat stance. "Let go of him or I'll blow your brains out."

"You'd shoot me for beating this prick's ass, Sam?"

"I'd shoot you for kicking a puppy," Sam told him. "You're just as useless as your lunkhead brother." He thumbed the hammer back on his gun and Arnold released his hold on Robert, who fell back into the booth, gasping for air.

"This isn't over," Arnold said, pointing his finger at Robert. "You won't always have your brother-in-law or your pet cop here to protect your ass. I'll be watching and waiting for that day."

"Go on, get out of here before I arrest you for assault and battery," Sam said, keeping the gun aimed at him.

Arnold spit on Robert's table and stormed out the door, muttering threats all the way. When he was gone, Sam holstered his weapon and asked, "Are you okay?"

Robert coughed and nodded his head, then took a drink from the glass of water the worried-looking young waitress brought him. As she wiped the table clean, he choked and coughed again, his eyes watering, and said, "I'm alright, thanks to you. I appreciate it, Sam."

The older man sat down across from him in the booth and, the excitement over, the rest of the diners went back to their meals, whispering among themselves. Robert ordered a pastrami on rye and French fries, and Sam asked for a ham sandwich.

"I'm damn sure glad you showed up when you did," Robert said after the waitress took their orders and left.

"It was good timing. I just happened to be walking by. But Arnold was right, I won't always be there. And he's not the only one you need to worry about. Do you have a gun?"

"I've got a shotgun and a .22 rifle," Robert said. "I haven't had either one out of the closet in a couple of years."

"If I were you, I'd get myself a pistol and carry it," Sam advised. "The Collett boys hold grudges and don't forget things very fast."

"Maybe I'll see if Lester has a handgun I can borrow for a while."

"As mad as he is right now, I'd stay out of his way if I was you," Sam said. "Just before I left the station, he was on his way out the door to a special emergency City Council meeting. He might do you worse than Arnold and Duane would."

Dog's Run

Sam looked around the dining room, then leaned forward and pulled something out of his hip pocket and passed it to Robert under the table.

"Here, keep this handy until you get one of your own."

Robert took the small semi-automatic pistol and slipped it into his jacket pocket and nodded.

"That's a Colt .380. My kid brother carried it all across Europe fighting the Krauts and it never let him down."

"Thank you, Sam. I owe you."

"No, I owe *you* an apology," Sam said. "Out there at the shooting the other day when you took that picture, I told you I thought better of you. I should have known you better than that."

"Hell, how many of us know our own selves? To be honest with you, I didn't know what I was going to do with the picture when I took it."

"For what it's worth, I think you did just the right thing," Sam said as the waitress returned with their orders.

Chapter 29

"Harvey Collett called and wants to see you right now," said Lillian, hanging up the telephone as Robert came through the office door. "He sounded really mad!"

"Well how about that, Mr. Harvey Collett himself wants to see little old me," Robert said. "I wonder if he wants to buy some advertising."

"More than likely he wants to shoot you."

"Naaa… Harvey's not the type to get his hands dirty himself. He'd have one of his henchmen do it for him. Fact is, Arnold Collett just tried to wring my neck."

"What happened? Are you all right?" The concern on Lillian's face was deep.

Robert told her, omitting the part about the pistol Sam Carpenter had given him.

"You need to tell Chief Smeal about this!"

"I think it's best I avoid Lester right now," Robert told her. "He's pretty steamed up about today's paper."

"Yeah, but still…."

"It will be fine," he assured her, heading back toward his office.

"Aren't you going to go see Mr. Collett?"

"Oh, I think I'll let him sit and stew for a while longer," Robert said. "I read an article in *Reader's Digest* a while back that said a little bit of stress is good for the heart. It gets the blood pressure up and is kind of like exercising."

"Well then I must be getting my exercise today!" Lillian said. "The darned telephone hasn't stopped ringing."

As if on cue, the telephone on her desk rang.

"See? This job comes with lots of extra benefits," Robert told her. "I think you may have lost some weight already and it's not much past noon!"

Lillian threw a pencil at his back as he walked away, then picked up the telephone receiver to hear the latest complaint or comment over the front page photograph.

***

When I wrote before about doin it in the back seat of Mr. Wilson's car, I guess it made me think of something bad. The thing that started me down the dead end I've come to. It's embarrisin even to write about it, but it happened so I guess I can't hide it from myself, now can I? That day I wasn't wantin to be with anybody because my stomach was crampin like it does just before I get my monthly. But Mr. Collett, he sent Arnold to get me. I told him I didn't want to go, but nobody tells Mr. Collett no, or Arnold either for that matter. I tried to explain that I wasn't up to that, but Mr. Collett, he just told Arnold to wait outside, then he rolled back that big old chair of his and told me to get to work. When I was done, Arnold was takin me back home and he handed me a bottle and said to take some giggle water and wash my mouth out. Now, I've listened to Arnold's lines plenty of times, so when he said a pretty girl like me shouldn't be carryin the taste of an old man around in her mouth, I knew what he was getting at and I just ignored him. But that just made him mad and he pulled that big old Packard of his uncle's into the cemetery and drove to the back and said it was time I showed him some appreciation for always givin me a ride. Like he did it out of the kindness of his heart and not because his uncle told him to! I didn't want to do nothing and told him so, but he just crawled in the back where I was and pushed me down on the seat. He was so rough with me it hurt! And then during it all Aunt Flo came to visit, and there was blood all over the seat when he got done with me. That set him off like a crazy man and he called me a nasty whore and hit me. Hit me hard. I started crying and he told me to shut up and hit me again.

Robert felt his lunch rising to the back of his throat and had to make a hasty trip to the bathroom, just managing to make it before he threw up.

"Are you all right?" Lillian asked from the other side of the door.

He flushed the toilet, washed his face in the sink, and then said "I'm fine, Lillian. I guess my lunch didn't agree with me is all."

"Maybe that *Reader's Digest* story about stress wasn't so true after all," she said as he cupped water into his hands and washed his mouth out.

Lillian eyed him skeptically as he came out of the bathroom.

"Are you sure you're okay?"

Robert had never felt *less* okay in his life, but he just nodded and walked back to his office, with Lillian close on his heels.

"Maybe you should go home and lay down for a while. I can handle things here."

"No, I told you I'm fine."

"You don't look fine to me. You look terrible."

"Well, thank you very much," he said. "You always know how to make a man feel better about himself."

"That's not what I mean, you know that. I'm just worried about you."

"I said I'm fine, woman. Stop being such a mother hen."

"So if you're not going to go home, what *are* you going to do?"

Robert shrugged his shoulders, took his straw Panama hat off the coat tree and put it on his head, then replied, "I guess I'll go have a visit with Harvey Collett.

Chapter 30

Harvey Collett ruled over his small town empire from the second floor of the Foster Building, a red brick structure on Main Street that held his dry goods store on the first floor. It was the only building in town with an elevator, although the lift was for the private use of Collett only. Visitors were required to ring a doorbell from the sidewalk and climb a steep flight of stairs once they had convinced Collett's secretary, over the intercom, that they had legitimate business worth bothering her employer about and she buzzed them in.

In addition to the store and a fuel oil company, Collett also owned a large amount of real estate upon which his construction company had built cheap housing to meet the demands of servicemen returning from the war.

For $100 down and the GI Bill to back them up, veterans could realize the American dream of home ownership, even if those homes were flimsy affairs that barely met building codes, if at all. Of course, it helped that Collett was a senior member of the City Council and knew how to use his money and influence to his advantage to skirt around troublesome things like that. What did it matter if doorjambs swelled in rainy weather and doors wouldn't shut tight, or if roofs leaked? For just a few dollars he'd be happy to send out one of his maintenance men to fix the problems. Sometimes, if the homeowner was lucky, the repairs lasted through the next storm.

Collett was a huge, heavy jowled man with roll after roll of fat stretching the buttons of his custom made shirts, and wide suspenders holding his trousers up. He seldom rose from his throne-like chair from the time he arrived at his office every morning at 7:30 sharp until he left late in the evening.

But that didn't mean he was lazy by any means. Collett was a shrewd businessman who had taken the run down dry goods store his maternal grandfather, Albert Foster, had started years ago and turned it into a thriving business. A business that would have supported several families comfortably, or at least those of Foster's three grandchildren, to whom he had bequeathed equal shares in his will. However, Harvey Collett did not believe in sharing, and before the flowers had wilted on his grandfather's grave, he was busy scheming.

His sister, Janet, was a flighty woman with no head for business. It had been easy for him to swindle her out of her share of their inheritance by convincing her that their grandfather had invested it in railroad stock on a line that went belly-up. Of course, Collett wasn't completely heartless. He gave his sister a steady job working in the store, even paying her a nickel more an hour than he did the other employees. He even allowed her husband to drive one of his trucks, delivering fuel oil in the wintertime and kept him busy doing repair work on the houses he held the notes on.

His brother was even easier to deal with. Harold wasn't as big as Harvey, nor was he as smart. In fact, Harold was as dumb as a pile of horseshit, and that was the name Collett always used when referencing him - Horseshit Harold. He married his brother off to a petite, good looking woman named Nancy Smith, and ensconced them on a farm outside of town. Far enough out that old Horseshit Harold couldn't wander into town often enough to get underfoot, but close enough that Collett could pay a visit on his sister-in-law when Harold was out working in the fields and bend her over the kitchen table when the mood struck him. To him it was a win-win-win situation. Horseshit Harold had work to keep him busy, and a woman the likes of which he'd never have gotten on his own. Nancy was living in a nice house that put her roots in Dog's Run to shame, and Collett, well didn't he deserve a little something now and then for bringing those two lost souls together in the first place?

He had been surprised that a woman as small as Nancy could even deliver not one, but two boys the size of her sons. To be honest, he didn't know if he or his brother had fathered Duane or Arnold, but the family resemblance was enough that nobody questioned it. As if anyone in Elmhurst would *dare* to do so!

Both boys were heavy bodied, heavy headed louts, but Collett felt a certain affection for them and had found their size and lack of imagination useful. When somebody complained too loudly about the shoddy construction of their home or didn't make their payment on time, or when some disgruntled employee started talking when they should keep their mouths shut, Duane and Arnold were very good about convincing them that silence was golden and prompt payment of their obligations was healthy.

At first Collett had thought getting Duane a job as a policeman was just a way to appease the young man when he had taken offense to finding his uncle and his new wife getting friendly on his couch, but it had actually turned out pretty well. Duane loved being a cop, and there were times when that badge came in handy. There were a few veterans who had seen enough combat not to be intimidated when Arnold showed up to collect their late payments or explain to them that they needed to quit complaining so much about petty little things like leaky pipes and cracking foundations. One of them had even stuck a war souvenir, German Luger, in the young man's belly and ordered him off the property. Stubborn fools like that soon found themselves pulled over some dark night, and when the cop and his brother were done with them, they usually had an epiphany and stopped being a problem.

And now here was that muckraking, newspaper editor sticking his nose in places where it didn't belong! Duane was an idiot, getting his picture taken that way, but the damn newspaperman didn't need to run it like he did. Collett would have loved to have the boys rough him up a bit to let him know how things worked around Elmhurst. But there was a problem. Two problems, actually. First, Arnold had accosted him in broad daylight, right there in the restaurant in front of everybody, which led to the showdown with Sam Carpenter. And then there was the matter of Lester Smeal. If there were two men in Elmhurst who Collett couldn't bully or buy, it was those two cops. And one of them was married to the newspaper owner's sister!

When Roxanne came into his office to tell him that Robert Tucker was there, Collett put away the ledger he was reading and said, "It's about goddamn time! Show him in."

Robert Tucker was an average looking man in every way. Not too tall or too short, too thin or too fat. He wasn't movie star handsome, though he wasn't unattractive either. Collett was sure he wouldn't have much trouble getting a woman's attention if he wanted to. From what he had learned, Tucker apparently hadn't wanted to since his wife had left him three years earlier. But he wasn't a queer, either. He just seemed to devote all of his time to his newspaper and his addlebrained mother. Collett knew all of this because it was his business to know what went on in his town. Knowledge was power, and he was the most powerful man in Elmhurst.

"Mr. Tucker, welcome! Please, have a seat." Collett heaved his bulk across the desktop to shake hands, then waved him to a chair.

He looked at Tucker over steepled fingers for a long moment, waiting for the other man to speak. Collett knew a thing or two about negotiation and the first rule was that whoever spoke first was at a disadvantage. But Tucker remained silent. Two long minutes ticked by, an uncomfortably long time in a situation like that. Finally, Collett couldn't stand it any longer. He put his hands on his desktop and said, "We have a problem."

"We do?" Tucker asked.

"Yes, we do."

The other man didn't reply and the silence started over but Collett broke it before it could stretch out again. He lifted a copy of that day's newspaper from a credenza to his side and laid it on the desk. "Can you explain this to me?"

"Explain it?'

"Yes, explain it."

"Well, sir, it's called a newspaper," Tucker said.

"I know what it is, smartass. I'd like you to explain this picture," Collett said, stabbing a thick finger into the page.

"What's to explain? A big ox of a cop standing with his foot on a man he just killed, grinning like an idiot. I think it speaks for itself."

"Now you listen here, asshole, I'm not in a mood for this bullshit!" Collett shouted. "You had no business being out there at that shooting scene in the first place, let alone taking that picture and putting it in the paper!"

"Really? Because when I was in school, my journalism professors told me that doing that *was* my business."

"Oh, you think you're pretty smart, do you?" Collett sneered.

"Well, I *did* go to school like I said, so yeah, I guess I must have at least a few smarts."

"Do you have any idea who I am? Any idea of the power I have in this town, you little piss ant?"

"Mr. Collett, I know who you are, and I know *what* you are," Tucker said, "and I'm sorry, but I'm just not impressed. Just like I'm not impressed with your two nephews. So how about you get to the point."

"The *point*," Collett bellowed, "is that you're done in this town, you son-of-a-bitch! I'm going to show you what happens when somebody pisses me off, and when I'm done, there won't be enough of you left to worry about."

Hearing his uncle's upraised voice, Arnold opened a side door and looked in. Seeing Tucker, he started toward his chair, fists balled and hatred in his eyes. Before he was two steps into the room, Tucker was on his feet and the small, blue steel semiautomatic pistol was in his hand, aimed at Arnold's belly.

"Call your dog off before I shoot him," he warned.

"How dare you pull a gun on me!" shrieked Collett. "I'll have your ass thrown so far under the jail that it'll take them a week to dig you out."

"I didn't pull it on you," Tucker said, "I pulled it on this mutthead. And if you don't tell him to stand down, I'm going to empty it into him. I mean it."

Arnold had stopped at the sight of the Colt in Tucker's hand, but stood poised to attack at any minute.

"Back off, Arnold," Collett said, and his nephew relaxed and dropped into a chair near the door.

"Gee, how long did it take to train him that well?" Tucker asked.

"You have absolutely no idea how far over the line you've stepped. You had better give your soul to Jesus, because I now own your ass," Collett told him.

"You may own a lot of people in this town, but you don't own me," Tucker said, lowering the gun but not putting it away. "Now, did you have anything else you wanted to talk about or are we done here?"

"Oh, *you're* done! That's for sure," Collett said.

"Good." Tucker said, crossing to the door he had come through and putting his hand on the knob. "I've got more to do today than wasting time with you and your pet gorilla there. Here's an idea for you, Mr. Collett. Arnold there doesn't seem to be too good at playing the role of a thug, so why don't you give him a couple of rags and some soap and water and see if he knows how to get blood out of the back seat of a Packard?"

Before Collett could reply, Tucker opened the door and left the office, tucking the pistol away in his pocket before Collett's secretary could see it. If Roxanne was surprised by the sounds of a loud argument coming from her employer's private office, the redhead behind the reception desk didn't show it, keeping her face in a *True Confessions* magazine as Tucker opened the outer door and went down the stairs.

***

Back on the sidewalk, Robert took a deep breath and tried to calm his shaking hands. He had had a few fights in his life and wasn't a coward, but he realized that he was probably fortunate that fate had kept him out of combat during the war. Two violent confrontations in one day were just about more than he could handle.

Chapter 31

By the end of the day the fallout from the newspaper's front page had resulted in the loss of four advertisers, dozens of telephone calls for and against Robert's decision to run the photograph, the suspension of Duane Collett from the Elmhurst Police Department pending further investigation of the Conrad Phillips shooting, and a letter of reprimand for Police Chief Lester Smeal.

"I know it seems bad right now, but maybe this was really a good thing," Elizabeth said to her husband, who had been in a black mood since the mayor had called early that morning.

"Don't try to justify your brother's actions to me," Lester said. "I can't believe that Robert would stab me in the back like that. A letter of reprimand? I've never had a letter of reprimand before he pulled this shit!"

"Les, you know the City Council had to do that to cover themselves with all of this publicity."

"Yeah, publicity that Robert brought on us!"

"Still, it doesn't mean anything. You're still you. Still the war hero that came home and made good."

"Shit, Lizzie, this country forgot its heroes the day the war ended. You know that."

"I don't know about that," she said. "You went into the Army a small town boy who was working at the greenhouse with his Daddy. Look at you now, the Chief of Police, living in this fine house and giving me and the kids this good life."

"I'm damn good at my job," Lester shot back, bristling. "Nobody *gave* me anything. I earned everything we've got."

"I didn't mean that, honey," Elizabeth assured him. "Yes, you *are* good at your job. You're the best. But there were a lot of men coming home from the war looking for jobs. You can't deny that your record helped get you on the force in the first place."

"Yeah, and now I've got a reprimand on my record, thanks to your brother!"

"Les, try to put your pride aside for a minute and look at the bright side. You've complained about Duane Collett ever since the day you pinned on a patrolman's badge. How many times have you said he's a disgrace to the uniform? But as long as his Uncle Harvey sits on the City Council and has so much influence in this town, there was nothing you could do to get rid of him. Now he's on his way out."

"He's suspended, that's all. Harvey Collett will figure out a way to make sure he keeps his job."

"I don't think so," Elizabeth said, shaking her head. "Not after what Robert did, sending it out to all those other big newspapers."

"Yeah, gave this town a black eye to the whole wide world!"

"Well, nobody ever died of a black eye, and maybe that's what it will take to make the rest of the Council stand up to Harvey Collett and say "no more." In the long run, maybe Robert did you and this town a favor."

"Sure, the man's a goddamn knight in shining armor," Lester snapped. "Maybe I should give him that fucking medal the Army gave me!"

"Please don't use that word," Elizabeth said. "This isn't an Army barracks or a barroom. The children might hear you."

Chastised, Lester watched the lightning bugs flitting across the yard and remained silent. From inside the house they could hear their children laughing at something on the RCA television Lester had bought the family for Christmas. Lester knew that Elizabeth was right. In the long run, Robert running that picture on the front page of the newspaper was probably the best thing that could happen to rid him of Duane Collett. But he still felt betrayed. Lester had learned about loyalty in the war. If a man couldn't depend on the people around him, he could end up dead in a hurry.

"It's bedtime, I need to get them settled. Will you come upstairs and tuck them in?"

"Yeah, I'll be along," Lester said.

Elizabeth got off the swing, then leaned down and kissed his cheek. "I hate it when the only two men I love in the world are at odds."

"You're always the peacemaker," Lester said. "But sometimes things don't work out the way we want them to."

"Les, I lost my Daddy when I was a little girl, and Mama's not

Mama anymore. She's still alive, but I lose more of her every day. Except for you and the kids, Bobby is all I have left."

"I'm not asking you to choose between the two of us," he said.

"Then you have to get past this and the two of you need to patch things up."

"Go take care of the kids," Lester told her. "Tell them I'll be up in a bit."

She looked at him a moment longer, than straightened up and went inside, leaving him alone with his thoughts.

***

Across town, Robert was reading an article in *Life* magazine about Captain James Jabara, an F-86 Sabre pilot who became the world's first jet ace, shooting down six enemy MiGs in Korea. It had been a long day and he was tired, but still wound up, having so much on his mind. He knew that sleep would be a long time coming.

He finished the article and checked the doors to be sure they were locked, not because he was afraid of somebody breaking in, but rather his mother breaking out while he slept. On the Wednesday before Easter Sunday she had snuck out before daylight and Ted DuPont had spotted her sitting on the steps of Trinity Church as he drove past in his patrol car. It was a cold morning and Dorothy had been shoeless and dressed only in a flannel nightgown, but she hadn't seemed to notice. She told the young policeman she was waiting for the Sunrise Service to begin. To prevent that from happening again, Robert had installed locks high up on the inside doors and made sure they were secured every night before he went to bed. Then he remembered the incident at the Blue Elk at noon and went to the bookcase in the living room and took the Colt pistol Sam Carpenter had loaned him from where he had hidden it on the top shelf and put it in his pocket. Feeling more secure, he turned out the lights and went upstairs.

He knocked on his mother's bedroom door and then peeked inside. She was curled on her side, snoring softly. Robert went to his own room, undressed and took a hot shower, then toweled off and went to bed. He read a few pages from a Frank Yerby book titled *Floodtide*, set in pre-Civil War Natchez, and surprised himself by feeling drowsy long before he expected to. Setting the book on his nightstand, he turned off the light and closed his eyes.

Robert had just fallen asleep when he felt somebody crawling into bed with him and naked flesh against his. Jerking awake, he sat up in bed and turned the bedside light on.

"Mama, what are you doing in here? And where are your clothes?"

"The kids are sound asleep. Make love to me, William."

Horrified, Robert jumped out of bed and said, "Mama, it's me, Robert, your son. Daddy's not here. He died a long time ago, remember?"

"Shhh, you'll wake them up," Dorothy said, holding a finger to her lips. "Now come back to bed. It's been a long time since we've done it. Who knows, maybe we'll make another baby. Would you like another baby, William?"

Robert held his hand over his mouth to keep himself from screaming as his mother cupped a breast with one hand and reached toward him with the other.

"Mama! Stop that and cover yourself. I'm not Daddy. Stop it."

Dorothy stared at him in confusion, then smiled. "I know what you want. Okay, we'll do it doggie style." She rolled over and thrust her rump in the air, then looked over her shoulder at him. "Come on, William, I want it as much as you do."

Robert fled the room, running down the hallway to the stairs, as Dorothy called his father's name.

Chapter 32

"What a rotten way to start the day," Floyd Mahoney said around the stub of an unlit cigar that he seemed to have been born with, as he swept up the last shards of glass that had once been the front window of the *Citizen-Press*. "Don't you worry Robert. My boy Freddie's cutting a new piece of glass right now and we'll have it installed before lunchtime."

Robert, who had spent most of the night lying awake on the couch, wanted to tell him that the day had started out rotten long before dawn, but he just nodded and said, "Thank you, Floyd. I appreciate the fast service."

The smell of smoke hung heavy in the air and the floor squished with water underfoot.

"Damn kids! Chief, you need to put a stop to all this hooliganism," Floyd said. "What's this town coming to when they're throwing bricks through front windows and setting fires?"

"This wasn't kids. You know it and I know it," Robert said, squatting to pick up what was left of a broken bottle and holding it to his nose. "This was full of gasoline. Kids don't throw Molotov cocktails."

"Neither one of us knows a damn thing," Lester said. "We weren't here and nobody saw what happened. Who knows what kids pick up in the movies and in magazines these days?"

"Come on, Les! Are you going to tell me…."

"I'm not going to tell you a damn thing! You wouldn't listen anyway."

Already tired and irritable, Robert felt his temper flare. "What's that supposed to mean?"

"You know exactly what I mean. I told you to stay out of this whole mess, but you just wouldn't listen, would you? No, you had to go down there to the Run and stick your nose in stuff that wasn't any of your business! Now do you see what's it's getting you?"

"Les, the news *is* my business! My job is to report what's happening in this town."

"Then maybe you'd better find a new line of work. Because this isn't working out too well for you, is it?"

Robert felt his face grow hot and he said, "Instead of worrying about me, how about you do *your* job, Les, and go arrest Arnold and Duane Collett for doing this?"

"I'm getting damned tired of you telling me how to do my job!" Lester shouted. "I don't have any evidence that Duane or Arnold did this. For all I know, it was kids just like Floyd here said. Besides, according to you, I've got bigger fish to fry, what with all these murderers you're seeing hiding behind every tree. So I guess I don't have time to worry about your little problem now, do I?"

He stalked out of the newspaper office, slamming the door so hard that Robert expected the glass to shatter just like the front window had. The Buick's big motor roared to life and the tires squealed as Lester sped away, cutting off a milk truck without a backward glance.

The two men stared after the police car in uncomfortable silence, then Robert shook his head and threw the broken bottle into a trash can.

***

Lester Smeal cursed and pounded the Buick's steering wheel as he raced out of town.

Damn you, Robert! How dare you tell me how to do my job? Brother-in-law or not, I ought to turn this car around and go back and kick your ass! You just won't let things alone, will you?

Lester knew that he was as angry at himself and the situation as he was with Robert, but that didn't change things. He was a man who liked to be in control, and it felt like things around him were starting to spin out of control. He needed to get a handle on this whole situation, and he knew just where to start.

***

The same pack of menacing dogs greeted the police car when Lester pulled into Rex Hooper's yard. He honked the horn twice, and when he didn't get a response from Hooper's shack, he hit the siren, quickly changing the dogs snarls into howls.

Dog's Run

"Rex Hooper! It's Chief Smeal. I want to talk to you. Call these damn dogs off!"

"Go away, Chief! Don't get out of that car if ya know what's good for ya!"

"I just want to talk. Call them off."

"I'll tell ya jist what I told that newspaper feller. I got nothin' to say, so git on out of here!"

Once a man has faced a banzai charge of suicidal Japs, a bunch of flea bitten curs wasn't something to be afraid of and Les wasn't in the mood to waste a lot of time shouting back and forth.

"You got two choices, Rex. I can kick the shit out of these dogs and come in there and talk to you, or you can call them off. What's it gonna be?"

"And then you'll gun me down just like that fat ass cop of yours done Conrad!"

"If I wanted you dead you'd have been dead a long time ago, Rex. Now call off these damn dogs. Because I *will* start shooting them any minute now."

"How do I know ya ain't gonna shoot me, too, once ya get in here?"

"Because I said I wasn't going to!"

"Why should I trust you?"

"Oh, Jesus H. Christ! I don't have all day for this shit! I'm leaving my gun in the car and I'm getting out! The first one of those dogs bites me, I'm gonna kick its head off and beat the rest of them to death with its body."

Lester pulled his revolver out of its holster and laid it on the seat next to him, then started to open the car door. The dogs' growling grew even nastier and a large black and white bitch reared up on her hind legs. Lester shoved the door open forcefully and it slammed into the dog's chest, knocking her over backward with a yelp. A smaller, short haired boxer mix lowered its head and hunched its shoulders as if to charge, but a sharp whistle came from the shack and Hooper called out, "You dogs git out of here now! Go lay down!"

As quickly as if the man had turned off a light switch, the dogs backed off and moved out of Lester's way as he made his way to the shack's door. When he got close enough, he saw Hooper standing a few paces back, aiming a shotgun at his chest.

"I'm not armed," Lester said, holding his arms out to the sides.

"Turn around so I know you ain't got a pistol stuck in your belt," ordered Hooper.

Lester did it, and then pulled his pockets inside out to show that all he had was a handkerchief, his wallet, a comb, and a pack of Wrigley's chewing gum.

"We're gonna have to draw the line if you expect me to strip down."

"You promise you ain't gonna try to take this here shotgun away and use it on me?"

"I might take it away and stick it up your ass if you keep pointing it at me," Lester said. "But I'm not gonna shoot you with it."

Hooper held the shotgun steady for another moment, then lowered the barrel and said, "I still don't trust you."

"Well, that's up to you," Lester said as he stepped inside, where the smell of alcohol and filth nearly overwhelmed him. "But I'm here to tell you that I'm gonna get to the bottom of Conrad's shooting. And I know you know something about it, or what led up to it."

"I weren't anywhere near where Conrad got himself shot."

"No, but you *were* parked with him out by the bridge the other night when that girl got herself killed."

"I got nothin' to say 'bout that."

"Come on, Rex, this ain't getting nobody nowhere. I need to know what you saw that night."

"Didn't see a damn thing."

"Bullshit! You people out here keep saying you want justice. Well I do, too, damn it. But how am I supposed to figure out what happened if none of you will cooperate? I don't have a damn crystal ball."

"I don't aim to get myself killed like Conrad did."

"Don't you get it, Rex? If Duane Collett really *did* murder your cousin in cold blood, keeping your mouth shut is the best way to get yourself killed! Because he knows you two were together that night, and even though he's suspended from his job, he's still running around out there."

"Well if he comes around here he'll be a dead man!"

"It wouldn't be any big loss to the world, far as I'm concerned," said Lester. "But I'd rather let the state fry his ass if he did murder Conrad."

"Ain't no *if* about it. He shot Conrad down like a dog!"

"How do you know that if you weren't there to see it?"

"I didn't have to see it," Hooper said, tears running down his cheeks, and Lester realized just how drunk the man was. "Conrad Phillips never had a fight in his life! He may not have been nothin' but a hillbilly moonshiner from the Run, but he was like a brother to me. And that damn Duane Collett gunned him down for no reason."

"If that's what happened, I won't rest until they sit him down in the electric chair down in Columbus. I promise you that."

"You really think they're gonna do anything to him for what he did?"

"I'll personally see to it," Lester promised.

Rex dropped into his chair and took a long drink from the jar of moonshine on the table.

"I ain't no war hero like you. Fact is, I'm a damn coward."

Lester sat across from him, pulled the jar to himself and took a drink. The liquor went down smooth and warmed his gut. Nobody made moonshine like Conrad Phillips did.

"I think all men are cowards a lot more often than they're heroes," he said, "and that includes me, too. Any man who was in combat and tells you he wasn't afraid is a damn liar."

"No, I was a *real* coward," Hooper said, shaking his head, his eyes ten thousand miles away. He lit a cigarette and Lester pushed the jar back toward him. Hooper took another drink, then wiped his eyes with the backs of his grimy hands.

"I was with the 77th Infantry Division at Leyte and Ie Shima and held my own. They killed us by the dozens before we ever finished wading ashore, but I kept on goin' forward. I saw some terrible things, Chief, and did some terrible things too. But then we went to Okinawa. I was part of a rifle platoon they sent out on patrol and I stepped off the trail to take a leak and 'bout then we got ambushed. They shot those poor boys to pieces, and then they came in with their bayonets to finish the job."

The tears were falling hard now, and Lester remained silent and let him get it out. "I ran! Ran like a dog. Instead of standin' my ground and fightin' back, I threw my rifle down and just ran. And I didn't stop runnin' until I come upon a field hospital. I stayed there for three days and all I did was cry like a baby. Finally some men came to get me. I figured they was gonna stand me in front of a firin' squad and I wouldn't a blamed them if they did. But they took me farther back behind the lines and I talked to a couple more doctors. Next thing I knew, I was declared unfit for combat and they had me emptyin' bed pans until the war ended, while good men, men I had served with, kept fightin' and dyin' on the front lines."

He took another long drink and passed the jar to Lester, who took a sip.

"You did one bad thing, but it sounds like you did a lot of good ones too," Lester observed. "The 77th was a hell of a unit. Saw a lot of action."

"All it takes is one time to make you a coward."

"I saw a lot of good men who broke down, one time or another. That didn't take away from what they did the rest of the time."

"Maybe not, but runnin' away like a coward takes away from everythin' a man did before."

"Tell me about what happened at the bridge that night, Rex."

Chapter 33

Robert had spent the entire day cleaning up the mess at the newspaper, hauling out burned papers and what was left of the front counter, and Lillian's desk and chair. It could have been worse.

Fortunately, Doodie McRae, the same man Lester had watched Duane abuse in an alley five years earlier, was sifting through a trashcan at the end of the block and had heard the sound of breaking glass, and then tires squealing as a car sped away. Seeing the flames, he left his wagon on the sidewalk and ran the two blocks to the fire station, where he woke up Seth Montgomery and told him the newspaper office was on fire.

The fire had charred much of the lobby and the false wall that separated it from the newsroom, and destroyed what was out front, but the volunteer firemen had extinguished it before it could do more damage. The monetary loss wasn't as bad as the time it took to clean up the mess.

Word travels fast in a small town, and several men and boys had showed up to help with the cleanup, including Doodie, who was excited when Robert took his photograph and said he was going to put it on the front page of the next edition.

"Then I'll be famous, huh? Just like Officer Collett?"

"Yeah, you'll be famous," Robert assured him. "But you're a hero. Nothing like Duane Collett."

"Well, ain't he a hero, too? He shot that bad guy."

Robert didn't know how to explain to, the simple man, that things weren't always what they seemed to be and that sometimes the bad guys wore badges too. So he just patted Doodie on the shoulder and said, "Let's just concentrate on you being a hero for now, okay?"

***

A blue Plymouth sedan was parked in the driveway when he got home, and Robert wondered if his day could possibly get any worse.

"Well, it's about time," said the thin, severe-faced woman sitting on the sofa, when Robert walked through the door. "Your poor mother has been sitting here alone, all day long, and who knows what kind of mischief she could have gotten herself into if I hadn't have dropped in?"

"Hello, Aunt Kathryn," Robert said. "It's good to see you, too."

She pinched her nose and waved her hand in front of her face. "You smell like a fireplace! Really, Robert, how can a man in your position walk around town looking like you are? You're filthy."

"We had a fire at the office," he told her. "I washed up the best I could before coming home."

"Well, it wasn't enough!"

Familiar with his aunt's displeasure with most things in life, Robert did not take her criticism to heart. But she was just getting started.

"I cannot believe that I'm the last to know that my only sister suffered such an accident almost a week ago!"

"Mama's fine, Aunt Dorothy. She just got a little confused and crawled up on that ladder. Mrs. Alexander, next door, comes over to make her lunch and checks on her several times a day."

"Obviously that's not enough, is it? If it were, your mother would not have nearly broken her neck in that fall. It's time we do something, Robert."

"Aunt Kathryn, everything is fine. She didn't break anything, all she got were a few scratches."

"Everything is *not* fine, Robert! She needs to be in a facility where she can get proper care around the clock."

Dorothy, who became agitated when people argued around her, sat beside her sister wringing her hands, looking from one to the other.

"It's okay, Mama," Robert told her, bending to kiss her cheek.

"It's *not* okay," Kathryn said, her voice rising shrilly. "Robert, I called your sister and told her to come over here so the three of us can discuss what to do about poor Dorothy. I'm her sister and I have a right to…"

Tears started brimming in Dorothy's eyes and Robert patted her hand.

"Aunt Kathryn, you're upsetting Mama. Please lower your voice."

"I will not," Kathryn said, jumping to her feet. "You listen to me, Robert Tucker! Either we find a way to deal with this, this *issue* together, or I will contact the welfare authorities and have them intervene."

Dorothy was crying now and had shrunk back into the cushions. Robert sat down beside her and put his arm around her shoulder.

"Oh, stop coddling her, Robert! That's the problem here. You insist on trying to keep your mother wrapped up in a protective cocoon where real life doesn't intrude. But you're not making this any easier. She needs professional care."

"What she *needs* is for you to calm down and stop upsetting her," Robert said, trying hard to keep his voice level when what he really wanted to do was to shake the old biddy and tell her to mind her own damn business.

Before she could reply, the screen door opened and Elizabeth came into the house. "Aunt Kathryn, what is going *on* in here? I could hear you yelling clear out on the sidewalk."

"I was *not* yelling," Kathryn said. "I was trying to get it through your brother's thick head that Dorothy needs to be institutionalized. The time has come."

Seeing her mother trembling and crying in Robert's arm, Elizabeth pointed toward the door and said, "*The time has come* for you to leave, Aunt Kathryn. You've got Mama all upset with your shouting."

"I am not *shouting*. Stop saying I'm shouting. I'm just…"

A woman married to a war hero and police chief, and the mother of two active young children, is bound to have some steel in her spine and Elizabeth was not one to back down from a confrontation when she knew she was right. She picked her aunt's purse up from the floor in front of the couch, grasped Kathryn firmly by the upper arm, and steered her out the door and down off the porch to where her car was parked in the driveway.

From outside, Robert could hear the women's voices but he ignored them and crooned softly to his mother to drown them out. After a while, Dorothy seemed to calm down and he felt her relax in his arms.

"Don't send me away, Bobby. Please don't do that to me! I'll try to be good and not get in any more trouble."

Robert kissed her forehead and held her close. "I promise you, Mama, you're not going anywhere."

He heard his aunt's car start up and a moment later Elizabeth came back in, her face tight.

"How is she?"

"She's okay," Robert said. "Thanks for showing up when you did."

"Aunt Kathryn has always loved sticking her nose where it doesn't belong," Elizabeth said. She paced the room, and Robert knew there was more she wanted to say.

"How about I take you in the kitchen and get you a bowl of peaches," Robert asked his mother.

"No, that lady will come back and steal me," Dorothy said. "I don't want to be alone."

"You won't be alone. Lizzie and I will be right here, Mama."

"Elizabeth? She's coming? When? I haven't seen her since she married Lester. Is she mad at me, Robert?"

"No, Mama, Lizzie's not mad at you," Robert assured her, trying to avoid his sister's eyes. "Come on, let's get you those peaches you and Lizzie canned a while back. You do love your peaches, don't you, Mama?"

"Yes, yes I do."

He led her into the kitchen, got her settled at the table with a bowl of peach slices, then went back into the living room. Elizabeth was standing in the doorway smoking a cigarette, the screen door propped open.

"Lizzie…"

"She's right, Bobby. I hate to say it, but the time has come."

"Please, Lizzie, not today. I've already had just about the worst day of my life."

"Then *when*, Bobby? We can't ignore the truth forever. Mama does need somebody to look after her. Maybe not 24 hours a day like Aunt Kathryn says, but to fill in when you're not here. You can't do it all, Bobby. And you shouldn't have to."

"Do you hear me complaining?"

"No, Bobby, you never complain. You're Mr. Noble himself. But that doesn't change the fact that you can't be by her side every minute of every day."

As if on cue, a loud crash and then a cry of pain came from the kitchen. They rushed to the sound to find their mother holding her wrist, blood streaming from her hand. A broken Mason jar and sliced peaches in heavy syrup were spilled at her feet.

"Mama, what did you do?"

"I'm sorry," Dorothy whimpered. "I wanted more peaches and didn't want to interrupt you and your girlfriend on your date, Bobby."

"Looked worse than it was. Only took four stitches to close the wound, but she'll be fine," Doctor Crowther said. "She'll be sore for a while, but there's no permanent damage."

"Thanks, Doc," Robert said. "We seem to be taking up your time on a regular basis lately."

The doctor dropped his head slightly and regarded him over the top of his glasses. "We had a conversation last week about…"

"Stop," Robert said, holding up his hand. "No disrespect, Doc, but a nurse or a companion or whatever you call it wouldn't have made any difference this time around. Lizzie and I were both right there in the other room when this happened."

The doctor nodded his head, then asked, "But what about next time, Robert? And there *will* be a next time. Will it be another fall off a ladder? Another cut? Or maybe she'll decide to cook herself dinner and burn the house down, with her in it?"

***

Once they had their mother home and settled in her bed, Robert and Elizabeth sat together in the living room, neither speaking for a long time.

Finally, Robert said, "Earlier you called me noble. But the truth is, I'm being selfish, aren't I? I'm not willing to let her go. Not physically, but the memory of her the way things used to be. That's not fair, is it?"

"It's not a question of fair, it's a question of acceptance, Bobby. You just can't seem to accept that the Mama who raised us is gone. Her body is still here, but *she* is gone."

"Not completely," Robert told her. "There are still times when she comes back."

"Fragments, Bobby" Elizabeth told him. "Fragments of time. And those fragments are getting smaller and less frequent every day."

Robert knew she was right. That Doctor Crowther was right. That even his Aunt Kathryn was right.

"I can't put her in a home, Lizzie. I just can't."

"I understand, Bobby. But there are alternatives. Why don't you go upstairs and take a shower. You smell like a walking pile of soot from cleaning up your office all day long. Meanwhile I'll fix you something to eat and we'll talk."

"Les and the kids…"

"Lester Smeal is a grown man. If he can keep the peace in this town and deal with drunks and hillbillies and the City Council, he damn sure can figure out a way to feed himself and two kids for one night! Now get yourself upstairs and get cleaned up."

***

"This is delicious," Robert said, slicing through a ham steak and spearing the severed piece with his fork.

"I just threw it together," Elizabeth said modestly, though the slight smile at the corners of her mouth showed she appreciated the compliment.

"Sometimes I forget what good cooking is, except when I have dinner at your place," her brother admitted.

"Well, there's always a place at the table for you anytime you're of a mind to drop in. You don't have to wait for an invitation."

"I know that, Lizzie. And I appreciate it."

Elizabeth raised her coffee cup to her lips and regarded her brother over the rim. "So what are we going to do about Mama, Bobby?"

Robert chewed for a moment, swallowed, and then said, "Doc Crowther said maybe we should consider a nurse or somebody like that to look after her when I'm gone. I'm just not sure I could afford it."

"Lester and I could pitch in to help with the cost."

"You've got enough to deal with, raising the kids," Robert said. "I'll figure out something."

"So we're back to Mr. Noble, are we? She's my mother, too, and my responsibility, too. We can contribute something to help cover the cost. I know you've done so much, but it's time, Bobby. I'm glad to see you're finally accepting that. I guess two doctor visits in less than a week is a bit much."

"There's more to it than that," Robert told her.

"Oh?"

He had been trying to put the embarrassing incident of the night before when his mother had come to his bed out of his mind, and though it was uncomfortable to discuss with his sister, he felt she needed to know. When he finished, Elizabeth looked at him with horror.

"Oh Bobby! I am *so* sorry." She reached across the table and took his hand. "I can't imagine… I'm just…" She wiped tears from her eyes and Robert squeezed her hand gently.

"I'll talk to Doc Crowther tomorrow and see if he can suggest someone."

"Thanks, Lizzie," Robert said. "There's so much going on right now…. I'm overwhelmed."

"If you need somebody to talk to, I'm here, Bobby."

Robert did need somebody to talk to. Somebody with whom he could hand part of the responsibility for the problem of what to do about Wanda Jean's diaries and all that they revealed. But those secrets were not the kind of things one shared with a woman, let alone one's sister. He just took his hand back and picked up his fork again.

Chapter 34

Elizabeth spent the night in her old bedroom and had their mother up and dressed and breakfast on the table when Robert came downstairs the next morning. As she did many mornings, Dorothy seemed like her old self, chatting happily about a robin that was building a nest in the elm tree outside the kitchen window and complimenting Elizabeth on breakfast.

"I just love poached eggs, and you always get them just right," she said, smiling at her daughter across the table. Elizabeth beamed, enjoying the temporary return to normalcy, even though she knew it wouldn't last.

"Do you need to get home and check in on Les and the kids?" Robert asked her as he finished his breakfast and carried his plate to the sink.

"I should. Mama, will you be okay while I run back home for a while?"

"Of course, dear, I'm not *that* old yet!"

"Fine then, I'll do that and maybe I'll bring the kids back with me in a little while."

"Oh, that would be wonderful. Perhaps we'll bake cookies. They do love my peanut butter cookies."

"Yes, they do, and so do I," Robert said. "So be sure to save some for me."

"You run along, both of you. I'll be right here when you get back," Dorothy assured them.

"Now, Mama, don't you turn on that oven until I get back," Elizabeth said. "Loretta needs to learn how to make cookies, too. We'll let her help you and she can learn from the master, okay?"

"That would be wonderful," Dorothy said, and Robert left the house while they were still discussing the great cookie bakeoff. After the previous day's difficulties, he hoped the pleasant breakfast was a preview of things to come.

Lester Smeal was not having a pleasant morning at all. He had not slept well, missing Elizabeth in the bed beside him, and his mind reeling with the problems that had descended on him since those two boys had come running into the Sunshine Café to tell him about finding Wanda Jean Reider's body.

How had so much gone to hell in just ten days? One minute he was sitting at the counter enjoying a meatloaf sandwich, and the next he had a dead woman on his hands, and a dead moonshiner killed by one of his officers. Followed by front page newspaper pictures of that officer posing over the corpse grinning like an idiot, a letter of reprimand from the City Council, reporters calling from all over the country, and folks right there in Elmhurst asking what he was going to do about it. Then some fool sets fire to the newspaper office. and not to mention the information he had finally managed to drag out of Rex Hooper. Now what the hell was he supposed to do with that?

Unused to not having their mother there when they woke up, the kids were restless and full of questions.

"Did you and Mama have a fight?" Loretta demanded to know while Lester tried to make oatmeal for breakfast.

"No, we didn't have a fight. I told you. Uncle Robert needed her help with your Grandma last night."

"Is Gramma gonna die?" Woodrow asked.

"No, she's not gonna die," Lester told him. "She's just…"

"Irene says she's crazy," Loretta said.

"She's not crazy. She just gets confused sometimes."

"She gets confused a *lot*," Loretta corrected him. "Most of the time she can't remember that Mama is her daughter and she keeps calling me Lizzie."

"Sometimes old people do that. It's probably because you look so much like your Mama did when she was a little girl," Lester told her.

"Do you really think so? Mama's so pretty."

"Yes, she is. She was always the prettiest girl in town and she grew up to be the prettiest woman around. And that's just what you're going to do, too."

"Will I have boobies like Mama when I grow up?" Loretta wanted to know.

Not much embarrassed Lester Smeal, but he felt his face coloring.

Dog's Run

The last thing he wanted to do this morning was discuss female anatomy with his daughter. Especially *her* anatomy! He was saved when the screen door banged closed and Elizabeth came into the kitchen waving her hand in front of her face.

"What's burning?"

Suddenly Lester became aware of the smoke coming from the toaster. Elizabeth pulled the handle of the Sunbeam up and plucked two charred pieces of bread out of the slots. Using a table knife she started to scrape the black off them over the sink, but gave up and threw them in the trash can instead.

"Here, let me do that," she said, taking the spoon that Lester was stirring the oatmeal with as the telephone began to ring. "Can you get that?"

"Good morning to you, too," Lester said, kissing her on the forehead, relieved to escape the kitchen and the conversation with Loretta about breasts, no matter who was on the other end of the telephone.

The caller was Buck Schroeder, minister of the small church in Dog's Run.

"I'm sorry to bother you at home, Chief Smeal, but can you come out here?"

"What's the problem, Reverend?"

"I'd prefer not to talk over the telephone. It's important."

Lester knew that discussing anything sensitive over the party line telephone was a bad idea, and that if Schroeder wanted to see him in person, he had his reasons.

"Give me an hour."

"Fine. I'll be here," Schroeder said, and Lester hung up.

Elizabeth followed him upstairs as he quickly shaved and pulled on his uniform.

"How did it go last night?"

"Robert's decided it's time to get some help for Mama."

"Is that so? I'm surprised, as stubborn as he's been about it. He's been kind of like an ostrich hiding its head in the sand when things come up."

"There's a reason," Elizabeth said, and told him about Dorothy coming to Robert's bedroom.

"Oh shit," Lester said as he took his gun belt down from the top shelf of the bedroom closet and buckled it on. "Is Robert all right?"

"It really shook him up, Les."

"I can imagine."

"Les, I know things are tense between you two right now, but he's your best friend and he needs you. Can you put aside your hard feelings and talk to him?"

Lester knew she was right and that he needed to forget his own bruised ego and be there for the man who was the closest thing to a brother he had ever known. He nodded as he pulled his Smith & Wesson .44 from its holster and opened the cylinder to slide in the fat brass cartridges with their heavy lead bullets.

"I have to go out to the Run to talk to that preacher fellow, but when I get back to town I'll drop in on Robert and we'll talk, okay?"

"Thank you," Elizabeth said, kissing him on the cheek. "I better get downstairs and make sure the kids finish their breakfasts."

"Yeah, well be prepared. Loretta wants to talk about boobies."

Elizabeth chuckled and said, "That child never ceases to amaze me. But she's getting to that age where she's curious. I guess it's time we had that talk."

"When you say *we* need to have that talk…."

"Don't worry, Mr. War Hero, I'll keep you out of this particular one. But remember, when Woodrow starts asking about peckers, it's all yours."

"Such language out of an fine, upstanding, churchgoing lady!" Lester said, pulling her close for a kiss.

Elizabeth grinned and stood on tiptoe to rub her pelvis against his. "Oh, you'd be surprised the language this lady can use. Especially when she had to sleep in her old room in her Mama's house overnight and not with her man. In fact, it makes her long for…," she leaned close and whispered in his ear.

Lester felt his face flush again and Elizabeth laughed at his discomfort, then gave his crotch another grind before pushing herself away. She paused at the bedroom door and looked back over her shoulder with mischievous eyes. "Hurry back from the Run."

Chapter 35

Buck Schroeder was a tall, slender man who sometimes seemed to be all angles and elbows. Thick, bushy white eyebrows, that reminded Lester of two caterpillars, crawled across his forehead and his ears resembled jug handles attached to the side of his head, which was covered by a few thin strands of white hair.

Lester had always admired the reverend for his dedication to serving the people of the Run, often in the face of strong opposition from those who considered religion an outside interference to living their lives the way they chose and not according to the rules set down in some book a thousand years ago. He was cutting the grass in the church's side yard with an ancient push mower, when the chief's car pulled into the gravel parking lot.

"Getting a head start on the heat of the day?" Lester asked as he climbed out of the Buick.

Schroeder nodded and walked over to shake hands. "Seems like by the time I get done it's grown back up again."

"Maybe you should get one of those ones with a gasoline motor. I saw one in the Sears and Roebuck catalogue that you can even ride on."

Pulling a blue bandana out of the pocket of his overalls, the preacher wiped his face, then shook his head. "The good Lord gave me a strong back and strong arms and legs to work with, so I guess I'll just keep doing it this way. Besides, for what one of those contraptions cost, I can help a few people in need. Newer isn't always better, my friend."

Lester looked at Schroeder's rusty, old Model A Ford and said, "I don't know, Reverend. Don't you think God might at least want you riding around to do his work in something better than that old jalopy?"

"Why, it's only twenty years old," Schroeder said. "It's got another ten or fifteen good years in it. That's probably as much as I do."

Lester knew that Schroeder was pushing 80, but the sturdy, old man had more energy than a lot of men half his age. He had spent most of his working life putting in long hours firing the boilers at the Haughton Elevator Company in Toledo and lived frugally with his wife, Amelia, in a small cottage next door to the church.

The childless couple devoted most of their time and money to helping the poor people who lived in the shanties and tarpaper shacks of Dog's Run. If somebody needed a ride to the doctor, help patching a leaky roof, advice on how to handle a problem child, or someone to pray over them as they lay dying, Buck Schroeder was there.

Amelia, a woman just as short and round as her husband was tall and lanky, was a midwife who had helped deliver two or three generations of babies in the cramped and usually dirty bedrooms of the Run, or occasionally on a kitchen table if she needed more room to work. She tried to teach hygiene and housekeeping skills to women who were usually pleased if they could fill a galvanized tub with water and oversee a procession of children, and sometimes even a reluctant husband, to use it for a Saturday night bath in the same water.

"You said you needed to talk?"

"Let's sit here in the shade," Schroeder said, leading Lester to a bench under a massive oak tree.

When they were settled, Buck drew his old pipe from a pocket and shook tobacco into its bowl from a leather pouch, then struck a wooden match with a fingernail and lit it, puffing out a cloud of smoke. When it was burning well, he shook the match to extinguish it and dropped it in the grass at his feet.

"Joe Cooper's wife came to see me yesterday. She said her daughter, Charlotte, is with child, and that Paulie Reider is the father."

Lester wondered if there was ever good news about the Reider family.

"How old is Charlotte now?"

"She'll be fifteen next month."

Lester knew a lot of girls from the Run who were mothers in their mid-teens and wasn't too surprised by the news. Nor was he surprised at the reverend's next statement.

"Stella Cooper says Joe's going to kill Paulie if he sees him."

Though he didn't know him, Lester couldn't blame the man. He imagined if some young buck were to get Loretta in trouble in a few years, he'd feel the same way. There were a lot of shotgun weddings in the Run, and they weren't unheard of in town, either.

"I reckon Cooper will calm down sooner or later. Paulie ain't much, but maybe being a father will straighten him out." Even as he said the words, Lester knew better. Paulie Reider was a punk, and any girl who depended on him was going to have a hard row to hoe.

"There's more to it than that," Schroeder said. "This wasn't a couple of kids taking things too far and now having to face the consequences. Mrs. Cooper says Paulie raped her daughter."

***

They found Joe Cooper hoeing his garden, chopping at the ground viciously and cursing under his breath. When he saw Lester and Reverend Schroeder standing at the edge of the garden, he dropped the hoe and stalked over to them, his shoulders squared defiantly.

"Whatever ya come to say, you're wastin' your time. God ain't gonna help Paulie Reider when I find him and the law can't protect him."

"Joe, this is Chief Smeal. He's…

"I know who he is," Cooper said. "I'll thank ya both to stay out of my business."

"Well now, I can't say as I blame you for wanting to teach Paulie a lesson," Lester said. "But if you go and kill that kid, then it becomes my business."

"We'll have to cross that bridge when we get to it," Cooper said. "I'm gonna do what I got to do and then you can do what you got to."

"And what good's that gonna do your wife and kids? Who's gonna pay the bills and put food on the table if you're sittin' in a prison cell?" Lester asked.

Cooper just glared at them, and Lester could feel the man's rage radiating outward, like heat from a potbelly stove.

"Joe, I know you're filled with hate right now," Schroeder said. "But the Lord says vengeance is his."

"Yeah, well the Lord ain't never had a daughter raped by a son-of-a-bitch like Paulie Reider!"

"No, but his son was hung on a cross for all of us."

"Save the sermon for Sunday mornin', Preacher."

"Listen Mr. Cooper, if he did this, killing's too good for Paulie Reider. I'll arrest him and stick his ass in prison, and he'll get his in there. A young punk like him, I guarantee he'll know all about what rape feels like by the end of his first day. And he'll know it every day for the rest of his life. Which probably won't be too long."

"It'd serve him right," Cooper said. "But how do I know that'll really happen? Who's to say some shyster lawyer won't get him off with a slap on the wrist?"

"No lawyer's gonna do a lick of work for a kid like him, with no money to pay their bill. Nothing in it for them. Let me talk to your daughter and find out what happened and I'll handle it."

"What if you're wrong? What if he *does* get off somehow?"

"He won't," Lester assured him. "But you and me both know how things are, here in the Run. You're not the only father out here. If he did get off somehow, it wouldn't surprise me at all to find him hanging from a tree limb some morning. And I'll be honest with you, if the law didn't do its job and it came to that, I wouldn't put very much effort into trying to find out who strung him up. But I'm asking you to let me do it the right way first."

Cooper stared at them a long minute, then said, "She's in the house. Don't know how much she'll tell you. My daughter ain't no tramp like that Paulie's sister was. Me and my woman, we raised our kids right. I ain't much for church goin' but we taught them right from wrong."

"Let's talk to her," Lester said.

***

Charlotte Cooper was a chubby girl with lifeless eyes and dull brown hair that hung listlessly around her shoulders. Lester suspected that she was slow minded, but her parents had taught her good manners and she addressed him as sir and tried to answer his questions, though she kept her eyes downcast. He wasn't sure if that was because of shyness or shame, but suspected it was a combination of both.

She didn't want to tell her story in front of her father or Reverend Schroeder, so they sat outside on a bench under the shade of an elm tree while Lester was inside with Charlotte and her mother. He hoped that the preacher could help calm the enraged father and keep him from hunting Paulie Reider down and doing something that would only add to the family's troubles.

"Now Charlotte, honey, you tell Chief Smeal what you told me about what happened," Stella Cooper told her daughter.

"I'm afraid to. Paulie said if I ever told anybody he'd hurt me. I only told you 'bout it because of that thing, Mama. 'Cause my friend hasn't come to visit the last two months."

In spite of his experiences in the war and as a policeman, Lester was raised modestly and wondered if every conversation he would have with a female that day would be about things that embarrassed him. But he hid his discomfort and said, "Don't you worry about Paulie Reider, Charlotte. I promise you that he'll never bother you again."

"Papa said he's gonna kill Paulie. Will he go to jail for that? I don't want my Papa to go to jail."

"That's why I'm here," Lester told her. "It's my job to make sure Paulie can't hurt you again and that your Daddy don't get himself into trouble by hurting Paulie. That's why I need you to tell me what happened."

"Go on, honey, it's okay," Stella urged. "Chief Smeal will make it all better."

Charlotte never looked up as she told her story. She had been taking a shortcut home through the woods from Reynolds' Store, where she had gone to collect the penny a bottle deposit on pop bottles she had collected along the side of the road, and used the money to purchase candy. Walking along the well worn path, she had encountered Paulie Reider, who demanded she share her candy with him. Charlotte had not wanted to, but she was afraid of the bully and handed him the paper sack containing Jujubes, Red Hots, Slo Pokes, and licorice.

"That's all ya got?" Paulia asked with a sneer. "How come ya didn't get none of them candy cigarettes?"

"I don't know," Charlotte had said with a shrug of her shoulders, just wanting to get back whatever candy Paulie would allow her to have and get home.

"Shit, candy's for kids," he told her, after taking out what he wanted and handing the bag back. "How come ya still act like a kid anyway?"

"I don't know," she replied again, wanting to look inside the sack and see what he had left her, but afraid to.

"Ya got tits, so ya ain't no kid," he said. "I bet ya got hair growing down there too, don't ya?"

Charlotte had blushed deeply, unaccustomed to such crude talk.

"Yeah, I bet ya do," Paulie said, stepping closer. He pinched her left breast and Charlotte had yelped in pain and slapped his hand away.

"That's naughty!"

"Naaa, that ain't naughty," Paulie had said. "Hell, don't you know nothin'?"

"I know that's naughty," Charlotte had told him. "Boys ain't supposed to touch girls there!"

"Sure they are," Paulie said. "That's what they're there for." He reached for her breast and she slapped his hand away again.

"Oh, ya like it rough do you?" Okay, that's good, too," he had said, and squeezed her breast forcefully, causing Charlotte to cry out in pain.

She dropped the candy and pushed him away and started to run down the path. But Paulie had caught up with her in just a few steps and pushed her down in the path, laughing at her as she flailed away, trying to fight him off.

"Shut up, ya noisy bitch," he had said as she screamed when he pushed her dress up and ripped her cotton panties off. Charlotte had screamed again, and Paulie had slapped her face, then reached in his back pocket for his knife. The blade flipped open and he had held the point under her chin. "Scream or fight me again and I'll cut your fuckin' throat!"

Terrified, Charlotte had lain still while he raped her, wishing herself dead, but afraid Paulie *would* kill her. When he was done, he had stood and pulled his pants up, laughing at her.

"Did ya like that? Yeah, I think ya did. All you women are nothing but whores, just like that sister of mine was. You play your cards right and I'll come by one of these days and give it to ya again."

Charlotte had rolled onto her side, overcome with pain and shame. Before he left her there, Paulie had knelt down and held the knife blade alongside her face. "This is just between you and me, bitch. Ya say a word about this to anybody and I'll cut yer eyeballs out, ya hear me? Then I'll find yer Mama and do the same thing to her I just did to you. I *know* she'll like it!"

Charlotte nodded, afraid to speak.

"Yeah, you remember that. Keep yer mouth shut. Or else."

Paulie had laughed again, then stood up and walked back down the path to where Charlotte had dropped the bag of candy. He picked it up and shoved it into his pocket, then called back over his shoulder, "Thanks for the candy. And the pussy!" as he sauntered down the path.

Charlotte had lain still until the sound of his laughter had died away, then ran home. Her mother was busy scrubbing clothes on a washboard when she came home and didn't notice Charlotte's tear streaked face. She had cleaned herself up and never spoken a word about what had happened there in the woods, afraid that if she did, Paulie would make good on his threats. It was only after she had missed her period twice, which Mama always called her monthly "friend" visit, that Charlotte knew something was wrong. She told her mother and the story came out.

    The people of Dog's Run were an independent lot, not given to running to the doctor anytime they got a sniffle or pain, or calling on the law when they had a problem. Joe Cooper had listened to his daughter's story, then picked up the shotgun that stood behind the front door of their little four room house and went looking for Paulie Reider. Fortunately for both of them, the boy was nowhere to be found. Stella Cooper had gone to Reverend Schroeder hoping he could help calm her husband down.

***

    When Lester dropped Schroeder off at the church an hour later, he was feeling a lot of the same anger Joe Cooper had displayed. Her mother had told Charlotte that he would make things all better, but Lester knew he couldn't make it better. Charlotte had already faced a dim future, growing up poor and slow minded like she was. But now she'd have a baby to take care of when she wasn't much more than a baby herself. And the best Lester could hope to do was find Paulie and see that he was punished, if he could keep her father from killing him first. For the sake of his wife and kids, Cooper had agreed to let the law handle it, but Lester knew that the man's patience could only last so long, and he needed to work fast. He drove to the Reider place on Roan Road.

Dog's Run

Chapter 36

"Mama, the law's here," Penny said, running inside to tell her mother they had company.

Alice Reider nodded without looking up from her ironing. "Let him in, then take your brother outside and let us talk."

"Is it about that man that was here lookin' for Paulie?"

"I 'spect so," Alice said. "The law don't come out here on social visits. Now let the man in and run along."

Penny opened the door and Lester Smeal came in, taking his hat off as he stepped through the doorway. David Lee looked up at the big lawman and said, "Are you gonna shoot that man that was here with the shotgun?"

"I sure hope I don't have to shoot anybody," Lester said.

"Go on, Penny, take your brother outside," Alice said.

"I don't want to go outside. I want to hear!"

"Don't matter what you want," Alice told the boy. "Now scoot!"

Penny took him by the hand and led him outside, David Lee protesting all the way.

"I figured you'd be along 'fore too long. I don't know where Paulie is. Haven't seen him in a couple days now."

"He's got himself in some big trouble this time," Lester said.

Alice sprinkled a shirt with water from an RC Cola bottle with a perforated metal head stuck in the mouth.

"It was always just a matter of time. I never expected him to come to no good."

"Joe Cooper's going to kill him if he finds him before I do," Lester told her.

"Can't say as I blame him. If it was me, I'd do the same thing. I should have smothered him the day he was born. The day he came outta me I knew he weren't no good. People say you can't tell that 'bout a baby, but I could with him."

"Any idea where I might find him?" Lester asked.

"Anyplace I could tell you, Joe Cooper's already been. Paulie knows he's lookin' for him so he's hidin' out. Or maybe he's done left town for good. Don't know and don't care as long as he don't come back around here. I got two kids left to raise. One's a halfwit and the other's sharp as a tack. I don't need him bringin' his troubles home for them to see."

"Miz Reider, I know you've had a rough few days lately and I sure don't want to add to your troubles, but if Paulie does show up…"

"Chief Smeal, I haven't had a rough few days. I've had a rough *life*, and nothin' you can do is gonna add to my troubles or make them any better neither. Reverend Schroeder, he always says that God's got a plan for all of us, and it's not for us to understand. I have to believe that. Because if I didn't, I'd walk out on that same bridge that my Wanda Jean jumped off of last week and I'd follow her right over the edge. So this here thing with Paulie, it's just one more part of God's plan, whatever that is. Now, if Paulie comes around here, the best thing I could do was shoot him myself and save Joe Cooper the trouble. But that ain't my way. I'll leave it for God to sort out and I'll let you know if he does come around. But I don't 'spect it. He's a rat and he knows the cats are on the prowl after him. Wherever he is, he's hid deep, and I hope the ground caves in on top of him and leaves him there. That may sound terrible for a mother to say, but that's the way I feel about it. I can overlook a lot, but he stopped bein' my son the day he laid his hands on that poor little girl out there in the woods."

There was nothing he could say to that, so Lester just nodded and left her to her ironing.

***

"Mama, is Paulie going to jail?"

"Jail or the grave, Penny."

"I don't want him to die! Is that man gonna shoot him?"

Alice pulled her daughter close and said, "Honey, the good Lord has a plan for all of us, just like Reverend Schroeder says. Now, we don't know what that plan is and it ain't our place to question his wisdom. But whatever happens with Paulie, you can't worry yourself about it. But I do need you to tell me if you see him sneakin' around here. Will you promise me that, baby girl?"

"Yes, ma'am."

"And I need you to promise me somthin' else, Penny. I need you to promise to keep yourself out of trouble. 'Cause the Lord, he's got a plan for you too. You're gonna leave the Run someday and go off to school. You ain't gonna be ironin' and cleanin' house for rich ladies like your Mama does, because someday you're gonna *be* one of those rich ladies!"

"But I don't want to leave, Mama! I want to stay here with you and David Lee."

"I know you do, Penny, but let's not worry about that now. The Lord and your sister, Wanda Jean, has provided a way for you to get yourself an education and have a good life away from all this mess here. And when you do, why, you can send for me and David Lee and we'll live in a grand house together. But your job 'tween now and then is to keep yourself out of trouble and be a good girl. I'm depending on you to do that. Will you do that for your Mama, Penny?"

"Yes, ma'am, I will. I promise. I'll make you proud of me someday."

"Oh, baby," Alice said, kissing her forehead. "I'm already as proud of you as can be. Don't you ever forget that."

***

Lester drove around the Run for an hour or so, but Alice Reider was right. Paulie knew he was being hunted and he had made himself scarce. Nobody had seen him, and even the crowd of juvenile delinquents he hung out with seemed to have no sympathy for somebody who would rape a girl like Charlotte Cooper.

Back in town, Lester sat down at his desk and opened the folded newspaper to see the front page story about the fire at the *Citizen-Press* office and a photograph of Doodie McRae, whom Robert was heralding as a hero for spotting the fire and summoning help before more damage was done.

Which reminded Lester that he had promised Elizabeth that he would talk to Robert. He picked up the telephone receiver and dialed the newspaper office.

"We need to talk," he told Robert when he came on the line. "Let's go for a ride."

***

They drove out to the abandoned quarry five miles south of town. Lester parked in the gravel lot where a well worn path led down to the water's edge and they unwrapped the sandwiches Lester had picked up at the café. Parked a short distance away was an ancient Dodge that some teenager had removed the fenders and cut the top off in an attempt to turn it into a hotrod. A few bicycles lay at the edge of the lot or were propped up on kickstands. Below them came the sound of youthful voices and splashing.

"God, when's the last time we were out here?"

"Been a long time," Robert said. "Before the war."

"It was a different world back then, wasn't it?"

"Maybe the world hasn't changed that much. Maybe we have. Listen to those kids. They're still having fun like we did way back then. Not a care in the world."

"Oh, we had plenty of cares," Lester said. "At least we *thought* they were cares. Remember when you and me used to double date and bring the girls out here to go swimming? Who was that girl you was dating back then? Patty somebody? Her family moved up somewhere around Detroit and you moped around for weeks with a broken heart."

"Patty Zabielski."

"That's right, Patty, from out in Polack town. Had those huge knockers. I don't know if you was in love with her or just her knockers."

"I was what, fifteen, sixteen? The whole world was centered around knockers back then."

Lester laughed and said, "I remember me and Lizzie was in the front seat of my Daddy's old Hudson at the drive-in and you and Patty was smoochin' so hot and heavy in the backseat. And Lizzie, bein' a good girl and all, she was trying to ignore what was happening back there. Most she'd let me do was a quick touch outside her blouse. And then Patty's brassiere come flying over the seat and landed right on her shoulder. She was mortified!"

They both laughed at the memory, the comfortable laugh of old friends with long shared histories.

"Tell you the truth, that was the first time I ever saw them and I squirted right then and there," Robert said. "You think Lizzie was mortified? I wanted to die!"

"Well, I did notice you kind of separated a foot or so right after that and things seemed to calm down back there," Lester remembered. "Not a word was said as we all just watched the movie, and there Lizzie sat for the next half hour with that brassiere just draped across the back of the seat and her shoulder. Damn thing was big enough to make a tent out of!"

"Well you can bet she gave me hell as soon as we got home," Robert said. "I like to have never heard the end of it."

"What do you suppose ever happened to old Patty?" Lester asked.

"Who knows? We swore we were going to write to each other every day after they moved away, and as soon as we got out of high school, I was going to drive up to Detroit and get her and we were going to get married and live happily ever after. I never heard a word from her after she left."

"Oh well," Lester said, "those things happen. By the first week of the school year you were head over heels in love with Christina Oswald. Talk about going from feast to famine, that girl was flat as a board! But you didn't seem to mind at all."

"Yeah, and then she left me for Richie Taylor because he had a car and all I had was the bicycle I used on my paper route."

"Life can be fickle," Lester observed. "Do you remember the chewing tobacco?"

"Oh God, don't remind me. I'm eating!"

"We filched a bag of Beech Nut from my old man and decided we'd be real he men."

"Stop," Robert pleaded, "you'll make me sick all over again."

"It tasted like crap, but neither one of us would admit it. You had a big old plug in your mouth and I was going like a bat out of hell down the road and hit those railroad tracks and I swear that old car went two feet up in the air. Blew a tire coming down and you swallowed that damned tobacco!"

Robert groaned at the memory, but Lester kept right on telling the tale. "I was changing that tire and just knowing that my Dad was gonna kill both of us for tearing up his car, and there you were on your hands and knees over in the grass puking your guts out!"

"If I could reach your gun I'd shoot you," Robert said.

"And along come Richard Shadlin and his dad, and do you remember what he told you?"

Robert groaned again, trying to shut out his words.

"He said if you felt something furry in your mouth to swallow it back real quick, because it was your asshole!"

"Stop before I start puking again!"

They laughed heartily, laughed until tears ran down their faces and washed away at least some of the stress both had been dealing with.

"That was what, 20 years ago? Maybe 25? And I still turn green when I see somebody filling their mouth with that stuff!"

When the laughter finally died, they sat in comfortable silence for a few minutes, listening to the teenagers having fun in the water.

"Lizzie told me about what happened the other night with your Mama. I'm sorry you had to deal with that, Robert."

"Me too. I keep thinking things will get better, even though I know they won't. Lizzie is going to talk to Doc Crowther today and see if he can suggest somebody to help out with her."

"Whatever it costs, we'll help," Lester assured him.

"Thanks, Les. Lizzie said so, too, but you've got kids to raise and educate. I'll figure out something."

"Bullshit. We're family and we'll do our part."

Robert nodded.

"Remember that, Bob. We're family. We may disagree and fuss at each other now and then, but family's family. We stick together through it all. I'd walk through hell for you, and I know you'd do the same for me."

"Thanks, Lester. I need that right now. I didn't run that picture of Duane to hurt you. I just wanted the town to know what he'd done."

"Lizzie says maybe you did me a favor in the long run. She says you made it hard for the City Council to ignore Duane, in spite of his uncle. I've tried to get rid of him for as long as I've been Chief."

"Do you think they will fire him?"

"Who knows? Harvey Collett swings a lot of weight around this town. I guess it all comes down to if the City Council's more afraid of the bad publicity or of pissing off Harvey."

Lester swallowed the last of his sandwich and washed it down with what was left of his Coca Cola. "There's more bad news out of the Run." He told Robert about the rape of Charlotte Cooper.

"I used to think this was just a nice, little town, an idyllic place to live and raise kids."

Lester shook his head. "I stopped thinking that about a week after I pinned this badge on my shirt. All a town is is the sum of the people who live in it. And people are the same anywhere, with all their good qualities and sins and secrets."

Robert knew all about those sins and secrets and was tempted to tell Lester about Wanda Jean's diaries, but once again he felt a need to protect her, though he wasn't sure *what* his silence was protecting her from.

Chapter 37

I just knew that when Arnold Collett did that to me, it wasn't goin to be the last time. I didn't want him to do it and I danged sure didn't want it to happen again. But I guess in his mind once he had me that way he owned a part of me, just like those other men. I guess the difference is that they paid for their part and he just took his. It weren't but a week later that I was comin out of the Western Auto Store where I went to look at a new alarm clock for my Mama and there went that big old Packard past me, with Arnold at the wheel and Mr. Collett in back. Arnold, he looked at me and then said somthin over his shoulder, and I was thinkin Mr Collett must have told him to pull over but they kept right on going. I should have known Mr. Collett wouldn't want to be seen pickin me up in broad daylight like that right there on Main Street. But an hour later when I started walkin back home here comes Arnold pullin up beside me and he rolled down the window and said "get in back." But instead of takin me back to Mr. Collett's office he drove right to the cemetery and pulled way in the back by Pauper's Field where they bury all the poor people whose family can't afford a proper funeral and all. I told Arnold no, but he just pulled over and went back to the trunk and come back with a blanket and told me to spread it out on the seat so I didn't make another mess like last time. I told him no again but he said to shut up and do what I was told or else there'd be one more dead hillbilly layin there, but I'd be on top of the ground and not under it. He said by the time they found me the birds would have pecked my eyes out and the coons and squirrels would have chewed the rest of my face off. That scared me more'n bein dead did! So I just did what he said and Arnold crawled on me and had his way. At least he didn't hit me this time. I guess he knew he didn't have to. Instead he just kept talking dirty while he was on top of me pumpin away. Calling me filthy names and tellin me he knew I wanted it and askin me how much more I liked it than with his uncle and all those other men. I can't explain it, but of all the times

I've done it and all the different men I've done it with, this was the most humiliating thing I've ever done. I felt like all those dead people from the Run, some of them my kinfolk, had come out of their graves and were watching what Arnold did to me. When he was done he just pulled his pants up and told me to get out of the car. He said I was his whore now and he'd have me any time he wanted and any way he wanted. Then he drove away and left me standin there in the cemetery.

There was a knock on Robert's office door and Elizabeth poked her head inside. "You busy?"

He slipped the diary into his desk drawer and waved her in. His sister sat in the chair across from his desk with an expression of frustration on her face.

"You're looking mighty vexed, Lizzie. What put a bee in your bonnet?"

"Oh, Mama! She said yesterday that she wanted to get her hair done, so I called and made her an appointment for this afternoon with Gloria Eldridge over at the beauty parlor. Everything was just fine at lunch, she was all dressed and ready to go, and was chattering away like a magpie all the way there. But once we got there she got real quiet and just nodded and smiled when Gloria and the other lady that works there were welcoming her and saying how good it was to see her again. Gloria got her in the chair and suddenly Mama started asking her who she was and who I was and why she was there.

"Bobby, Gloria has been cutting and styling Mama's hair since we were little kids, but suddenly Mama said she didn't want to be there and wanted to go home. The next thing I know she just got up out of the chair and walked right past me and out the door with the drape hanging around her neck. She was half a block away before I caught up with her, headed down the sidewalk toward home. I couldn't convince her to go back to the car with me, or to take the darned drape off, so we walked back to the house with her wearing it. I was so frustrated it was all I could do not to just yank it off her and march her right back to the beauty parlor like I would a child playing hooky from school. When we got back to the house she wanted to go outside and mow the grass, and when I told her you had already mowed it, she wanted to know when we were going to the beauty shop! I finally got her settled in for her nap, then went next door to ask Mrs. Alexander to keep an eye on her while I walked back downtown, took the drape back to the beauty shop, and picked up the car."

"I'm sorry, Lizzie."

"How do you do it, Bobby? Day in and day out like you do, and still run a business? I've only spent part of the last two days with her and I'm about ready to pull my hair out!"

"Well, go see Miz Eldridge. I hear she's got a cancellation. Maybe she can fix what you have left."

"It's not funny, Bobby," Elizabeth said, tears in her eyes.

"I know it's not," he told her, "but what else can you do but laugh or cry? And crying makes your makeup run and you get those raccoon eyes."

His attempt at humor only made matters worse and the tears Elizabeth had been trying to hold back flowed freely. "I just can't do it, Bobby. I try but I can't. I'm a terrible daughter!"

He came around the desk and knelt down in front of her chair, pulling her close and feeling her hot tears soak through his shirt as she cried. "It's okay, Lizzie. I know how difficult Mama can be sometimes."

"I try so hard, but I just don't have your patience."

"It's okay," he said again.

"No, it's *not* okay," Elizabeth sobbed. "Darn it, Bobby, it's not! And it's never going to be okay. Mama isn't a child but she is one. The only difference is that eventually a child grows up and Mama never will. I can't paddle her and send her to her room when she misbehaves, and I don't want to. She's my mother, damn it. But instead, I have to be her mother! I just can't do it."

"Did Doc Crowther give you any names to check out for help with her?"

Elizabeth pulled away and fished in her dress pocket for a tissue to wipe her eyes, then nodded her head.

"He gave me five names. One was a lady who sounded older than Mama and was so hard of hearing that she couldn't understand me on the telephone. Another said she's due to have a baby in two months and wouldn't be able to work after it was born. The other three are supposed to come by this evening. Can you be there at six? I really need your help in this decision."

"I'll be there," he assured her, and Elizabeth wrapped her arms around his neck and pulled him close again as a new round of sobs shook her body.

"I love her so much, Bobby! I want to be a good daughter. I really do."

"You *are* a good daughter."

"I wish I was like you, Bobby, I really do. You're always so patient with her and you never seem to get upset. I feel like I have absolutely no patience at all."

"Sure you do," Robert assured her. "If you didn't, you'd have beat Les over the head with his billy club years ago."

Elizabeth chuckled in spite of herself and pulled back. "Speaking of that reprobate husband of mine, did you two get a chance to talk?"

Robert nodded. "We did. We drove out to the quarry this afternoon. I think we both needed that."

"The quarry? Gosh, how long has it been since we were out there?"

"It's been a long time. Since before the war."

"You need to find yourself a nice woman, Robert. We could go out there on a double date, just like the old times. It'd be fun."

"Well, let me see if I can find me a gal that wears the same size brassiere as Patty Zabielski did and we'll do it," he promised.

Elizabeth blushed at the memory. "Oh Lord, that was the most uncomfortable night of my life!"

"Well, it wasn't too comfortable for me sitting there behind you, either," Robert told her, and they both laughed out loud.

"I didn't know if I was going to get boobie cooties or something," Elizabeth said and laughed again. She wiped more tears from her eyes, but this time they were tears of happiness.

"I love you, Bobby"

"I love you too, Lizzie. Now why don't you go fix your makeup, and I'll see you at the house this evening."

As Elizabeth started to leave, she turned in the office doorway and said," Please don't ever leave me, Bobby. I'm losing Mama so fast, and if I lost you too, I couldn't stand it."

"I'll be here," he promised, "I'm not going anywhere."

***

"Well, that was fun," Robert said as they watched the last of the potential companions for their mother waddle down the sidewalk. An obese woman who had spent the entire interview wheezing and complaining that her knees would never be able to handle the two steps up to the porch, let alone the stairs to the second floor.

Elizabeth closed the front door and leaned her back against it, as if to keep any of them from returning.

"So which one did you like best? Her or the one with the little dog that peed on the couch, or the first one?"

"Was she the kleptomaniac?"

"I liked her. A five finger discount here and there doesn't necessarily make her a bad person," Robert said.

"Oh, you can't be serious, Bobby? She has a police record, for heaven's sake!"

"Well, that might come in handy, Sis. If she could shoplift a pot roast or some lamb chops now and then it could help offset what we pay her."

Elizabeth shook her head and asked, "Seriously, Bobby, who are we going to find? Some gum chewing teenager who will ignore Mama while she sits there on the couch reading movie star magazines?"

"I've got an idea," Robert told her.

Chapter 38

For the second day in a row, the telephone interrupted breakfast. It was Doc Crowther's nurse, Margaret Hughes.

"Chief Smeal? I'm sorry to bother you at home, but you need to come over here to the office right away."

"Please tell me my mother-in-law didn't jump off a roof using an umbrella for a parachute," Lester said.

"No, it's Doodie McRae. And he's hurt real bad."

***

Doodie had been beaten so badly that he was hard to recognize. His face was battered terribly, his nose and jaw were broken, both eyes were swollen shut, and his smashed lips looked like two strips of raw, bloody steak. Doodie had never been one for dental hygiene, but what few teeth he had left had been broken or knocked out.

"My God, what happened to him?" Lester asked.

"Don't know," the doctor said. "Warren Pratt and his boy were going fishing and found him laying on the side of that dirt road that goes out past the river. He thought a car had hit him. He didn't want to leave him while he went for help, so they brought him here."

"How bad off is he?"

"He's been unconscious since they brought him in. Looks like he's got some broken ribs, and I'm worried about a punctured lung. But the worst of it, that I can determine so far, is that he's got a skull fracture, and I don't know how much damage that's done. He needs to be in a hospital, but as bad off as he is, moving him might kill him. I'm surprised them bringing him here didn't already do it."

"This wasn't no car accident, was it, Doc?"

Crowther shook his head as he pulled the sheet off to reveal livid bruises on Doodie's torso. "Back's just as bad as the front and sides. I'd bet you dollars to donuts those were made by boots. Somebody beat and kicked this poor man almost to death. Who would do a thing like that, Chief?"

Lester tried to keep his rage in control as he said, "I've got a damned good idea."

***

Chickens scattered as Lester pulled the Buick off the road and into the driveway of Harold Collett's farmyard. A large, black mongrel, chained to a tree, raised its head long enough to bark and then decided that it had done all that was required to announce the arrival of the visitor. He laid his head back down on his paws and ignored Lester as he walked across the yard and climbed the steps to the porch.

From inside he heard the sound of Lefty Frizzell on a radio, promising somebody that if they had the money, he had the time. He rapped on the screen door with his knuckles and a moment later, a small woman with blond hair rolled in curlers came to the door.

"Morning, Mrs. Collett. I'm looking for your sons. Are they here?"

"What you want with them? They ain't done nothin' wrong."

"I didn't say they did. I just need to talk to them."

"How come you fired Duane? He's a good boy. He didn't deserve firing."

"I didn't fire him, ma'am. The City Council suspended him pending an investigation of that shooting out in the Run the other day."

"I know you've had it in for Duane ever since you joined the police force. And I know you cheated him out of the Chief's job. And now you're trying to railroad him for killing that hillbilly, when what you should be doing is pinning a medal on him."

"It's out of my hands, Mrs. Collett. The City Council makes the decisions on who gets hired and fired."

"Well you damn sure ain't gonna do anything to help him, I know that!"

Lester knew the conversation wasn't going anywhere, but he asked again, "Like I said, I need to talk to Duane and Arnold. Are they here?"

"No, they're not and I don't know where they are. They're grown men and it's not my job to watch over them."

Lester nodded, "Thanks for your time, ma'am."

"Don't come around here bothering me again," Nancy Collett

warned as he turned away. "All I gotta do is pick up the telephone and call my husband's brother, Harvey, and you'll be makin' your livin' pickin' up trash alongside the road with one of them sticks with a nail on the end of it!"

Lester was tempted to tell her that he was sure Harvey Collett already knew all about picking up trash, but he held his tongue and walked back to his car.

***

Duane lived in a war surplus Quonset hut, one of several that Harvey Collett had bought cheaply and converted to living quarters. The front half was a living room and kitchen, and a cheap partition separated a bedroom and bath in the rear. The door was propped open by a brick and Lester could see Duane's wife, Marcella, sitting in a chrome kitchen chair at the table, smoking. When he knocked, she turned her head and saw him and waved him in.

"How you doin' this fine morning, Chief?"

"I'm fine," Lester told her. "A little early to be hitting the sauce, ain't it?"

"What, this?" Marcella asked, picking up the glass of amber liquid next to her ashtray and taking a sip. "It's never too early when you're married to Duane Collett. Fact is, Chief, it's probably the only thing that keeps me from taking his gun and blowing his head off while he's asleep. Or mine."

He could tell that though it was still morning, she had been drinking for a while. "Well, the world wouldn't miss him," Lester said. "But I'd hate to think of you blowing that pretty little head of yours off."

"Do you think I'm pretty?"

"Course you are. You're a damn fine looking woman."

At one time she had been, with her dark eyes and thick black hair, and a figure that made a man take notice as she walked past him on the sidewalk. But the combination of alcohol, cigarettes, and life with Duane Collette, had taken their toll. There was a hardness about her that took away from her physical beauty, an ugliness creeping in more and more every year that no amount of pancake makeup could cover up.

She lowered her head and looked at him. "Yeah then, if that's so, how come you never made a pass at me?"

"Well, because you're married and I'm married, and things like that never work out well. Somebody always gets hurt."

"Nobody gets hurt if nobody else knows."

"Somebody always finds out."

"Not always," she said, taking a drink and grinning slyly at him. She leaned forward, her loose fitting cotton blouse revealing her breasts, which were not clad in a brassiere. "For instance, nobody knows that every once in a while when Duane is on the nightshift, his Uncle Harvey comes over and keeps me company."

"See there, now three of us know it," Lester told her.

"Three? Oh hell, Duane's known about it forever," she said, waving the glass at him. "In fact," she leaned closer and Lester could smell the whiskey on her breath when she giggled and said, "Duane, he encourages it. Tells me to keep old Uncle Harvey happy and we'll never have to pay rent!"

Lester didn't say anything, and Marcella took another drink and said, "He's a pig."

"Who, Duane or Uncle Harvey?"

"Both of them," she snorted. "Take your pick."

"Do you know where Duane is?" Lester asked her.

"Haven't seen him in a couple of days," she said as she refilled the glass. "He comes and goes." She snorted again and said, "Just like good, old Uncle Harvey."

"How about Arnold?"

"Arnold? No way! I've got my standards."

"No, I mean, do you know where Arnold is?"

"Did you try Uncle Harvey's office? He's usually somewhere close."

"You take care," Lester told her. "And go easy on the booze, Okay, Marcella?"

"You're leaving? Stay a while!"

"I don't think so."

"Stay!"

"Sorry, I need to find Duane and Arnold."

"You don't know what you're missing, Chief. I can do things. Things you'll really like. Things that that prim and proper wife of yours never even heard of."

"I'm sure you can," Lester said. "And I appreciate the offer. But I'm going to have to pass."

"Then screw you! Do you think I need you? I can have any man I want."

As Lester walked out the door, the glass crashed against the wall beside him, the remainder of the whiskey in it splashing the white paint that covered the hut's wall and curved ceiling.

Driving away, Lester couldn't help but feel repulsed by Marcella, not attracted. He remembered her as a pretty, smiling woman who always seemed to laugh at life. He didn't think life had given her much to laugh about in the last few years.

His job exposed him to a lot in life that most of the good citizens of Elmhurst could never imagine. Most police officers had opportunities to cheat if they were so inclined. Lester had strayed once in his marriage, a foolish mistake he deeply regretted and vowed would never happen again. But Marcella's cavalier admission of her affair with her own husband's uncle, and the revelation that Duane not only knew, but encouraged it, made him feel sick to his stomach.

Chapter 39

Alice Reider was ironing when Robert knocked on the door. It was a never ending job that seemed to take up much of her waking hours, which began before dawn and ended long after her children were asleep.

"If you're here to ask about Paulie, I'll tell you what I told that poor girl's daddy and Chief Smeal. I ain't seen him, and I don't want to. I'm a God fearin' woman and I have put up with a lot from the men in my life, but what he did… I'm done with him."

"That's not why I'm here," he told her.

"Is this about those books of Wanda Jean's?"

"No, ma'am. I'm still going through them and…"

She shook her head and said, "I get to thinkin' that maybe I should have just burned those things when I found them. What's done is done and digging up dirt from the past ain't gonna bring my baby back to me."

"No, ma'am, it won't," Robert told her, "and if that's what you want, I'll bring them back to you. But I read what your daughter wrote in them and…"

"Stop," Alice said, holding her hand up. "Whatever's in them, I trust you to do what you feel is right. But I don't want to know, sir. I know what my girl was to the rest of the people in this town, but she was still my baby, Mr. Tucker. I want to remember that cute, little thing that picked daisies and asked me to put them in a jar of water, and played with her cut out dolls over there on the floor."

Robert nodded and she asked, "So what is it that brings you out here to the Run, Mr. Tucker?"

"I'd like to offer you a job."

***

"Alice Reider? Are you nuts, Bob?"

"Hear me out on this, Lester. She's a good woman, she's a hard worker, and she…"

"And she's a hillbilly from the Run with a fugitive son, a dead daughter who was the town slut, and two no 'count husbands."

"She's also the mother of a soldier laying over there in the cemetery who died fighting for this country," Robert told him. "And she's got another daughter who's smart as a whip and has the makings of a good kid. And more than that, I trust her. I think she'll be just the right person to take care of Mama."

"I don't know, Bobby," Elizabeth said. "She's not exactly what I had in mind."

"Then who would you prefer, Lizzie? The fat woman with the bad knees, the one who can't even housebreak a dog, or the klepto? Or maybe one of those high school kids you talked about with her nose in a magazine?"

"There must be somebody…"

"If there is, we haven't found her yet."

"It's only been two days since we agreed to get some help."

"You wanted me to find somebody, Sis. I did."

"How do you plan to make this work, Bob? I thought you were talking about a live in situation. Are you going to move that woman and her two kids in with you? And don't forget, that little boy of hers has a whole set of problems of his own."

"Let's just try having her look after Mama during the day and the three nights a week I have to work late printing the newspaper and see how that works out. If it does, and if it gets to the point where we need somebody to live in, we have the attic, that I finished off when I was in college. That's where I had my desk and studied. The boy can sleep up there, and Mrs. Reider and the girl can share Lizzie's old bedroom."

"What is it about this woman, Bobby? Why do you feel compelled to save her?" Elizabeth asked.

"I'm not saving her, Lizzie! I'm trying to solve a problem. Okay, maybe you're right, but damn it, all her life, all anybody has ever done is kick her. Maybe it's time she got a break."

Robert turned his neck from side to side, listening to the little cracking noises inside. Wishing they would give him some relief from the headache that seemed to have begun the day Alice Reider walked into his office and gave him Wanda Jean's diaries. Since then, it had not let up.

"I don't like it one bit," Lester said. "Nothing good ever come out of messing with those people out there."

"Just because somebody is poor and lives in the Run, that doesn't make them bad. You always see just the bad side, Les. Yes, there are some shiftless people out there. I don't deny it. But there's also a lot of hard-working, decent people who never come to the attention of the police. When the war came along, a lot of men from the Run signed right up and did their duty. And you and I both know that there were some people from right here in town, good people, who found ways to avoid service. Tom Hockabee, from our graduating class, was just fine to play football and baseball back in school, but suddenly he had a back problem and got himself declared 4F. Gary Michaelson claimed he had to stay home to take care of his aging mother and got himself a deferment. And we both know that Sandra Michaelson is as healthy as a horse. And there's kids that come from the Run who were never in a bit of trouble and work hard and go on to make something of themselves. If you remember, just last month, I had a story in the paper about that Hawkins boy, who never missed a day of school from first grade all the way through high school. He was a straight A student and he got himself an appointment to West Point. They're not all bootleggers and wife beaters."

Lester lit a cigarette and blew a cloud of blue smoke into the air, then shook his head. "I know all that, Bob. Let's look at this woman in particular. One husband dead, driving drunk, the other in the state pen for murder, and that Paulie! Not to mention Wanda Jean. Her track record ain't all that impressive."

"I'm not denying that. But like I said, she's also got a son who died over there in Korea and that other daughter is a good kid. If nothing else, Les, isn't the memory of that dead soldier at least deserving of giving his mama a chance?"

They were all silent for a moment, then Elizabeth asked, "So when does she start?"

"She's going to come by tomorrow morning after church to meet Mama and we'll see how that goes. Mama seems to be at her best in the early part of the day. I'd like you to be there. We don't have to make any long term decisions right this minute. She'll come in for a couple of hours every afternoon while I'm at work, since that seems to be Mama's bad time. And she'll stay the evenings I have to print the newspaper so it's not such an abrupt change for Mama, like moving somebody in out of the blue. You know how she gets sometimes when things happen too fast around her."

"I have to tell you, Bobby, I have some serious reservations about this. What if…."

"I think it's damn foolishness," Lester said, interrupting his wife. "I know you need to find some help for your mama, but I'm not sure you've really given finding someone, the right person, enough time."

"What's foolish, Les? No matter what her two husbands and kids have done, if you talk to anybody in this town that has hired Alice Reider to do housework or ironing, they'll all tell you she's a hard worker and as honest as the day is long. Would I like to find somebody with formal nurse training and experience working with somebody like Mama who's willing to accept what we can afford, and live in? Of course I would! But the chances of that happening are slim to none, and Slim just left town on the morning train."

"I have to admit that Emily McCleskey and Sharon Treplett are both always saying that Mrs. Reider does a great job for them and I've never heard a word of complaint," Elizabeth said. "I guess we can try it and see how it works out."

"That's all I'm asking," Robert said.

"And what happens if that older son of hers shows back up and steals you blind, or worse?"

"Well, I guess if he shows up, that would be up to our police chief to arrest him for what he did to that poor girl out in the Run." Robert said, "You said, yourself, that you think Paulie's long gone."

"He'd better be," Lester said. "If he does show his face anywhere around here, Joe Cooper is going kill him on sight. Promise me this, Robert. The first time you see a problem with this woman being there at the house, you put a stop to it and send her packing, okay?"

"You have my word on it," Robert replied. "Thanks for trusting me on this. "I think things are going to work out fine."

As he said those words, Robert had no idea just how wrong the future would prove him to be.

Chapter 40

Doodie McRae died Saturday night without regaining consciousness.

Lester had just finished breaking up a family fight out in the Run, and was turning brothers Alan and Matthew Woodbury over to night jailer Harold Cote to lock into separate cells when the call came from Doc Crowther.

"I did all I could for him," the doctor said. "I decided to take the risk of sending him into the hospital in Toledo, but he was gone by the time the ambulance got him there. Maybe I shouldn't have done that, Chief. He was so bad off I didn't think he could survive the trip, but he needed more than I could give him here."

"Don't second-guess yourself, Doc. I know you did your best for him. I want an autopsy done in Toledo and a full report."

"I'm just a small-town doctor, and I've seen a lot of things in my time. But I've never seen anybody abused like that poor man was. It just isn't right, Lester. Whoever did this to him should burn in Hell."

"When I get my hands on them, they will. I can assure you of that," Lester promised.

***

There was no doubt in Lester's mind that Duane and Arnold Collett were responsible for Doodie McRae's murder. Ever since the fire at the newspaper office, people had been patting Doodie on the shoulder and slapping his back, telling him what a good job he had done in discovering the fire and spreading the alarm. Doodie, who had always lived on the fringe of society in Elmhurst, liked the attention and enjoyed being a hero. So it was only natural that he would embellish the story. He had told the usual crowd of hangers on, at Randy's Barbershop, he had seen the arsonist and hinted that he was working closely with Chief Smeal toward an arrest. When word got back to Lester about Doodie's boasts, he had questioned the man, and Doodie had begun crying and admitted he had invented that part of the story.

"Please don't put me in jail, Chief. I was just making stuff up because everybody liked me and I was a hero. I'm sorry."

"Nobody is going to put you in jail, Doodie, but you can't go around lying about things like that. Whoever started that fire might believe it and come after you."

"Why would they come after me?"

"Because they might want to shut you up so you can't testify against them."

"What's that word mean? Testerfied?"

"Testify. It means to go into court and swear on a Bible that what you say is true."

"Doodie don't swear, Chief. I did when I was little and my Mama washed my mouth out with soap and told me never to swear again. I didn't like that soap!"

"Look, I just don't want you to get hurt, Doodie. There are bad people out there that could hurt you if they believe that you really did see who started that fire."

"But they wouldn't be allowed to do that, right Chief? Hurt me? Because I'm a hero and people are supposed to respect heroes, huh?"

Lester wanted to tell him that people only respected heroes as long as they needed them, and then they quickly forgot.

"Besides, I'm a policeman, too."

"You're a policeman, Doodie?"

"Uh huh," Doodie had said with a proud nod of his head.

"Are you telling fibs again, Doodie?"

"No, sir, I am! Don't you remember? You made me a policeman."

He pulled back the front of the long, grimy raincoat he wore winter and summer to reveal the tin badge pinned to his shirt. "See, I'm a policeman just like you!"

It had been at least three years earlier that Lester had indeed given Doodie the school safety patrol badge that he had found in a box of things left by his predecessor, Chief Gray, upon his retirement. Lester had done so after Doodie took it upon himself to stand on the side of the road waving his arms to slow down cars driving past the school.

"What are you doing, Doodie?" the chief had asked.

"I'm tryin' to make people drive slower 'cause this here is a school and I don't want no kids to get runned over," Doodie had told him.

"I saw a thing on the newsreel at the movies yesterday about school crossing guards keepin' little kids from getting runned over and I want to be one of them. Little kids ain't always careful around cars, Chief. They need somebody like me to look out for them."

"Well, that's very good," Lester had said, "but it's Sunday, Doodie, and school doesn't even start for another month."

Doodie had wrinkled his head in thought for a moment, then smiled broadly and said, "I'm making it a habit for them to drive slow by the school. I learned about habits from the nuns when I was at that place for kids that don't have no Mama or Papa that they sent me to in Toledo after my Mama died. They said habits can be good or bad and if you have good habits, that's a good thing. But if you have bad habits you should practice to make them better and that if you practice hard enough, why, them bad habits get turned into good ones! So that's what I'm doing Chief, I'm given' those people in those cars practice to make good habits for when the little kids go to school."

"I guess I can't argue that," Lester had admitted. "You keep on instilling those good habits in folks, Doodie."

"Yeah, that's what I'm doin'. I'm stillin' good habits and people."

Lester had remembered the badge, and the next time he saw Doodie at his post by the school, he had pinned the badge on him. Doodie had raised his right hand, and Lester had sworn him in as a special, auxiliary crossing guard. With a proud grin that stretched ear to ear, Doodie had returned his salute, smartly, and gone off to keep the streets of Elmhurst safe for school children.

Now Doodie was sitting in his office wiping tears from his face with the back of a dirty hand and asking, "Do I still get to be a policeman, even though I told a fib?"

"Yeah, Doodie, you still get to be a policeman," Lester had told him, then pointed a warning finger and said, "But no more telling lies, okay? Because that's what we call conduct unbecoming an officer and you don't want to get in trouble for that now, do you?"

"No, sir," Doodie had assured him. "I'll be good, Chief, I promise!"

Lester had sent him on his way, with no idea that the damage had already been done and that word of Doodie's boasting had already made the rounds from the barber shop to the pool hall to the local taverns, setting in motion the terrible events to come.

***

Lester made the rounds looking for Arnold and Duane until after midnight, but they were nowhere to be found. Harold Collett was more hospitable than his wife had been when Lester went back to the farm, but said he had not seen either of his sons in two or three days. He dreaded going back to Duane's and having another encounter with Marcella, but when he knocked on the door of the Quonset hut and nobody answered, he looked through the screen and saw her laying slumped over the same table where he had left her hours earlier.

Lester had gone in, wrinkling his nose in disgust at the empty whiskey bottle and cigarette butts scattered over the tabletop and the pool of urine under her chair.

"Marcella. Marcella, wake up!"

He slapped her face lightly, calling her name until she finally opened one bleary eye. "Who's that?"

"It's Lester Smeal. Have you seen Duane?"

"Not here," she said, the eye drooping closed.

Lester shook her by the shoulders but got no response. He picked up her glass from where it had fallen on the floor and rolled away, filled it with water at the sink, and splashed it in her face.

"Whaa the hell? You tryin' to drown me?" She slurred, managing to get both eyes open this time.

"Duane? Have you seen him? Or Arnold?"

"You came back," she said with a smile, then burped, the smell of rancid alcohol and cigarettes turning his stomach. "Knew you'd be back. You want some, don' you?"

"I need to find Duane and Arnold."

"How you want it, Chief? Standin' up? Layin' down? In my mouth? Or the back door? It's all the same to me. I stopped feelin' anything a long time ago."

"Goddammit woman, don't you have any respect for yourself at all?"

"Come on," she said, reaching out towards him.

Lester took a step back, out of her reach, "Get yourself cleaned up and get in bed. You're a disgusting mess."

"Yeah, well maybe you're just too damn picky. Thas' okay, there's plenty more want a taste of this honey."

Lester knew there was nothing to be gained by trying to talk to Marcella. Duane and his brother hadn't been there, and she had sunken too deeply into the cesspool of her life to redeem. He left her there at the table where he found her, and by the time the Buick pulled out of the driveway, she had passed out again, escaping to the relief that only oblivion could give her.

***

"How dare you come to my home in the middle of the night like this, questioning me like I'm some common criminal!" Harvey Collett had shouted, when Lester pounded on his door a little after midnight. "The City Council is going to hear about this, Chief Smeal, you can rest assured about that!"

"Arnold and Duane," Lester demanded again. "Where are they?"

"I have no idea," Collett said. "I'm their uncle, not their babysitter."

"If you know where they are you'd better tell me," Lester warned. "Otherwise, you'll find yourself sitting in a cell right next to them."

"You listen to me, you obnoxious blowhard," Collett had shot back, "I don't give a tinker's damn what kind of medal they gave you back in the war. This is my town and you're a joke! I own this town and if you push me, you'll regret the day you were ever born."

Lester wanted to smash the fat man's doughy face, to pummel him and knock him to the ground and then kick the life out of him like Arnold and Duane had done to poor Doodie McRae. He knew that while Collett may not have had a direct hand in what had happened to Wanda Jean Reider and Doodie, he was involved. But he managed to control his anger.

"You'd better think real long and hard about how much you want to try to protect those boys," Lester warned him. "Because I am going to find them and I'm going to see that they're punished. And if you think they have any loyalty to you at all, you're a fool. They're both going to start singing the minute I throw them in a cell, and you're going to go down with them."

"Get out of here," Collett sneered. "Go write a speeding ticket or beat up on one of those hillbillies out in the Run while you can. Because this time tomorrow it's all over for you."

Lester played his trump card.

"I'll make it real easy for you tomorrow morning," he said, grabbing the older man and spinning him around to push his face against the doorjamb. "You won't even have to drive into town because you'll already be there. You're under arrest for the murder of Wanda Jean Reider."

"Are you insane?" Collett bellowed. "That little whore committed suicide by jumping off the bridge over Dogs Run."

"I have a witness that saw your Packard stopped on the bridge and who will swear that he saw the driver hit Wanda Jean and then throw her off the bridge."

"It wasn't me," Collett said. "I don't even drive that car. Everybody knows that Arnold is my chauffeur."

"Does he drive you over to his brother's house and wait outside while you screw Marcella, too?"

"Listen to yourself. You've lost your mind! Maybe it's that battle fatigue from the war that I keep hearing about. Maybe you need some kind of psychological help. Do you think anybody's going to believe this crazy story of yours?"

Lester ignored him and snapped handcuffs on his wrists. Collett was so big that he had to use two pair, one loop of each on a wrist and the other two locked together behind the fat man's back.

Collett cursed and shouted as Lester led him out to the Buick and shoved him in the back. "You've gone way too far this time, Smeal! Get these things off me and get out of here, and the only thing you'll lose is your job. But if you do this, you'll be just as dead as that moron Doodie McRae."

"Instead of making threats, you should spend your time telling me where to find those two," Lester told him. "Otherwise, save your breath, because you're going to need it when they set your fat ass in the electric chair down in Columbus."

Chapter 41

"Mama, this here is Mrs. Alice Reider. She's come to visit with you for a little bit," Robert said.

"How do you do? It's nice to meet you," Dorothy said.

"My pleasure, ma'am," Alice replied. "You have a lovely home, Mrs. Tucker."

"Why thank you. Are you new in town, Mrs. Reider?"

"No, ma'am, I live out in the Run. But your son has been tellin' me that once in a while you need a little help 'round here, and I was hoping you'd consider lettin' me help out now and then."

"Oh, I get by fine," Dorothy told her with a dismissive wave of her hand. "But Robert and Elizabeth worry about me a lot. I get forgetful at times is all. They're always making a mountain out of a mole hill."

"Ain't that just like children, no matter how old they get?" Alice asked. "But that's better than some I know who don't have time for their Mama at all, once they get older."

"Do you have children, Mrs. Reider?"

"Why, yes I do. Seven of them. And please call me Alice, ma'am."

"Seven? My Lord, what a handful! Maybe I should be coming around to help you out."

"Well, I'm 'fraid four of them have passed on," Alice said.

"Oh, you poor dear," Dorothy said, patting her hand. "I just cannot imagine losing one of my children. Would you like a cup of tea, Alice?"

"That'd be mighty fine, ma'am."

"Let's you and me go in the kitchen and get acquainted. And please call me Dorothy."

Robert and Elizabeth watched them walk down the hallway to the kitchen, chattering away like old friends. "What do you think, Liz?"

"I have to admit, Mama seems to have taken right to her," his sister said. "I won't lie to you and tell you that I'm still not skeptical, but I'm willing to give it a try and see what happens."

"Now, if we can just get Lester to at least keep an open mind about it," Robert said.

"Les has his own problems right now," Elizabeth told him.

"I heard about Doodie at church," Robert said. "And did he really lock up Harvey Collett?"

"Yes, but he's out already. The mayor and Judge Hathaway and Mr. Collett's lawyer were down at the jail getting him out by daylight."

"Les is really on a roll. I'd have loved to have been a fly on the wall to see that!"

"It's not funny, Bobby. I'm afraid for him," Elizabeth hugged her arms together as if to ward off a shiver, in spite of the warm day. "He feels such a sense of, I don't know, rage? I have to be honest with you, Bobby, I'm afraid if he does find Duane and Arnold, he might just shoot them on sight!"

"What time did he get home last night?"

"It was sometime in the wee hours of the morning," she said. "And then by 6 o'clock this morning the mayor was on the phone shouting at him and he went back down to the station to meet him and the lawyer. He's supposed to go to a special meeting of the City Council at 2 p.m. today. I told him to clean up and get some sleep, but he's so fired up that all he can do is pace back and forth like a tiger in a cage. I've never seen him this way before, Bobby."

They were interrupted when Dorothy called from the kitchen, "Bobby? Lizzie? Would you like some lunch? Alice and I are going to make grilled cheese sandwiches."

Neither sibling had an appetite.

***

Lester wasn't the only one seething with rage. Harvey Collett was beside himself with anger and frustration as he drove toward town. Locked up like a common criminal? Made to sit in a filthy jail cell with some stinking hillbilly from the Run, sleeping off a drunk? He not only wanted to see Lester Smeal fired, he wanted to gouge his eyes out, to wrap his fingers around the police chief's neck and watch his face turn purple as he squeezed the very life out of him. War hero? Smeal was going to learn that Harvey Collett wasn't some slant-eyed Jap hiding behind a palm tree on some no name island somewhere. If Smeal thought he had been in a war before, he had another thought coming!

Dog's Run 207

Arnold and Duane were to blame for this whole mess. How could those two stupid mules have done something so incredibly foolish? First Wanda Jean, and then Duane had killed that hillbilly for talking about what he had seen that night at the bridge. Like anybody would have believed him anyway. Just a moonshiner from the Run. But no, Duane had to shoot him, and then get his damn fool picture on the front page of the newspaper, posing like he did.

He had told them to throw a scare into the newspaper publisher, but instead of having a quiet little talk with him in some dark alley, Arnold had accosted him in a restaurant full of people, and then they had tried to burn the damned newspaper office down. And they couldn't even accomplish that! The next thing he knew, Tucker had put that imbecile Doodie McRae's picture on the front page and the retard had gone around town spreading all kinds of rumors about knowing who had started the fire.

Collett had told his nephews to relax, that if Doodie actually *did* know anything, he'd have told the whole wide world about it right away and Lester Smeal would have already been knocking at their door. But Duane and Arnold just had to hunt him down and work him over. And now he was dead, Duane and Arnold were on the run, and Smeal was pounding on his door in the middle of the night and hauling him off to jail.

At least he could do something about that! Collett had enough power to accomplish anything he wanted in Elmhurst. Sure, the City Council might have suspended Duane after he killed that hillbilly and then allowed himself to be photographed like he did, but that was just for show. If those two boys would have just done what he told them and kept a low profile, everything would have been fine. But what could you expect from a pair of thickheaded clods who didn't have the sense of a sparrow between the two of them? Collett wasn't sure what he could do to get his nephews' tits out of the wringer, but the first thing he was going to do was get rid of Lester Smeal. And when this was all over, that muckraking newspaper editor would get his, too!

Speaking of tits, Collett had hoped to at least blow off a little bit of steam with Marcella before he went to the City Council meeting, since Horseshit Harold was always such a Bible thumper and had hauled himself and Nancy off to church, like he did every Sunday morning. He'd have much rather worked Nancy over, because even though she was older than Duane's wife, he still found her attractive and she was always receptive. Marcella had been drinking more and more all the time, and had gotten surly. Sure, she'd do whatever he told her to with no argument, but a man appreciated a smile and some respect now and then, too. When he found her laying in a pool of her own piss and shit, it was all he could do not to gag. He'd never touch her again.

He missed Wanda Jean. That girl knew exactly what it took to make him happy, and in the long run, it was a lot easier to just hand her some money when she was done and send her on her way. Arnold had screwed that up for him, too! Collett had wanted to beat his brains out when he found out Arnold had raped Wanda Jean. Not that the big lummox had any brains to spare anyway. And then the money went missing, and she was the only one that could've taken it. Arnold and Duane didn't have the imagination or the guts to pull off something like that, and his secretary was so busy reading her silly magazines that she wouldn't have noticed the key to Fort Knox if someone would have laid it on her desk.

***

"What are you doing here, Robert?"

"Thought you might need a friendly face. Besides, this is news. Big news."

"Well stick around, because the shit's going to hit the fan here. By the time this is over I may need to get a paper route from you, because if Harvey Collett has his way, I'm going to be out of a job."

"Are you having second thoughts about arresting him last night?"

"Hell no! However all this shakes out, I know it all comes down to him pulling the strings. And whether they fire me or not, I'm going to prove it and see him behind bars to stay."

"Just know I'm behind you all the way, Les. Family, remember?"

"I know I can count on you. It's those yayhoos in there I'm not sure about."

As he spoke, the Town Clerk, Wallace Hegelmeyer, poked his head out into the hallway and said, "The Council is about ready to begin."

Robert followed Lester inside and took a seat in the front row.

Chapter 42

Even with such short notice, word had spread quickly and there was a crowd of people in the Council chambers. They had come to enjoy the show of the town's most powerful citizen pitted against their hero police chief. Harvey Collett, as part of the Council's investigation, was seated in the front row instead of his usual chair behind the dais.

Mayor Louis Fisher was in a foul mood as he rapped his gavel to begin the proceedings. "I want this room cleared. This is a sensitive matter that needs to be discussed. Anybody who doesn't belong here needs to get out now."

"We ain't going anywhere," said a voice from the back of the room.

"And just who are you?" the mayor asked irritably.

"Anthony McClellan."

"Well, Mr. McClellan, I'm afraid you're wrong. You are going to leave and so is everybody else who doesn't have a reason to be here."

"I've got a reason. I'm a citizen of this town and I pay my taxes and I fought a Goddamn war for the right to do what I want in my own country."

"Officer Shaver, clear the courtroom," the mayor ordered.

Before Billy Shaver could react, another man stood up. "According to the Constitution of the United States and the laws of the State of Ohio, this is an open meeting and you can't make anyone leave."

"Who the hell are you? Some lawyer?"

"Yes, sir, I am. My name is James Barrett. I was a Captain with the Judge Advocate General's Corps during the war and I just opened a law office on Crestview Street last month. And I happen to live in one of Harvey Collett's housing developments."

"Well, Mr. Barrett, I have news for you. You are going to vacate the premises or else I'll order you arrested. Everybody get out of here that don't belong!"

Robert stood up, camera in hand, and said, "Just so you know, Mr.

Mayor, this is going to be on the front page of Tuesday's newspaper. And it's going out to all of those same wire services that you all heard from last week. I think they're going to find this latest development from Elmhurst very interesting."

"And let me remind the Council of one other thing, if I might," Barrett said, still on his feet. "All of these people here are voters. And I believe that at least three of you are up for re-election in November. As are you, Mr. Mayor. Do you really want to take this that far?"

The mayor looked stricken, and went into a huddle with the other five councilmembers. There were mutters of cover-up and conspiracies going through the crowd, which was growing louder all the time.

"All right, they can stay," the mayor said angrily when the huddle broke up. "But," he said, pointing a warning finger at Robert, "don't think I'm going to forget this, Tucker!"

Robert quickly raised his camera and caught the mayor's gesture, then lowered it with a grin and said, "I'm counting on it."

"Gentlemen of the Council, esteemed citizens, we are here to discuss recent events in this city and Police Chief Smeal's abusive actions last night toward one of the most prominent citizens of our community."

He went on to remind the Council of the series of violent events that had taken place in the last two weeks, describing Lester as incompetent to handle a major criminal investigation. Then, the mayor claimed, Chief Smeal had lashed out at Harvey Collett, blaming him for what he believed were the crimes committed by Arnold and Wayne Collett, the nephews of the aggrieved community leader.

"There is absolutely no reason to believe that either officer, Duane Collett or his brother Arnold, had any involvement in the recent tragedies. Yet, Chief Smeal, in an effort to settle old grudges, has gone on a vendetta against them. He's been to their parents' farm demanding to know where they are, and last night he arrested Councilman Collett here on trumped up charges just to wield the power of his position with the police department. I'm asking for the immediate dismissal of Lester Smeal, and the launching of a full investigation into his recent actions."

The mayor and Harvey Collett may have believed that they had a stranglehold on the Town Council, but the one thing they hadn't counted on was public opinion. Duane Collett's picture on the front page of the newspaper, standing over the body of the man he had killed, had already made Elmhurst look like a redneck Georgia town. If they thought that a temporary suspension was enough to make the bad publicity go away, the presence of so many citizens, voters, in the council chambers, along with the threat of even more scrutiny from the national press, was more than they had bargained for.

"Lester Smeal has served his country and this community with honor," said Arthur Friedman, who recognized several of his customers in the crowd. "I think we need to think long and hard before we go disparaging his reputation."

"I agree," said Orville Hastings, whose two sons had both come back from the war and bought homes from Harvey Collett under the GI Bill. Homes that were falling apart around them as Collett turned a deaf ear to their complaints. "Maybe it's time we think long and hard about the direction this community is going. It's not like the old days; things are changing and we need to change with them."

Harvey Collett glared at Hastings, who ignored him with a turn of his patrician head. *Go ahead and turn away from me, you son of a bitch. Those two sons of yours may think they had problems before, but they have no idea,* Collett thought. And as for Friedman, that little Jew must have forgotten that Collett's mortgage company held the note on his building. But he'd damn sure be reminded when that note was called due the first thing Monday morning!

"Chief Smeal, what do you have to say for yourself?" the mayor asked, trying to cut off further comment from the councilmembers. "Can you give us one reason to justify your actions last night toward Mr. Collett?"

Lester stood up and faced the Council and the large American flag hanging on the wall behind them. "I'm not in the habit of discussing open investigations in front of the whole world. But since it seems like this here's Show and Tell day, I have a witness who saw Harvey Collett's Packard stopped on the bridge over Dogs Run and saw a man from that car assaulting Wanda Jean Reider and then throwing her off the bridge."

The room burst out in chaos as people gasped and began talking excitedly among themselves. The mayor rapped his gavel once, twice, a third time, and shouted, "Silence! Silence! I will have this room cleared if you all don't quiet down right now."

Not wanting to miss a moment of the show going on before them, the crowd quieted down.

"Who is this witness? Where did he come from?"

"I'm not at liberty to say," Lester told him. "We've got enough people dead around here lately and I'm not going to jeopardize his safety by naming him. Once I have Arnold and Wayne Collet in custody, and re-arrest Mr. Collett here, I'll file my charges and it will all come out in court."

"I want this person's name and I want it now," the mayor shouted. "Otherwise I'll hold you in contempt and you'll be the one sitting in a cell."

"You couldn't possibly hold me in more contempt than I do you and this kangaroo court you're trying to run," Lester told him. "You have no authority to try to lock me up. Now, if you want to call Judge Hathaway down here and he orders me to tell you, *he* can charge me with contempt of court. Because I'm still not going to tell you and have somebody else killed. But I think he needs to remember that *he's* up for reelection this year, too."

The room exploded in noise again and the mayor pounded his gavel, trying to be heard above the crowd, who ignored him. Finally Lester turned and yelled, "Everybody calm down and shut up. Let's get on with this."

The room grew quiet again as they responded to his authoritative order, waiting to hear what would happen next.

The councilmembers were back in the huddle, and when they broke apart this time, Lester knew he had won the battle.

"Okay, Chief Smeal, we're dropping this for now. But this isn't over. No, sir, it's a long way from over!"

***

"What the hell was that all about?" Harvey Collett demanded, cornering the mayor as the meeting broke up. "What just happened here?"

"What could I do, Harvey? You saw the mood of the crowd, they still think that goddamned Smeal is some kind of hero. And there were a lot of new faces in the crowd. That lawyer fellow was right, those are *voters*, Harvey. The councilmembers may have a lot of respect for you, but that only goes so far. They want to keep their seats when election time rolls around."

"Respect, my ass," Collett spat, "That bunch of turncoats need to fear me. Me, instead of that bunch of malcontents sitting in front of them! I can *buy* all the votes I need. Just like I bought you, Louie."

Before the mayor could reply, Collett shouldered past him and stalked out the door.

Chapter 43

Even with Lester's victory over the mayor and Harvey Collett, Sunday dinner was not a celebratory event. Dorothy and the kids talked happily about everything from Woodrow's tree house to Loretta's latest infatuation, which was with horses. But for their part, Robert, Lester and Elizabeth were subdued, aware that the maelstrom swirling around them could be lethal.

Robert had an uneasiness about him, partly from his newsman's instinct that the biggest story of his career could break at any moment, but also because he felt compelled to do something about the information revealed to him in Wanda Jean's diaries, though he still didn't know what the right thing was. Lester, who was a man of action, fidgeted. He was physically exhausted and mentally strained. He knew he needed sleep, but all he wanted was to be out on the street looking for Duane and Arnold.

Elizabeth was no fool, she knew her husband's work could be dangerous, but she had always felt Lester more than capable of dealing with anything that came along. But now she felt a real threat not only to his safety, but to the very life they had created. Looking around her at the people she loved, sitting around the table, she wanted to freeze that moment and hold onto it forever. For somewhere, buried in the deep recesses of her mind, she felt a fear that it all could be snatched away at any moment.

***

Dorothy had been more like her old self than at any time in recent memory, insisting that she help the children do dishes and clean up after dinner. She told them about her new friend, Alice, and regaled them with tales of their mother and uncle's escapades as children.

"It's such a nice evening," Elizabeth said, as she rocked gently beside Lester in the porch swing. When he didn't respond, she nudged him gently in the ribs with her elbow and said, "Honey, you're falling asleep. Why don't you go upstairs to bed?"

He roused himself for a moment and said, "I'm just resting my eyes" then dozed off again.

"Come on, you, I'm taking you upstairs to bed. You're dead on your feet," she told him, standing up and hooking her arm under his to pull him out of the swing.

"You can take me wherever you want, but I don't think I'm going to do you much good right now," Lester said. "Give me a few hours sleep and I'll make it up to you."

"In your dreams," Elizabeth said with a smile as she steered him toward the door. She paused long enough to tell Robert, "I'll be back, you sit tight."

Robert lit a cigarette and watched the fireflies dancing in the yard. From inside the house came the pleasant voices of his mother and the children. While far off in the distance, a train whistle howled its mournful song, a conflicting sound, but one that seemed to fit the mood perfectly.

***

"Did you get him to bed?" Robert asked his sister when she rejoined him.

"He was sound asleep by the time his head hit the pillow," Elizabeth said, returning to the porch swing. "Poor man's been running on willpower and stubbornness for days now."

"Well, Les has a mule streak a mile wide in him. We both know that," he told her.

"I'm worried, Bobby. What's happened to this town? It feels like things are spinning out of control and we're all going be sucked down into the vortex."

"Vortex? That's a $5 word if I ever heard one. Are you doing that "word a day" to increase your vocabulary thing from the *Blade*?"

"I'm serious, Bobby. I've never seen Les like this before."

"Lester likes to be in control," he told her. "And he has a strong sense of right and wrong. When he sees something that's not right or somebody that's crossed over the line, he has to make it right. That's just who he is, Sis. That's what makes him a good policeman and a good man. This is all going to blow over. Les will catch those two and no matter how much pull Harvey Collett used to have in this town, there's not a damn thing he can do to save them. I saw that today in that meeting, Lizzie. The balance of power is shifting. There's a whole new generation, *our* generation, that's fed up with the way things have always been. Those men that took the beaches in the South Pacific and beat the Krauts back in Europe, they're not willing to just take a backseat anymore."

"It's more than that," she said, "It started a few months ago. Something's been eating at his insides, Bobby. He's been moody and quiet one minute, and the next he's grabbing me and dancing me across the living room like we were at the Junior Prom. The other night, before everything went crazy around here, the kids had gone to bed and I was knitting, and Les was in his chair reading a *Field & Stream* magazine. I looked up and he was just staring at me, and there were tears in his eyes, Bobby! In all the time I've known him, I've never seen Lester Smeal cry. I asked him what was wrong, and he just said, "I love you so much.""

"Most women would cherish a tender moment like that," Robert said.

"Most women aren't married to Lester Smeal," Elizabeth responded. "Not that he has ever hesitated to show his love for me and the kids, but it's always been in that oafish schoolboy clown way of his. Les would rather say "I love you" while he's tickling you or picking you up off your feet and swinging you around the room. That's just more his style."

"He's always been a contrary combination," Robert admitted. "Trying to decipher whatever goes on inside that big lug's head would keep Freud awake at night. Just do what you've done all along, Lizzie. Love him and thank God for every day. He may not be perfect, but he's a damn fine man."

"Promise me it's all going to be okay, Bobby. I'm scared. I don't know why, I know it doesn't make sense. But there's this dread deep inside of me. I can't explain it, maybe part of it's seeing Mama slip away more and more all the time. When we lost Daddy, it hurt so much. But at least he was gone and we had his memory to hold onto. With Mama, she's still here but she's going, too. I think watching that happen hurts even worse."

Robert left his rocking chair and moved to the swing and pulled her into his arms. "It's going to be okay, Lizzie. Sooner or later Les is going to catch those two maniacs and put them away, and this town will get back to normal."

Robert was an honest man, but if he had to admit it to himself, he wasn't sure if he really believed what he was telling her.

Chapter 44

Except for her immediate family, the men who would miss the comfort of her arms, and the women who were threatened by her very existence, the death of Wanda Jean Reider went unnoticed for the most part. Aside from the brief furor created by the front page photo of Duane Collett standing over his body, the death of Conrad Phillips did not seem to make much of a ripple in the collective psyche of the good people of Elmhurst.

But Doodie McRae's murder enraged everyone, from the checker players at the barbershop to the morning coffee crowd at the Sunshine Café, and the veterans drinking at the American Legion hall. Doodie may have been an outcast when he was alive, but he was a *town* outcast, one of their own, not one of those people from Dog's Run.

He may have been different, and yes, he was the occasional butt of jokes by some, but still, Doodie was one of them. Everyone knew Doodie for his always happy smile and his willingness to help. If somebody was unloading a truckload of produce at the Saturday farmers market, or raking leaves, or got their car stuck in the snow, there was Doodie, ready and eager to help out, hoping only for a smile or kind word in return. If you were an older citizen or not able to get around well, you could expect Doodie to be there with his snow shovel clearing your sidewalk after a winter storm. Though you might have to air the kitchen out after you invited him in for a cup of hot chocolate, in return for his hard labor, he would refuse to take even a penny for his work. "No, ma'am, Doodie don't want your money. I just like helping people. It's the neighborly thing to do, ain't it?"

***

There was a tenseness that Lester could only compare to that which he had felt among soldiers the night before storming an enemy beachhead. People in Elmhurst were angry and on edge. He could feel it just driving down Main Street, as the eyes followed his Buick, craning to see if there was a prisoner in the back seat.

No matter what Harvey Collett wanted to believe, the community was beginning to turn against the empire he had built. No one seemed to question whether or not Duane and Arnold were responsible for Doodie's death. People had seen their bullying ways too many times and turned their heads. It seemed like everyone knew somebody or had a story about somebody that Duane had pulled over in his police car and roughed up, simply because it was a slow night and he was bored. Arnold's hulking presence looming over someone who was a day late on their mortgage payment to Harvey Collett, or who had the audacity to complain about the ramshackle home he had built and sold them, was well-known around town.

***

Harvey Collett, seated at his desk, could feel it, too, and he didn't like it. He was a man who was used to being in control of everything around him. He pulled strings and people jumped. He liked making people jump and he'd be damned if he was going to let Lester Smeal, or those two idiot nephews of his, or the City Council, try to take that power away from him. If he could find those two boys, he'd shoot them both himself.

Hell, that might be the best way to handle it! Yeah that's right, they had gone rogue, and as much as it pained him, he had to do what was necessary to protect himself and the community, when they showed up at his office seeking refuge. That could work. The community wanted a hero? Harvey Collett could be that hero!

He didn't care if they were kin, even if they were his own sons, which he knew was entirely possible. He didn't get where he was in life by being maudlin about things like that. Now, where were they? They weren't smart enough to hide forever and they would turn up sooner or later. But he didn't have time to wait for later. He reached for the telephone on his desk and began calling in markers.

***

I know what I am and while I'm not particularly proud of it, I can't go back and change the past, can I? But stealing that money, that was somethin else. Mama didn't raise no thieves. Well I guess that ain't true either, is it? Look at Paulie. That boy would steal the pennies off a dead man's eyes if he had the chance. But I never stole anything until that night. I knew when that big old Packard stopped out front and Arnold honked the horn that he wasn't taking me to see Mr. Collett, no matter what he said. Don't ask me how, but I just knew it. There was somethin' about the way he acted, just like he did ever since what happened in the cemetery that night. He just had this, what do they call it, arrogance? Yeah that's the word, arrogance. He had this arrogance about him. But then I thought maybe I was wrong because instead of going to the cemetery he drove back into town and we parked in the alley behind the furniture store and he unlocked the back door and we went inside and up in Mr. Collett's private elevator like we always did when he wanted to see me. But he wasn't there and Arnold grinned like some big old ape and said "Surprise." He said one of these days that old man was gonna die because how long could his heart keep on pumpin' away keepin that fat old body of his goin'? And he said that when that day come it was going to be Arnold's turn to sit behind that desk and he wanted a taste of what it was gonna be like. Well, he may think he's gonna be the big cheese someday, but it weren't that night. I don't know if it was 'cause he was nervous about doing it there or what, but he couldn't do it. He tried but that limp noodle of his just wasn't up to the job. He made me do that one thing hopin' that might help but even that didn't. Finally I couln't help it, I just laughed at him and that really set him off! He hit me a bunch of times and it hurt, I ain't lyin' about that. But it was worth it just to see him humiliated for a change. Finally he smacked me in the nose and the blood went flyin' all over the place and that made him even madder. He told me to go into the old man's bathroom and get somethin' to clean that mess up with. And that's when I found the money.

Robert was almost through the last of Wanda Jean's diaries, and he looked forward to finishing them more than he had the end of his Army enlistment or his college days. Those had both come with the anticipation of a new beginning and a chance to move forward with life. Then he had known what his next step would be and what he could expect to happen. He wasn't sure what he was going to do with what was in those pages. Part of him wanted to throw them in the incinerator and forget they ever existed. But even though he couldn't explain it to himself, he felt like he owed this dead woman, he had never even known, an obligation to be her voice in the world she had left behind.

The night before, he had told Lizzie that when her husband saw something that was wrong, he felt a duty to make it right. Now Robert understood that need in his friend. But what was right? He knew that if he exposed the men who had used Wanda Jean as a no more than sordid plaything, lives and reputations would be ruined. And for what? It wouldn't bring her back or make people think any better of her. They wouldn't see her as a victim, but a pariah, just as she had been in life. Did *she* even see herself as a victim? Robert didn't think so from how he had come to know her in the words she had written. But then again, Doodie McRae had not known that *he* was the reason some people laughed when he shambled past, pulling his old wagon behind him.

He picked up the diary again, paused, and sat it back down and pulled his watch out of his vest pocket. Almost four. He picked up the telephone on his desk and called home.

"Mrs. Reider? It's Robert. How's Mama doing?"

"She was a might addled the last hour or so, wantin' me to go out to the garden with her to pick cutworms off the tomato plants. I told her they hide in the daytime and only come out at night. Then a bit later she wanted to make popcorn strings to put on the Christmas tree. I told her we might do that after supper and got her to lay down for a spell."

"This is going to be one of my late nights," Robert reminded her. "I've got to finish up the paper and we'll start printing about nine. You sure those two children of yours are going to be okay?"

"You don't worry about that, Mr. Tucker. They're sleepin' at my sister Georgia's. She's got six youngins of her own, so two more ain't even goin' get noticed in that crowd."

"If you need anything, you just give me a call. Once we start printing, I won't hear the telephone ring, but my sister Lizzie's number is right there on the pad next to the phone. You call her if you need to."

"Ain't goin' be any need for any of that," Alice told him. "Your Mama's a sweet thing and she sure can't be as hard as gettin' one of those drunk husbands of mine to settle down if she does get cantankerous. Course, I used the rollin' pin on the second one a time or two. I don't 'spect it'll come to that with Miss Dorothy."

Robert said goodbye and hung up, then walked out into the main office. "I'm going to go down the street and get an early dinner before you head home," he told Lillian.

Dog's Run

"I can stick around as long as you need me," she told him. "Nobody's waiting at home for me except a one-eyed cat and an empty house."

"Maybe we ought to start one of those lovelorn columns and put you in it," Robert suggested. "Find you a good man. I bet there's some lonely farmer somewhere out in Kansas or Nebraska that would love to have himself a mail order bride like you."

"The only two good men who ever walked this earth were my Daddy and Jesus, and they're both long gone, not that I could have married either one of them. Present company excepted, of course."

"Why Lillian Jackson, are you propositioning me?"

"And what if I was?"

Robert didn't know how to respond to that, and Lillian laughed at the look on his face. "Shoot, Robert, you wouldn't know a proposition if it crawled right up on your lap and made itself at home. Besides, I'm holding out until you get that convertible car you've been talking about."

He laughed and walked out the door. It would be the last time he laughed in a very long time.

Dog's Run

Chapter 45

Harvey Collett slammed the telephone down in frustration. Damn it, he had been on the phone most of the day putting the word out to every source he had, threatening, promising and cajoling, whatever it took to get the job done, but nobody had seen Arnold or Duane. None of the pool hall owners, bartenders, junkyard mechanics, and two-bit whores within a fifty mile radius, had anything to tell him. He was sure nobody was holding out on him. They knew better than that! But he needn't have worried; his nephews were close and would come to him before long.

***

Robert had finished his dinner and the waitress was placing a thick wedge of coconut pie in front of him when Lester slid into the booth.

"Afternoon, Chief, do you need a menu?"

"No, thanks, Darla," he said, shaking his head. "Just coffee."

As she left the table, Lester picked up a spoon and helped himself to a bite of the pie.

"I'll buy you a slice if you're broke." Robert offered.

"Naa, it tastes better if it's yours. Besides, you need to learn to share. Sometimes you act like an only child."

"Well, be glad I'm not. My sister's about the only woman in the world who'd put up with you."

"That's the truth," Lester agreed, "and while we're sharing, do you have any room for a news item?"

"Tell me you caught up with Duane and Arnold."

"No, but I just got a call from the police down in Wheeling, West Virginia. They got Paulie Reider locked up down there. He stuck up a gas station and stabbed the old man running it. They caught him trying to get away in a stolen Ford."

"The fellow he stabbed die?"

Lester nodded. "Poor old guy was gassed in France during World War I and had a hard time ever since. Just don't seem fair, does it?"

"What happens to Paulie now?"

"I expect they'll electrocute him, when it's all said and done."

"Poor Mrs. Reider. Have you told her yet?"

"Yep. Just came from your house."

"How'd she take it?"

Lester shrugged his shoulders. "I can't tell with that old lady. She just thanked me and said she knew he'd never come to no good. I do have to admit, she had the place looking good. She was beating rugs on the front porch when I showed up, and your mama was taking a nap. Maybe you were right about her after all."

"I'm always right, Robert said, scooping up the last bit of pie before Lester could steal it. "It sure seems like God picked her to pile a lot of trouble on, don't it?"

"Seems that way."

"Any word on Duane and Arnold?"

"No, but they're close," Lester told him. "I can just feel it. You still got that little peashooter Sam gave you?"

Robert nodded and Lester said, "Well, keep it handy. And if you see either one of them, shoot first and ask questions later."

"You think it's going to come to that?"

"Well, I don't see them two surrendering peacefully anytime soon, and they got nothing to lose at this point."

Robert paid his bill and left a tip, and they walked outside together.

"Guess I'll get back to work and try to wrap up things before Scotty blows his top."

Lester put an affectionate hand on his shoulder and said, "One of these days, when things settle down and get back to normal, we need to go fishing, Robert. It's been a long time. I enjoyed sitting out there at the quarry the other day talking."

"Me, too, Les. And you're right, we need to catch us a mess of fish and have Mama and Lizzie fry 'em up. Just the thought of that makes me hungry. And I just ate."

He turned to walk back down the street to the newspaper office and Lester climbed into the Buick and pulled away from the curb.

***

Dog's Run

It was 9 o'clock when Robert finished laying out the last page of the newspaper, which gave him an hour to spare before press time. The front page would have a photograph of Doodie McRae and the story of his murder, and the report of the citizens standing up to the mayor at the emergency City Council meeting, with an angry Mayor Fisher pointing his finger at the camera.

"It's about time," Scotty said, looking at the mockup, then shook his head. "Damn shame about that boy. He was an idiot, but a good hearted one. Used to poke his head in here every once in a while and look over my shoulder, asking questions. I kind of liked him."

"I didn't think you liked anybody, Robert said, with a smile. "Are you telling me that there's a soft spot somewhere inside that crusty old heart of yours?"

"Only godamned soft spot around here is the one in your head," growled Scotty, "now get the hell out of here so I can work!"

"Do you want me to set the headlines for you?"

"I *need* you to get out from underfoot before I put a boot in your ass. That's what I *need*."

"Okay, I'll be up in my office if you do need me," Robert said.

"Well stay there, because you're about as useless as a priest's hard on down here."

***

"You sure this is a good idea? Why don't we just point the nose of this son-of-a bitch west and not stop until we get to California?"

"How far do you think we'll get in a ten year old stolen car with half a tank of gas? Use your head, Arnold. The only one left who can tie us to any of this is Rex Hooper. I should have figured that if that goddamned Conrad was out there that night, Rex would have been with him. They was always together. Once he's dead, people can think whatever they want. But that's all they can do."

"What about your boss?"

"Smeal? I'd love to blow him right out of his shoes with my .38, and I will, sooner or later. Him and that brother-in-law of his both. But that may take a bit longer. Uncle Harvey can tell us what's best about that."

"Uncle Harvey's really pissed off," Arnold said. "I should have never taken that bitch up there to his office."

"You shouldn't have messed around with her at all. Then none of this would have happened."

"Well I did, and you can't change the past. And if you'd have ever crawled between those legs of hers, you'd know why I had to. What's done is done and that's that."

"I wish we could find that money. That'd go a long way toward making things up to Uncle Harvey."

"If we found out where she hid it, we could just get it and go on to California. Do you think we should go back to that shack she lived in and look for it again?"

Duane shook his head. "We turned that place upside down and it weren't there. We stick to the plan. We get rid of Cooper and then go see Uncle Harvey and see what he wants us to do next. Besides, if we *did* find that money and double-crossed him, California wouldn't be far enough away to hide. I'm not worried half as much about Smeal as I would be Uncle Harvey. If we went all the way to China, he'd start digging a hole and not stop until he popped out on the other side of the world right next to us."

Duane slowed the car as they turned off Alexis Road and into Dog's Run.

Chapter 46

Seein' all that money in that cloth sack when I looked under the bathroom sink for somethin' to clean myself up with made my knees shake! I had almost three hundred dollars saved up and I'd been figurin' to take that money and go away to Hollywood to get in the movies. But I knew it'd break my poor Mama's heart if I left so I was puttin' it off until the right time. Mr. Leander, my homeroom teacher in ninth grade, said that we all need to make goals in our lives. I remember him sayin' that goals was like a roadmap to our future and that if we didn't have no roadmap how was we goin' to get to where we was goin'? So I set myself a goal of $500. I figured if I had me $500 I could take Mama and Penny and David Lee and we'd all go to Hollywood. Who knows, maybe I could even get Penny a job in the movies. Look at all those kids in the Our Gang movies. I bet she'd fit right in and we'd both be movie stars. So I slid that sack of money under my dress and tucked it inside my drawers, hopin' that it didn't make too big a bulge and that Arnold wouldn't want to try again with me. But I didn't have to worry about that. He didn't say a word he just sat there drinkin' his uncle's whiskey while I cleaned the proof of what he did to me up, then we went down in the elevator and back out to the alley. He still didn't say a word, just got in the car and drove away, leavin' me standing there.

***

Rex Hooper's pack of dogs began barking the minute the brothers set foot on the property and they froze behind a tree.

"Shit, Duane, you didn't tell me about the damn dogs!"

"I don't think they'll do anything but raise hell."

"Yeah, or eat us alive!"

"Stop being so damned scared of your shadow. They're just dogs. If we have to, we'll shoot them, too."

"How many bullets you got in that damn gun of yours? There must be twenty of them. You going to beat the rest to death when it's empty?"

Before Duane could answer, the cabin door opened a crack and Rex Hooper warned, "Whoever's out there, you better git 'fore I let them dogs eat you!"

"See, I told you," Arnold said as the dogs began barking and growling even louder.

"Shut up! He'll hear you," hissed Duane.

"I said, git! Whatever those dogs leave of you, I'm goin' blow to hell with this shotgun," Hooper called.

Duane should have known that his former position meant nothing to the man inside the shack, but he was too used to the weight his badge carried and tried to rely on it still.

"Rex Hooper, this here is Officer Collett with the police department. I need to talk to you. Call off your dogs."

"You go to hell, you murderin' bastard," Hooper shouted back, firing the shotgun in the direction of his voice. The tree protected them from the buckshot, but not from the dogs, who charged them in a snarling mass of fangs and claws.

"Run!"

The brothers' size may have helped them intimidate the people who crossed their path or who their uncle sent them after, but against the four-legged threat bearing down on them, it was a hindrance. Duane managed to kick one away when it grabbed the leg of his pants and made it to the stolen Mercury just as another lunged at him, sinking its teeth into his calf. Duane cursed and shot the dog, then jerked the car's door open and jumped inside.

"Help me," he heard his brother scream as three of the dogs tried to pull him off his feet. Arnold was still thirty feet away, and the sight of him with a dog hanging onto each leg and another with its teeth deep in his left arm enraged Duane. He started the car and aimed it at the dog pack, feeling the right front tire thump over one and hearing a howl of pain that could have come from the dog or his brother. Duane stopped beside his brother and leaned across the seat to open the passenger door.

"Get in!"

Arnold kicked and beat at the dogs and finally managed to throw himself onto the seat, one dog still determinedly hanging onto his leg. "Go! Go!" he shouted.

But Duane's foot had slipped off the clutch, stalling the car's engine. He cursed again and started it just as another dog clamped onto the same leg, blood spurting as it did. Arnold shrieked in pain, and Duane stomped the accelerater to the floor, steering with one hand and holding onto his brother with the other to keep him from falling out. Rex Hooper's shotgun roared again and more buckshot rattled against the rear end of the car as it tore away from the scene.

The dogs had fallen away, and once they were out of the shotgun's range, Duane stopped the car long enough to get Arnold upright in the seat and the door closed.

"Jesus Christ, you're bleedin' everywhere," he said.

"It's hurts, Duane! Hurts bad."

Two of Arnold's fingers were hanging by bloody strips of flesh and his hand and legs were shredded.

"Here, drink this," Duane said, shoving the bottle of whiskey they had been sipping from for the last hour to his brother.

Arnold took a deep drink, then coughed, "Shit, Duane. Now what?"

"I need to get you to a doctor."

"No, no doctors. The minute we show up at a doctor's office or hospital, the police are gonna be all over us."

"Then what, Arnold? You're gonna bleed to death. Or else die of rabies. Should I get you to Mama? See if she can patch you up?"

"No, Smeal's probably got somebody watchin' the farm. We need Uncle Harvey. He'll know what to do."

"We can't show our face in town!"

"It's dark and nobody knows this car. Just park in the alley behind the store and we'll go in the back way. Nobody will know we're there."

"Are you sure?"

"Yeah, I'm sure. Uncle Harvey will know what to do."

***

I heard somebody in a movie say that money is a curse and I didn't understand it back then. But I do now. I should have known that Mr. Collett and Arnold weren't just gonna pretend they didn't know that money was missin' and sure enough, the next day Arnold showed up demandin' it back. I played innocent and told him I didn't know what he was talkin' about and I think if Penny and David Lee weren't here he'd have started beatin' on me again. But instead he left and came back again later with that brother of his. Like I was gonna be impressed with that tub of lard, policeman or not! I just told him I didn't know what they was talkin' about and then said I'd be happy to call Chief Smeal and have him give me one of them there lie detector tests to prove it. Well that made them stop and think again! I guess they didn't want the Chief involved. So they left, but tonight Arnold was back again, all fired up and tellin' me that if I just gave him the money back that was the end of it. He was almost beggin' me! But the way I figure it I earned that money. I started earnin' it the first time Mr. Bigelow laid me across his desk back there in high school and I been earnin' it ever since.

***

It was almost 10 o'clock and Harvey Collett was hungry and tired. He wanted to go home. He wanted to eat. He wanted to strangle somebody. He wanted to have Wanda Jean here on her knees doing what she did best. But that was over, thanks to Arnold. So instead, he waited.

Having the money stolen had infuriated him, but looking back, if he had to admit it, he had only himself to blame. He had gotten careless. He was counting the monthly mortgage payments Arnold and Duane had collected, over eleven grand, when Roxanne knocked on the door to tell him that Carmen was there to see him. He had been looking forward to that and had quickly stashed the moneybag in the cabinet under the bathroom sink before telling Roxanne to send her in.

Carmen was a good looking, Polack broad, married to another Polack, Eddie Karkowski. A big, dumb ox that had managed to get his legs crushed while he was unloading boxcars at the railroad yard in Toledo. Now he couldn't work and they were three months behind on their mortgage. Normally Harvey would have foreclosed and put them out on the street, but he told Arnold to have Carmen come see him when he served her a final notice. Not because he had any sympathy because her husband was a veteran, and now a cripple. Tough shit, those were the cards life had dealt him. But Carmen was a big titted woman, like a lot of the Polacks were, and he liked big tits.

So when she showed up at his office last month crying and pleading for more time, Harvey had told her maybe they could work something out. And they did, right over there on the couch against the office wall, and again, here on his desk. When he was done and she was getting dressed, he had told her that she had bought some time. The debt was still there and he wanted his money. But if she came to his office a couple of times a week and took care of business, he'd give her some time to figure something out.

Of course, he knew that she wouldn't. How could she? She was just a dumb Polack cow, and sooner or later he'd get tired of her and find somebody else to occupy his time. When that day came, he'd throw them out of the house and sell it again. There was always somebody wanting a good deal on a house. But for now, he was enjoying her tits and that big, round Polack ass.

Harvey had a lodge meeting to get to and he was running late after his latest encounter with Carmen, and he had forgotten about the money. But what the hell, who would have ever thought it would turn up missing? *Nobody* had the guts to steal from Harvey Collett, or was that crazy! But somebody had.

At first, for the briefest of seconds after he discovered the money was missing, he had wondered if Arnold had been that crazy. But he dismissed that notion quickly. Arnold was a lot of things, from stupid to lazy to ugly, but the one thing he wasn't, was crazy. He had broken enough heads to know what Harvey Collett did to people who pissed him off.

It didn't take Arnold long to confess the whole, stupid mess with Wanda Jean, and he was crying as he begged his uncle to forgive him, promising to get the money back. While the sight of the big lump of shit crying like a baby as he stood there with his head hanging had disgusted him, Harvey was surprised to find that hearing about the rape had aroused him.

"Go get my money," he had ordered his nephew. "You have 24 hours to get it back here on my desk and I don't want to see you until you've got it. Then I'll decide how to punish you. Now get out of here. And send Roxanne in on your way out."

He didn't really like screwing Roxanne. She was too passive and just laid there with her eyes closed until he was done, never moving or even making a grunt, so he didn't do it often. But he had a meeting at the bank in an hour and didn't have time to wait for Carmen or one of the other women who tried to pay their debts with their twats to answer his summons.

The sound of the elevator coming to life as it made its way up from the closed store downstairs interrupted his thoughts. Harvey glanced at the clock on his desk. 10:05. He opened a drawer on his desk, took out the short barreled, Colt Banker's Special, placed it on his desktop, and covered it with a newspaper. It was time to deal with his nephews.

Chapter 47

To tell you the truth, part of me wishes I never would have taken that money. But I did and what's done is done, and I know I can't just give it back and act like it never happened 'cause it did. And even if I did give it back, Mr. Collett and Arnold and Duane ain't gonna just let it go. No, there's gonna be hell to pay no matter. So I'm gonna do the only thing I know to do. I'm goin' to leave and go on out to Hollywood like I planned to do in the first place. I don't have time to explain it all to Mama and try to convince her to come with me on such short notice 'cause she can be so stubborn. But as soon as I get myself situated out there I'll buy a house and send for her and the little ones. But in the meantime I need to know that they're gonna be alright and that somebody will look after them in case Arnold comes back. And there's only one person I know I can trust. Chief Smeal is a good man, and that one time with him, it weren't like with all those others. It was different and he treated me real nice. And when we was done I felt like it was the only time I had ever enjoyed it. But I don't think he did, because he had this look about him, like he'd just lost his best friend or somethin'. I tried to get him to tell me what was wrong, but he just said it was a big mistake and he loved his wife and it could never happen again. And it never did, though I'd have done it with him any time, all he ever had to do was ask. But he never did. He didn't offer me any money and I didn't want any, but now I need something from him and he's the only one I can turn to. I know he won't let me down. I'll go explain it all to him tonight. Then when everybody goes to church tomorrow I'll leave Mama a note to let her know that as soon as I can I'll send for them and we'll live happily ever after, just like in the movies.

Robert stared at the last diary entry, horrified by what he had just read. His stomach roiled and he felt the vomit rush to the back of his throat. Not for the first time, since he had started learning Wanda Jean's secrets, did he barely make it across the hall and into the bathroom in time.

No! Lester, how could you? How could you do that to Lizzie and the kids? Why would you?

He wanted to scream. He wanted to find Lester and pound out his rage against him. He wanted to crawl inside a hole and die. Nothing, not the death of his father or the breakup of his marriage, or watching his mother's mental faculties slip away more and more, had ever left him feeling so empty, so betrayed, as reading about Lester's involvement with Wanda Jean.

For days, Robert had felt his disgust and anger building toward the men who so casually used Wanda Jean, and now he had to face the fact that his own brother-in-law, his best friend in the world for as long as he could remember, was one of them. And what about his wife and children? How could they mean so little to Lester?

***

The elevator opened directly into Harvey Collett's office, and he swiveled his chair around to face it. He was momentarily taken aback by the blood covering both of his nephews, when the door opened.

"What the hell happened?"

"That damn pack of dogs out at Rex Hooper's place mauled Arnold," Duane said, helping his brother to the couch. Harvey started to tell Arnold not to sit down on the expensive piece of furniture and get blood all over it, but what did it matter? Soon enough there'd be blood everywhere, anyway.

"What have you idiots done now? Why were you out there in the first place?"

"Because he's the last one that can tie us to any of this," Duane said. "We thought if we could shut him up, it would all blow over."

"Who the hell ever told either one of you that you could think?" Harvey thundered. "Between the two of you, you don't have enough brains to form a complete sentence, let alone plan something like this."

"We was just tryin'….."

"Shut up! Do you two realize what a mess you have created? It was bad enough killing that woman and then that damned hillbilly. But we could have gotten past that. Nobody cares about that trash from the Run. I was working to get us past that. But then you had to beat that retard to death! Now everybody in town's acting like he was the baby of the family or something, and calling for blood. And my money's still gone!"

"That idiot was tellin' everybody he knew, who set fire to the newspaper office. We had to shut him up, Uncle Harvey."

"Don't you think if he really saw something, he's have already told Smeal? He was just talking to get attention."

"Please, Uncle Harvey, I'm hurt bad," Arnold interrupted, grimacing with the pain. "Them dogs about eat me alive. I need a doctor."

"Shut up and let me think for a minute. You're whining like a baby."

"I just want it to stop hurtin,' 'cause I can't take much more!"

"No problem. I can stop it from hurting," Harvey told him, and shot him between the eyes with the Colt.

***

"What the hell's the matter with you? You look like you seen a ghost," Scotty said when Robert walked down the stairs to the pressroom.

"Are you ready to start printing?" Robert asked, woodenly.

"Ten more minutes. You okay, Bobby?"

"Uh, yeah. It's been a long week. I just want to get this issue out and go home and get to bed."

"You should hire some kid to help me on printing day. No reason in the world for you to be here."

Both men knew that no matter how much help Robert hired, there was no way he'd miss a pressrun, short of a death in the family. No small town newspaper publisher worth his salt would miss the thrill of seeing the first copies of a new issue come off the press. Each one was anxiously awaited, like the birth of a child they had created, and who could not be there for that? No, Robert would be there, even if the revelation of Lester's infidelity *had* hit him as hard as a death in the family. In a lot of ways, it was. Life as he knew it had stopped existing when he read that last entry in Wanda Jean's diary, and he couldn't picture what tomorrow would be like.

"Go upstairs and sit down for a few minutes," Scotty told him. "The way you look now, you'll fall into the press and I'll have to stop what I'm doing to drag you out of the way so I can work. Go on, get out of here. I'll buzz you when I'm ready."

***

"What did you do? You killed Arnold," Duane screeched, staring at his brother's mangled head in shock.

"No, *you* did," Harvey told him, the plan changing and a new one forming as he spoke. It would come in handy to still have at least one of his nephews around. There were still debts to collect and muscle needed to keep people in line. And Arnold had shown he couldn't be trusted.

"You killed him!"

"He was bleeding to death anyway, you damn fool. Now listen to me. I've got it all figured out. You killed that moonshiner in the line of duty, just like we've said all along. But Arnold killed the girl and the retard and you had nothing to do with it. You've been looking for him ever since, to bring him to justice, brother or no brother. You heard about the thing out at Hooper's place and tracked him here. When you tried to arrest him, he resisted and you had to shoot him. Hell boy, you're going to be a hero. I wouldn't be surprised if the City Council doesn't fire Smeal and make you chief when they hear how you broke this case wide open."

"You killed him," Duane repeated a third time. "Why did you have to kill him?"

"I just told you why, you damn idiot! This is all going to work out fine. Just keep your mouth shut and tell it like I laid it out for you."

"You bastard, you killed Arnold! It's not enough that you've been screwing my wife all this time, but now you killed my brother!"

Harvey realized that his latest scheme wasn't going to work. Who knew Duane would have any familial loyalty? Fortunately for him, Harvey never let such syrupy nonsense slow him down. Back to the original plan. Both boys had to go.

If Harvey had been surprised to learn that he had underestimated Duane's feelings for his brother, he was even more surprised by what happened next. Before he could turn the gun toward his nephew, Duane had his own revolver in his hand and flame shot from the barrel. The 158 grain lead slug tore Harvey's tailored Hathaway shirt and plunged

Dog's Run

though the fat surrounding his belly, to lodge deep inside the big man. He dropped the snub nose Colt, and clutched at his midsection with both hands.

"What have you done, you fool?"

"Something that was long overdue," Duane said, "And this one's for what you've been doing to my Mama." He shot his uncle again, and as the world started to go black around him, Harvey heard his nephew say, "And this one's for my Dad." It was the last thing he ever heard.

Chapter 48

Lester was sitting in the chair across from Robert's desk, holding Wanda Jean's diary in his hands, when he went back upstairs to his office.

"You bastard, I ought to kill you," Robert told him.

Lester set the book down and said, "I wouldn't blame you if you did."

"How could you do it, Les? I thought you loved Lizzie."

"I do. More than anything in this world."

"Then, why?"

"I wish I could tell you why it happened, Robert. It just did. It was back in early March. Lizzie and me was having trouble. She was so upset with how your Mama was going downhill, and she kept saying she was afraid it was going to happen to her, too, someday. She just shut me out. I'd try to talk to her and tell her that just because your Mama was fading away didn't mean she would, too. But she'd just shrug her shoulders and not say anything. It was like she was lost in her own world, and I couldn't drag her out of it."

"So instead of comforting her, you go find the first piece of ass that comes along?"

"It wasn't like that, Robert. I come across Wanda Jean walking down by Swan Creek, one evening, and it was raining cats and dogs. I offered her a ride, and she was just so nice to talk to. Nobody ever saw that side of her. They just saw what was on the outside, but she was good inside, too. It was like she knew I was hurting and she asked me what was wrong. It's not easy for a man like me to say what he's feeling inside. Everybody expects me to be the strong one, but for some reason I didn't need to be strong with her. I can't explain it and I'm damn sure not trying to excuse it."

Lester avoided Robert's eyes and looked toward the ceiling of the office. "We must have sat there talking for a couple of hours, and the next thing I knew, she leaned across the seat and kissed me. And then, well, it just happened. It only happened that once, but that was one time too many."

He lowered his head, and Robert could see the pain in his eyes. "I swear, it was just that one time. And nothing you can think about me can be worse than I already think of myself."

"So now what, Les? Do you expect me to just pretend it never happened and forget I even read about it?"

"I don't know. I really don't, Robert."

Robert opened his desk drawer and threw the first two diaries on the desktop. "I've been reading these and they just make me sick, Les. Everybody from the high school principal to half the business owners on Main Street have been with that girl since she was a kid. My first inclination was to publish the diaries and expose all of them."

"You'd be destroying a lot of reputations and families, if you did."

"I didn't destroy anything, Les! Don't try to make me the bad guy here. I wasn't the one messing around with that girl! Maybe the people of this town need to know how many sick bastards we have living among us."

"You're right," Lester told him. "I wish I was as good as you, Robert. But I'm not."

"Don't offer me platitudes, Les."

"That's a college boy word. I don't know what it means."

"It means… never mind what it means."

"So what are you going to do?"

"I don't know, Les. I really don't. You're right. If I do print the diaries, a lot of people will get hurt. Not just the men who were sleeping with Wanda Jean, but their families, too. They don't deserve that. But do I just keep quiet and let it go? Don't those wives deserve to know how treacherous their husbands are? How they've betrayed them?"

The telephone on Robert's desk rang, and he picked it up. "What?"

"Mr. Tucker? This here's Harold Cote over at the police station. Is Chief Smeal there? I need him."

Robert handed the telephone to Lester, who listened and said, "I'm on my way." He hung up and lunged out of his seat. "Somebody reported hearing gunshots coming from Harvey Collett's office."

He started through the door, but paused and turned back. "Robert, you're a good man. The best man I've ever known. I won't ask you to try to protect me if you do decide to tell what you know from those diaries of Wanda Jean's. If you did, you could never look yourself in the mirror again. You've got to do what you think is right. All I ask is that, if you do decide to print it, you let me tell Lizzie myself, first. She deserves that."

"She doesn't deserve any of this," Robert told him.

"You're right. And you don't deserve to be in the position you are right now. But there it is, and I don't envy you for it."

Their eyes met and held for a long time. Both men knew that whatever Robert decided, the friendship they had both treasured for so long was over. "I've got to go," Lester said.

Alice Reider had told Robert when she gave him Wanda Jean's diaries, that she knew he would do the right thing. Now Lester had said the same thing. But even with everything that happened and what he now knew about his community, Robert still didn't know what the right thing was.

As he heard the front door of the newspaper office close behind Lester, the buzzer on Robert's wall sounded and he stared at it uncomprehendingly for a moment, until it buzzed again. Then he started down the stairs to the pressroom.

***

Duane Collett stayed off the sidewalk, following the alley away from the Foster Building and the dead men he had left there, reloading his revolver as he went. Duane may not have been a genius, but he was smart enough to know that things had spun so far out of control that there was no going back, even before he shot his uncle.

He didn't believe for a minute that even Uncle Harvey could pull off the story he had proposed, and the sight of his dead brother had been enough to let him know that if push came to shove, his uncle would throw him to the wolves in a heartbeat. He could always hire more muscle to collect his debts and keep the disgruntled homebuyers in line. So it was time to clean house and collect some debts of his own, and Duane knew just where he was going to start.

The back door of the newspaper pressroom was propped open to allow the night air in, and Duane went down the concrete steps from the alley and slipped inside. Scotty MacLean, the old pressman, was bent over, doing something to the ancient printing press and looked up as Duane approached.

"Who the hell are you and what do you want?"

Duane smashed his wooden nightstick over the old man's head, the leaded center giving it enough power to crush his skull with one blow. Scotty crumpled at his feet and Duane stepped over him, in search of his real target.

He found Robert on the other side of the room, with an armload of blank newsprint. Upon seeing the blood-spattered former policeman with the revolver in his hand, Robert dropped the paper and dashed around the back of the Linotype machine just as Duane fired. The bullet smashed into the wall behind him.

"No use hiding, asshole. It's just you and me and there's nowhere to run."

Robert crouched down, afraid to poke his head up enough to see, but knowing he couldn't stay where he was. All Duane had to do was follow him around the Linotype and shoot him like a trapped rat.

He looked toward the open door leading outside, but knew he'd never make it. The stairs leading up to the office were no better a choice.

"Come on, I don't have all night," Duane said. "I still need to find your buddy, Smeal, and take care of him, too."

Robert decided the office steps were the best choice, but he couldn't force himself to leave what little cover he had and make a dash for them. He pulled Sam Carpenter's small .380 semiautomatic pistol from his hip pocket. He was familiar with the old Remington single shot .22 rifle and the 20 gauge Ranger repeating shotgun his Mama had bought him from the Sears catalogue when he was a boy, but the only time he had fired a pistol was during his Officer Basic Training course when he joined the Army. And he couldn't hit anything then.

"Well lookee here, Mr. Newspaperman went and got hisself a pipsqueak little old pistol," Duane said, stepping around the end of the Linotype. "After I shoot you, I'm gonna stick that thing up your ass and pull the trigger, just for fun."

Robert didn't take the time to aim, he just pointed the gun at Duane and pulled the trigger. The sound of the firing pin falling on an empty chamber seemed incredibly loud in the pressroom, and Duane grinned evilly.

"You need to pull the slide back to chamber a round, asshole. How the hell did you ever live this long without somebody killing you?" He thumbed back the hammer of his .38 and said, "It don't matter. It's all over now."

Dog's Run

"Drop the gun, Duane, or I'll kill you!"

Both men turned toward the sound of Lester Smeal's voice. The police chief was standing on the raised landing that led from the office stairs to the pressroom, his big .44 held in both hands.

Upon seeing his longtime enemy, the man wearing the badge that rightly should have been his, Duane forgot all about Robert and charged, firing blindly at the exposed man.

Lester's gun roared in response, but the shot went wild as he stumbled backward, clutching his abdomen, where blood flowed out from between his fingers. He started to raise the .44, but before he could, Duane shot him again, the bullet tearing through his lung.

Lester slumped down against the wall, dropping his gun. "Die, you bastard," Duane shouted gleefully, mounting the three steps to the landing. "They can fry me in the electric chair and I'll die smiling, knowing that you'll be in Hell waiting to greet me!"

He pointed his revolver at Lester's face and said, "Goodbye prick."

The little .380 wasn't much of a gun, and Robert may have been a terrible shot, but luck was with him and his shot hit Duane in the side. He screamed in pain and rage and turned toward Robert, swinging the gun in his direction. As he did so, Lester used the last of his strength to kick out, catching Duane's leg just above the ankle and knocking him off balance. He stumbled and dropped his gun, then scrambled down off the landing after it.

Robert pulled the trigger on the pistol again, only to realize that the gun had jammed, his first empty shell casing sticking out of the half closed slide like a stovepipe. He ran across the open space to the landing and jumped up beside Lester, who opened his mouth to speak, but only bright red frothy blood escaped from his lips.

"Les? Oh shit!"

Lester looked up at him, trying to communicate with his eyes what he couldn't say with words. A sound came from Duane's direction and Robert turned to see him reaching for where his gun lay under a worktable. Robert grabbed the .44 from where it had fallen from Lester's limp hand and aimed at the other man's chest as he straightened up and pulled the trigger. The heavy slug knocked Duane off his feet and the life left his eyes as he crashed against the Linotype.

Robert dropped the Smith & Wesson and turned his attention back to Lester. Lester's eyes were closed and his breathing shallow. He managed to open his eyes halfway when Robert called his name, and tried to move his lips to speak.

"Les!"

"Do the… right… thing…."

The words were no more than a whisper.

"Hang on, Les!"

The police chief tried to speak again, but nothing came out but more bloody bubbles.

"Les! Don't you dare die on me!"

But it was too late. With one final, raspy breath, he was gone.

Robert became aware of sirens growing louder, rapidly. He wiped the tears from his eyes with the back of a bloody hand, then picked up Lester's gun one last time. He walked over to where Duane Collett's body lay, and rolled him over to expose his side, then aimed carefully at the bullet hole the little .380 pistol had made and pulled the trigger. Then he went back to hold his friend. That was where Ted DuPont and Billy Shaver found him.

Chapter 49

Citizen-Press - June 18, 1951

Police Chief Killed In Shootout

Elmhurst Police Chief Lester Smeal was killed in a wild shootout in the *Citizen-Press* printing shop Monday night. But before the brave lawman died, he managed to slay his assailant, Duane Ray Collett, a renegade Elmhurst police officer who had been suspended by the City Council in the wake of the shooting of Conrad Phillips last week. *Citizen-Press* editor and publisher Robert Tucker told police that shortly before the shooting, Chief Smeal revealed that he had evidence that implicated Duane Collett and his brother Arnold James Collett, as well as City Councilman Harvey Collett, in the recent murders of Elmhurst residents Wanda Jean Reider and Donald "Doodie" McRae. Arnold Collett and Harvey Collett, who was related to the brothers, were found dead in Harvey Collett's office during the investigation following the shooting at the newspaper. Acting Police Chief Sam Carpenter said it is believed that Duane Collett was responsible for shooting those men as well, and the assault on Colin "Scotty" MacLean, a *Citizen-Press* employee, who remains in critical condition at a Toledo hospital. Mr. MacLean is expected to survive his injuries. Robert Tucker, in speaking of the death of Chief Smeal, who was married to his sister, said, "Lester Smeal was the best man I've ever known. When he tracked Duane Collett to the newspaper pressroom, he threw himself into the line of fire to protect me. And though he was mortally wounded, he still managed to engage and dispatch the assailant before he succumbed to his wounds. He was a hero in wartime, and he died a hero."

Epilogue

Citizen-Press - June 3, 1962

Reider Graduates With Honors

Elmhurst resident Penny Reider, daughter of Mrs. Alice Reider and the late Raymond Reider, graduated magna cum laude from the School of Journalism at Ohio State University today. Miss Reider, 21, has worked as a summer intern for the *Citizen-Press* for the last four years, and was a high school correspondent while attending Elmhurst High School. During her college career, she won numerous awards for her investigative reporting, including a series on class prejudice among the residents of her hometown. *Citizen-Press* editor and publisher Robert Tucker, and his wife Lillian, who is the office manager at the newspaper, said, "We could not be more proud if Penny were our own daughter. We've watched her grow up in the newspaper business, and look forward to her returning to Elmhurst to work with us someday." Miss Reider said that day will have to wait a while, since she has accepted an offer to work with the Associated Press and requested an assignment to Vietnam, to cover America's increasing involvement in the conflict there. "I'm a reporter, and that's where the news is," she said. "I can't wait to get over there and cover the story."

Dog's Run

If you enjoyed *Dog's Run*, take a look at this sample from *Big Lake*, the bestselling first book in Nick Russell's popular *Big Lake* mystery series.

****

Prologue

While the rest of the world may see images of cactus, barren rock mountains, vast deserts, and the Grand Canyon when thinking of Arizona, there is another, lesser known topographic character to this southwestern state. The Mogollon Rim is a massive upthrust shelf of mountain country, stretching nearly 200 miles, from Prescott in the central part of the state, and on into New Mexico to the east.

Here lies the world's largest Ponderosa pine forest, snow capped peaks climbing to over 9,000 feet, dozens of lakes filled with trophy rainbow and brown trout, and the White Mountain Apache Indian reservation. The forests are home to bear, mountain lion, elk and deer. The dozen or so rustic small towns scattered along the Mogollon Rim have experienced a growth surge in recent years as crime weary residents, fleeing the smog and stresses of big city life, have discovered the high mountain paradise.

Stretching along the base of the Rim, as it is called locally, is another little known secret outside the state's borders - the Salt River Canyon. This smaller version of the Grand Canyon, a deep gorge winding nearly 50 miles long, is as scenic as its famous big brother, but has been tamed by U.S. Highway 60, a two lane thoroughfare meandering more or less east-west across the state. Between the pine country of Show Low and the high desert of Globe, Highway 60 dips southward briefly, to cross the Salt River Canyon in a series of hairpin turns and steep downgrades.

The highway is a major route for travelers and commerce between the high country and the rest of the state. As Highway 60 descends off the high country of the Rim, the terrain changes from alpine to desert, majestic pine trees are replaced by mesquite and cactus, and sagebrush takes the place of grassy open meadows.

Chapter 1

Early on a Monday morning in late November the canyon was deserted, weekend visitors to the high country back at their desks in air conditioned offices in Phoenix and Tucson. A lone hawk rode the thermals through the canyon, sharp eyes alert for prey. Below, a small ground squirrel cautiously peered out from under a prickly pear cactus, wary of danger. Sensing none, after a long scrutiny it scampered across the inside lane of blacktop. The hawk, alerted by the movement, began a downward plunge, razor sharp talons extended in its dive toward an easy meal.

Unaware of the danger from above, the ground squirrel suddenly paused as a low growl and slight vibration simultaneously alerted its senses, telegraphing danger signals to its brain. With a frantic scrambling of nails on pavement, it made a hasty u-turn and retreated hurriedly back to its cover, seconds before the hawk could pounce on it. Frustrated, the winged predator reversed its plunge as the sound of a heavy engine grew louder.

Casually steering the armored car with one hand, Phil Johnson stuck a cigarette between his lips and thumbed the striker on his old Zippo lighter, a well worn souvenir he had carried every day since picking it up in a Saigon post exchange back in his Army days. Through a blue cloud of tobacco smoke, he looked sideways at his partner and grinned. "So, you gonna take that little teller, Tanya, to lunch while we're in the city?"

Mike Perkins' face reddened. "Come on Phil. You know I'm married. I don't mess around."

The driver leered, enjoying the younger man's discomfort. "Yeah kid, but that'll change. That little gal sure has the hots for you. Ever notice that every time we make our drop off at the bank, she makes it a point to check us in? And she's always giving you the eye. I tell you...

a man would be pretty dumb to pass that up. Great ass and everything else that goes with it."

"Yeah, maybe so. But a man'd be even dumber to mess up what I've got at home. When you got prime rib waiting on the table, why stop for a hotdog?"

Johnson chuckled and nodded his head. The inside of the truck had warmed up, and he took off his uniform hat and hung it over the barrel of the 12 gauge pump shotgun mounted vertically in a rack attached to the dashboard, then shrugged out of the heavy jacket he had worn when they began their route two hours earlier in the high country. Perkins reached over and guided the wheel with one hand to make the chore easier for his partner. "Thanks, kid," Johnson said as he pushed the jacket onto the seat beside him and reclaimed the steering wheel. "Guess I can't argue with you on that one, Mike. I just wish that little cutiepie would give me the chance, since you're going to disappoint her"

"I'll put in a good word for you," said the younger guard. "Maybe you can..."

"What's this?" interrupted Johnson as they rounded a curve, nodding toward a Jeep Wagoneer pulled into a scenic turnoff, its hood up. "What's she doing way out here?"

" Pull over."

"Hey kid, you wanna get us fired? You know we're not supposed to make any unauthorized stops."

"Bullshit, Phil! Pull over. This doesn't make sense."

The armored car pulled in beside the Jeep and stopped. Perkins opened his door and stepped down onto the ground. "What are you doing here?" he asked the woman who stood next to the upraised hood.

Before she could answer, a figure slipped around the back of the armored car and a sharp crack broke the early morning air. The bullet slammed into the back of the young guard's head and pitched him face forward down into the dirt, blood spraying the side of the armored car. The woman shuddered for an instant, then looked into the face of the gunman. "Come on, we don't have time to waste!"

Phil Johnson holstered his Smith & Wesson .38 and looked down at his dead partner, awestruck. "Damn! Twenty years in the Army and I never killed anyone...."

"Hurry up, baby," the woman said. "Someone might come along any time."

Stepping over the body, she hustled the guard to the back of the armored car. His hands shaking, Johnson fumbled a set of keys off his belt and unlocked the two sets of locks, then swung the doors open. Inside, neatly stacked, were twenty canvas money bags, each secured by a metal hasp. The receipts of a long ski weekend in the mountains, destined for the holding bank in central Phoenix.

Throwing open the rear tailgate of the Jeep, the man and woman quickly transferred the money, alert for the sound of an approaching car. The job only took a few moments, and when the last bag was in the Jeep, the woman wiped perspiration from her forehead with the back of her hand. "Let's get going. Mexico's waiting."

Johnson grabbed her by the back of the head and pulled her face close to his for a kiss. "Oh, girl! It's going to be so good."

"Not if you don't move your ass," she urged. "Get busy so we can get out of here."

Johnson walked back to the body of Mike Perkins and bent over. He hesitated, then took a deep breath and, grabbing him by the boots, dragged the dead man to the back of the armored car, trying to avoid looking at his mangled head. Grunting, he managed to manhandle the body through the steel doors, all the time fighting down nausea. "Come on, damn it," said the woman nervously.

Johnson crawled inside and dragged his partner's lifeless body in far enough to be able to close the doors. Then he stepped over the corpse and started to climb out of the armored car. The sight of a snub nose .38 revolver in the woman's hand stopped him. "What the..."

"Sorry, baby," said the woman, a smirk distorting her features. "But with all this money, a dirty old man like you would just slow me down, don't you think? Thanks for the help." Johnson's scream was cut short by three quick gunshots. He tumbled backward onto the body of the man he had killed. A heavy weight settled in his chest and it became impossible to keep his eyelids open, no mattered how hard he struggled.

Before his life's blood had stopped pumping out of him, the Jeep was gone and silence once again filled the canyon. The hawk, soaring high overhead, watched the Jeep's progress until it disappeared around a curve, then went back to the hunt.

Made in the USA
San Bernardino, CA
15 March 2015